RESCUED

THE GREAT ESCAPEE SERIES

BONNIE LACY

FROSTING ON THE CAKE PRODUCTIONS

Endorsement for Released, Book 1 ~

"A curmudgeonly ex-con senior citizen, a little girl named Bea, and her addict mother. An unlikely trio crosses paths on the road to redemption from their pasts in small town Nebraska—with a little help from above. With true-to-life grit and characters you love to love (and some you love to hate), RELEASED is a fresh slice of hope in a world of injured souls."

—Tosca Lee, NYT bestselling author of Progeny

To Jan
My sister by blood
My sister in crime
My sister in Jesus Christ
The Boss

Colossians 2:12 - Message - "Going under the water was a burial of your old life; coming up out of it was a resurrection, God raising you from the dead as he did Christ."

ONE

June 11, 1937 ~ Osceola, Nebraska ~ Journal of Dr. Walter Stevens, Professor of Agriculture ~ University of Nebraska ~ Assistant Henry Green on my personal payroll. Found a new pool today—really a cave. Drove camper through Nebraska on Highway 92. Great new road west from Omaha and my '35 Ford pickup pulled just fine. Stopped in Osceola—Henry's hometown—for early lunch at Thelma's Eatery and Diner. Home-cooked food. Pie! Even had new candy bar—"3 Musketeers." Package of three little bars. Henry got two and I ate one—too full of roast beef and pie to eat more. Up and coming little community. Decided to stretch our legs and walk our meal off. Left camper parked at Thelma's.

Railroad tracks and the highway divide the town. Fine Court House. Businesses seem to be on the

South side of the tracks. There's a street named Gospel Ridge on the North side. No wrong side of the tracks here.

Beautiful June day. Low humidity, though the sun was brilliant. Drawn to the park. Heard water gurgling from somewhere. Everywhere else is dry. Our ongoing drought studies show horrible devastation. Found a pool under RR bridge, right at the East edge of the city park. Impossible. The creek bed is cracked and flaking. How could there be a pool? Measured about nine by twelve feet of surface, very clear water. No visible bottom. Signs posted: "Keep Out," and "Witch hole." Frayed red plaid shirt tied to one—warning flag. Henry found a branch about ten feet long. Drove it into the pool several places. Couldn't touch bottom. The last time, the branch just disappeared. So many questions.

Present Day ~ "Here it is. Want to show this to Michael." Clarence Timmelsen tucked the faded newspaper article into his black T-shirt pocket. Oh-oh. The pocket had torn away from the shirt, leaving a small hole at the seam.

He could wear it today and toss it tonight. Great way to do laundry—shirt gets dirty and full of holes—throw it away. Rosita, the laundry lady at Hillcrest

Nursing Homes, would like that. She was always commenting on how little laundry he had. Probably because he hadn't started wetting the bed … yet.

Michael should be here by now. Clarence checked his watch. Probably should stick around and set up his law office, but he needed to escape again. Looked like a beautiful day.

He walked into the office from his bedroom. Kind of a nice commute.

Two rooms—bedroom and office. It felt like a high-end hotel compared to one cell in prison.

Carol had helped frame his law diplomas and certificates so he could hang them. The top left row was …

He rummaged in the closet for the tool box, found a ruler and measured from the ceiling … yup … off.

The maintenance guy would come running if he heard a hammer pounding. Any other day, Clarence might feel like antagonizing him—but not today. That's why he would leave the hammer in the tool box.

He'd had his breakfast of eggs and toast. Coffee with Mrs. Hatly and Harold. Always good to start the day with friends.

He'd been at Hillcrest Homes for six weeks, but he could still hear the mess-hall in prison—it had imprinted on his brain. The sound of trays clattering bounced off walls, feet shuffled—or stomped, and underneath it all, a legion of male voices rumbled. You never knew when, not if, a fight would break out. Clarence had usually sat by himself to keep out of trouble. Only stainless-steel trays and spoons in his part of prison—probably because they still thought he'd killed his wife. Annie.

At Hillcrest, he had knives, forks and spoons. And dinnerware. Napkins. Even music to eat by— sometimes a lady brought her keyboard and serenaded them. And he had the company of sweet little Mrs. Hatly. And Harold. Well, Harold was Harold. Him and his always-upside-down American flag pin on his lapel.

Breakfast was Clarence's favorite meal. The rest of the food was edible. What he wouldn't do for a big juicy steak once-in-a-while instead of casseroles all the time. At least he didn't have to cook or clean up.

Hard to believe it had only been, he checked the complementary Hillcrest calendar, six weeks since he had been kicked out of prison. So much had happened since then. He stared out the window, and a visual of memories growing up in Osceola played over his mind: building the library with Dad, going to the Clynder law offices—that might have been where law started for him, and Annie—in the library, in the restaurant, at their wedding.

All had crashed to a halt at the accident. He

blinked, tapping against the glass, emotion building. Even now. He tapped harder. Sixty years later.

He moved his hand--or hammering a nail in a wall wouldn't be the only thing the maintenance guy would have to fix.

The required law documents were hung. Almost impressive. The complimentary picture of Jesus was still in the bottom of his closet. He'd come a long way from the jerk he'd been in prison, even in six weeks, but he still wasn't ready to build a shrine to Him.

The cleaning woman, Mrs. Gustafson, alerted him when he needed to bring Jesus out of hiding on inspection days. She was a gem. Always brought him goodies from home. Her home baked cinnamon rolls were the best. If she slipped him one, he quietly closed the door to his room and locked it. He didn't unlock until he had licked all the frosting from his fingertips.

Annie smiled at him from a faded photograph in an antique frame Carol had scrounged up for him. She was his inspiration to keep on living. She would have wanted him to live a life that mattered.

He was still working on that.

The frame with bright balloons bouncing all over it held his Little One, Bea, and her mommy, Katty.

Katty had gone through rehab and was almost

finished with an online school to be his assistant. He was so proud of her. She was a top student.

He opened his fists and studied the scars on the palms of his hands. Angry-looking burns. Still tender. All worth it to save Bea.

He kissed his fingertip and planted it on Bea's cheek.

Family.

His reflection in the mirror satisfied him for a workday. Shoulder length gray hair slicked behind his ears—it had grown fast since the last administrator of the home demanded he cut it. Couldn't do much about bushy eyebrows, but his bright blue eyes surprised even him today. Sky blue.

He flicked off the ceiling light.

"You got important places to be, Mr. Timmelsen?"

Clarence jumped and turned toward the gritty voice speaking from near the closet. "Who's there?" He cleared his throat. His voice was husky but never that husky. "What do you think you're doing here?"

"Moved in last night. Next door."

Clarence flipped on the light again.

A man stepped from the corner of his room. Deep wrinkles on dark skin. White spiky hair. Black piercing eyes. Strange black suit—no collar on the black shirt.

"Well, you didn't move into my room. Go back to

yours." Clarence stiffened. "Who gave you the right to be in here, anyway?"

The man smiled. "You did."

"What?" Clarence pounded his chest. "I did?" He pointed in the man's face. "You can't just walk into someone's private room."

Sinister smile again.

Who the hell was this guy? Some evil relative of Phil Daynton? Probably somebody from the loins of that bastard, Judge Green. "Who are you—the devil? You must be a long-lost relative of John's from the grocery store. He's from the devil, too."

The man grinned. "I'm from everywhere. I'm from next door. I'm from the next town over." Teeth flashed white against his mottled skin. "I'm from your heart. I'm from the same country you are, Mr. Timmelsen."

Clarence's inner furnace boiled over. A vise grip tightened around his head, making it throb. "Well, Mr. Everywhere," yelled Clarence, pointing, "get the hell out of my room!"

Carol Neeton, the Director of Nursing, rushed into the room. "What is all the yelling about?"

Aide Lisha Hall, followed her, stethoscope trailing from her pocket, pounding her ample chest like a racer who had just finished a sprint. Only she wasn't a sprinter.

"It's him! He's in my room!" Clarence pointed at

the man. Only … he wasn't there. He twisted left and right. "Where'd he go?" He opened the door to his bathroom. "He's gone." He tore at his bedcovers, pillows flying. "He was just here!"

Carol looked at Lisha.

"Damn it! I'm not crazy. This guy just appeared in the corner there. He has white hair, dark skin and it's all wrinkled." He looked from Lisha to Carol. "I'm not kidding. He said he moved in last night, and that he's my neighbor."

"We did have a guy move in just next door, but he's limited to bed rest." Carol shook her head. "I don't think he's your man. He won't be wandering the halls, huh, Lisha?"

"Not in this life, Mr. Clarence." Lisha flipped the stethoscope around her neck. "You can peek in his room and see if it's him."

"Yeah. Reminds me of that old man that was shitting in my bathroom the day I checked in. What was his name? Thompson? He dead yet?"

"Clarence, that's not the way we speak about the deceased." Carol held the door for him and walked into the hall.

Clarence followed her into the room next door.

The room, Room 202, was pretty much like his. Walk in the door. Bathroom to the left with built-in closet. Window on the far wall. Bed this side of the window. Even the nightstand and chest of drawers were of nursing home issue—just like his.

Except Clarence had two rooms. One, his bedroom, Room 206. The other, Room 204, was his office with a desk, some chairs, and a bookcase. Even his office had another bathroom. He guessed for those emergency moments when a guest needed to go at the same time he needed to.

The man on the bed didn't stir. He didn't blink. He stared at the wall above the dresser—at the calendar maybe.

"Man, his room is emptier than mine. He just has a calendar. Not even a picture of Jesus."

Lisha's nostrils flared. "Oh, yeah. Been meaning to talk to you about that. It don't count hangin' it in the back of yer closet, right Miss Carol?"

Carol leaned over the bed. "Mr. Wainwright? It's your nurse, Carol. How are you doing today?" She checked each tube and the oxygen meter.

No sign of life except open eyes. And a pointer finger, with an oxygen monitor clipped to it, tapped up and down on the blanket. Dark skin all right. White hair. Seemed like the same man, but—

"So you can see, Clarence, Mr. Wainwright is not capable of moving more than that finger. Seeing him in your room is impossible. Not sure what or who you saw, but it can't be this man. He did move in last night." She turned to face him. "You must have heard them. Or dreamt it. That I give you."

The guy was a vegetable. Skin and bone. Still … something about those eyes.

Clarence stepped closer to the bed and leaned toward Carol. "What's his name?"

"Mr. Wainwright."

"Mr. Wainwright. Sorry about the mistake. But I swear you were in my room just now. I don't know how …." He shook his head, jingled change in his pocket and faced Carol. "In prison something like this happened. Old man died and left behind his demons. Bet this guy's demons got loose and came in my room." He leaned over the bed. "Better keep your old demons to yourself, buddy. I got enough of my own."

"Clarence!"

"Just bein' honest, Carol." Clarence blinked and wiped his eyes. Hand over his mouth. He gagged. "Damn, he stinks. Smells dead."

"Shh. Come on. Time to go. Give him his peace."

As they stepped to the door, Clarence glanced over his shoulder. "Creepy old man."

Mr. Wainwright's eyes were no longer burning a hole in the wall, but staring straight at Clarence, with a wicked, rheumy look.

Clarence grabbed Carol and Lisha. "Look. He moved his eyes."

Carol turned. "He did. Wow."

Lisha stepped back into the room. "Hi Mr. Wainwright. You feelin' better? Had a little comp'ny?" She patted his arm. "Dang. This guy got no meat on him at all."

Clarence muffled his mouth. "You should give him some of—"

"Shush, Clarence. Is he okay?" Carol reached into her jacket pocket and pulled out a pen. "Check his vitals. I'm sure with moving and all, he's probably disoriented and uncomfortable." She walked to the door. "I'll check his chart to see what's on order for him."

Lisha wrapped the blood pressure cuff around his bony arm and proceeded to pump it up, holding the stethoscope in place on his arm. She let the air out slowly but pumped it up again. This time she took even more time to release the air. "Huh. I can't get a reading."

She cocked her head toward Clarence. "Could you get Miss Carol for me?"

"Sure." He had started to leave the room when Carol whipped in with a clear plastic med cup, filled with bright pink liquid.

"I'm not sure he can swallow, but at least it's liquid." She lifted it to his mouth. "Mr. Wainwright, I have some Tylenol here for you." She hesitated. "Wow he's cold." Back to the man. "You seem uncomfortable, and this might help you relax. It's tough changing homes and beds and all." She started to part his lips with the cup and spoke to Lisha. "You get his temp yet?"

Mr. Wainwright's eyes shifted again. They turned black. His body became even more rigid. His eyes focused on something behind them.

Clarence took a step back as Michael appeared behind them at the door. "Michael. Hi."

A thick guttural growl came from the direction of Mr. Wainwright's bed.

Clarence jumped.

Pink medication splattered from the medicine cup onto Carol's hand and his gown. "Mr. Wainwright. You need to calm yourself."

The man shuddered and hissed. His eyes seemed to spark as Michael stepped into the room.

Clarence slowly stopped to look at Michael again. Then back to the body on the bed, still hissing and spitting. Back at Michael. Shivers skittered up his spine like a flea race in a circus. The room grew colder.

Michael seemed to grow taller the longer Clarence looked his way. Oh-oh. Angel costume. Wings started to sprout.

Lisha finally found her tongue. "Michael … uh, he don't like you." The whites of her eyes were visible surrounding the brown. Goosebumps lined her usually smooth brown skin.

Carol yelled close to his ear. "Mr. Wainwright? Mr. Wainwright!" She patted his cheek. "Snap out of it!"

Clarence shivered.

This was no man.

TWO

June 11, 1937 ~ Journal of Dr. Walter Stevens ~ Henry had dinner tonight at his brother's in Osceola. He came back to the camper drunk and angry. Seems his brother reneged on some promise to make him law partner. He stood by the pool a few minutes, then stripped down. I teased him—the women of Osceola wouldn't like a man that smelled like fish. Argued with him. Even wrestled him down, but Henry knocked me back. Slammed me against the rock wall. Stubborn. Stupid. Had him by the ear—before he went under. He gasped and seemed to shudder, sucked in water, and shoved me away.

He never came back up.

Present Day ~ Noell Carpenter stretched to her tiptoes on the concrete step and peeked through the diamond-shaped window in the front door.

Sigh. God, how does Gamma live in this?

She closed her eyes.

Breathe.

The familiar terror rose in her chest. She swallowed it down and checked through the window again. The front porch had been enclosed years ago —originally planned for a sunroom. But as Gam had walked back and forth, in and out, things had piled up. Until the new room was packed. A narrow path trailed through the mess—from the entrance to the door leading into the living room.

Piles of clothing. Boxes stacked high. Full shopping bags, cardboard. It had maybe started out fairly organized—with flattened cardboard boxes, labeled totes of clothing, old games—all categorized. An old duck from a grocery store bath soap display crowned one pile. It was a wonder it hadn't slid off the pile of magazines it reigned over.

Another item caught her eye. Always did. Every time she peeked in the front door, or when she tiptoed past the piles into the house, it stood out from the rest of the hoard.

It was an antique coffee cup with a business name on it—an advertisement giveaway back then, she guessed. She could read it from outside the door.

"Osceola Times ~ Your favorite Paper with Up-To-Date News." There was a chip out of the bottom rim. Noell liked to imagine the newspaper editor slamming it down on his desk, declaring the newest article to be the best of the century. Someday she would ask Gam if she could have it.

She opened the screen door, propped it with her foot and pushed the wood inner door, careful to ease it against the ceiling-high stack of newspapers behind it. Didn't want to start an avalanche. She might be the one buried.

Gamma called from inside. "You there, Sweetie?"

Sigh.

"Yeah, Gam. Give me a minute." She slipped her backpack off her shoulders. "Or two."

Now to unzip her backpack. One zipper ran over the top to the sides. One zipped across the front. Another at the bottom. She pulled a sheet of paper towel out and carefully unfolded it, laying it on the front step beside her feet and set the backpack on it, making sure the backpack didn't overlap the paper.

Step one: done.

Next, she shook a plastic shopping bag, crackling in the breeze. Standing flamingo-style, she slipped her foot out of her thrift store boot and pulled a new white bedroom slipper from the backpack. Her feet went on autopilot: into the slipper and into the house with that foot. The boot went inside the plastic shopping bag.

Only the other boot was stuck. A strategically placed brick beside the doorway became her boot puller. The boot came loose, fell on the step and bounced onto the sidewalk below.

Sigh. Some days it was so easy.

Not today.

A tear plopped onto the canvas backpack, darkening the blue fabric.

Deep breath.

She pulled the other slipper on, stepped down and retrieved the wayward boot.

She had been tired before, but now …

She stepped inside the porch. The sight of the piles of boxes—some leaning, one exploding across the side of the only path through—always made her gasp.

She had seen it all before. She peeked inside before entering everyday—ever since she had grown tall enough to see through the little window in the front door.

She stood just inside and waited, her eyes pinched shut. Her breathing became short gasps.

She knew what was coming. It happened every time she entered the house. Some days were just worse than others.

First one pile of magazines appeared to slide her

way. Then the stack of boxes marked "Clothing" she had tried to stabilize the day before, toppled. Putrid piles of hoarded junk floated toward her, opening her forever nightmare. Everywhere she glanced—the clutter, the boxes, the clothing—morphed into water crashing into her.

Something grabbed her foot; the slipper floated away. She choked and struggled to breathe. The more she thrashed and kicked, the more she was pulled under—under the water and trash.

Even though the water appeared murky and cloudy, yellow eyes glared at her; an evil grin taunted her—daring her to break free. She tried to pry her foot loose, but grimy fingers grabbed her hand.

She kicked with her other foot and the hand transformed into Mommy's hand, the face changed into Mommy's—eyes terrified, mouth open in a muffled scream. The face disappeared; the water receded. Boxes and clutter on the porch once again.

She coughed and sputtered. "Oh God! Oh God! Take away that nightmare!" Couldn't let Gam see. She wiped at the water on her face. Water. Always water.

It was just a … dream, right?

The only memory she had of her mom was always a terrifying dream. If she told Gam, Gam would cry. Every time she woke from that dream—from the first time till now, she prayed, "Jesus make me strong. Jesus, take away the dream. Jesus, please take away the scaredy-cat in me."

She did it now. "Jesus please take away my fears and take away that dream."

Whew.

The slipper had landed on top of the magazines.

How did that happen if it was just a dream? She shook her head, her chin jutted out. She would not cry—at least not now.

She hopped over to the slipper, shoved her foot in and slung the backpack over her shoulder, reading the antique mug as she walked by.

Something didn't smell right. Gam always insisted that no critter could find its way in. The house was tight. Noell wasn't so sure. Something smelled … dead.

She opened the door to the living room.

"My baby's home!" Gam sang it out and shuffled to her, using a walker. Step into it. Pick it up. Move it forward and start over. Almost a dance. Almost.

"Gam." Noell hugged her and dripped on her plaid shirt.

"I didn't know it was raining." Gamma tipped her head to look out the window. "You're all wet."

"I know. Sprinklers." No sense freaking Gamma out. Noel was already there herself. No sense in having them both terrified.

Some days she could feel Gam shrinking. Today

was one of those days. But the smaller she seemed to grow, more love poured from this woman who had taken her in years ago.

"How was the job hunt, dear?" Gamma gravitated back to her spot—the only clear spot on the sofa. That piece of furniture was her pride and joy. She had paid cash for a $3,000 Italian leather sofa way back when. And now magazines, newspapers, documents obscured the beautiful red upholstery. The clutter probably protected the leather.

"Not great. I have some prospects, I think. The hospital was interested. The newspaper office didn't have any openings, but she said I would be perfect for their office." She shrugged. "I'm not sure what that means."

"They like you and see that you are smart. That's what that means." Soft grey curls fell away from her face. Gam was the oldest grandma that looked the youngest, in spite of the walker. Her hair was longer, naturally curly, her eyes were snappy behind glasses and her mouth was snappy, too. She was a pretty lady despite her age of seventy-eight. She even dressed younger. She lived in jeans.

And she was fun to talk to—share a girl joke or two, but no place to sit. Not a place for anyone to enjoy Gamma's company.

After the nightmare Noell had just experienced, she needed some Gamma.

"How about the city office? Any openings there? I used to love working there. And I'm sure you would be welcome on my recommendations." She straightened. "I won awards there and bonuses." She pointed to Noell. "You could too."

"Well, I'll put my application in there, too, so we'll see." She shrugged. She moved to the stairway. "Need anything before I go upstairs, Gam? More water? A snack?"

"No. No, I'm fine. I just had a cookie." She popped her head up. "Made some fresh today. Help yourself. Take them upstairs with you."

Noell headed to the kitchen, opened the refrigerator door, counted to five, and scooped up two cookies. It was okay. They were fresh. Besides. Gam made them. She waved at Gam as she took the stairway, two steps at a time, and opened the door to her bedroom.

Ahhh. Breathe. She stepped inside and silently closed the door behind her.

She leaned against the back of the door and surveyed her room. Pristine. Sparse was a better word. Only two mementos sat out on her desk: the only thing reminding her of Mom—a baby bracelet. And Gam's Bible. That antique cup would look good next to the Bible.

She slid her backpack off her shoulders and kicked off her slippers. There was only one place she ever felt okay about doing that, and it was here in her room. The bed was made. Neat freak. No clutter. Closet door was closed.

She changed clothes and plopped down on her bed. What a day. Somebody had to hire her. She had to get out of here and find a place of her own. She dreamed of where she would live. Something with a little space. It would take money. She had saved ever since she was old enough to sweep Gamma's floors before all the hoarding had begun. Paper routes. Babysitting. Scooping snow. Lawn mowing.

She had even worked for Mr. Hardesty in his body shop. At first, she answered the phone and did minimal bookwork, but as he got to know her and she stuck around, she learned how to repair dents, touch-ups, detailing. She figured how to take apart an inside door panel one day when Mr. Hardesty was away. The customer had been in a hurry, and Noell tinkered until she fixed the door handle. Pretty proud of that one.

She should call him and see if he needed any help. He'd had to replace her when he needed more help, and she was still in school. They'd both been bummed.

Her phone buzzed. She kept the ringer off so Gam wouldn't worry or get startled. Gam still had the landline going, so she was okay with Noell having her own cell phone. Besides, Noell paid for it herself. All good.

"Hello?"

"Yes, is this Noell Carpenter?"

"Yes. This is she."

"This is Dottie at Osceola Community Hospital. I'd like to let you know you have a job here if it still works for you."

Noell sat up. "Cool. That's great."

"You'll need to come in for training tomorrow, okay?"

"Yeah, sure … I mean, yes, of course." She slid to the edge of the bed. "What time do you want me there? What should I wear? Do I need to bring anything?"

Dottie laughed on the other end. "How about nine tomorrow morning? Just wear casual and we'll get you set up with a uniform, depending on what department you end up in. We have several opportunities open, so we'll see where you fit. Okay?"

"Yeah. Yes. Sure."

"And we'll do some lab testing, blood work and urine testing. Drug testing. It's just routine. We do it on everybody, even the doctors."

Pictures of blood smears and needles spun in front of Noell's face. Her mouth went dry. Sweat seeped under her shirt. She cleared her throat. "Um, what opportunities are open, if I may ask?"

"Oh … what we call the bedpan brigade and housekeeping. Nothing too strenuous, although you do need a car to drive back and forth. Or a bike. Whatever it takes to get around, back and forth."

"I can ride a bike. But bedpans? What will I do with bedpans?"

Laughter. "People poop and pee in bedpans, so you'll be helping patients use them and when they are done, you dispose of the poop and pee."

"Dispose of it? Um … where? How?"

"Into the toilet. We have nifty sprayers hooked into the toilet, so you don't have to use your hands to clean it out. Just spray away. Sometimes you need to wipe the bedpan out if it's especially … gooey, but not usually."

Noell belched and fell back onto her bed, her phone slid onto the floor.

"Really easy. Well, I'll see you tomorrow … you there? Still interested? Noell? Are you still there?"

Noell covered her mouth and gagged. She scrambled for the phone, but the bathroom called her first.

"Noell? Noell?"

She leaned over the sparkling clean toilet in her private bathroom and threw up. Gah. Dottie said good-bye. The phone buzzed.

Guess the hospital won't work out.

THREE

June 12, 1937 ~ Journal of Dr. Stevens ~ Thelma gave me a mug from the diner. Nice lady. Probably felt sorry for me. Emotion is surprising me—hadn't known Henry all that long.

He had been a good assistant. Some problems had become apparent, but everybody has problems. There was a child somewhere he'd never gotten to raise. He had leaned toward the eccentric but …

I slept by a pool last night.

Why did I ever let Henry go in any pool?

In Arizona, Henry had helped make a major discovery—one upper pool connected to another below —at the bottom of the hill. He swam all that way underwater, but as he reached the lower pool opening, he became entangled in vines and almost drowned.

Chilly last night in Osceola. Heard raindrops on

the trees for a time, but it never hit the ground. Just a tease. Called a dry thunderstorm.

I slept by the pool instead of the camper, in hopes Henry would show up—somehow. Hope beyond all hope.

Can't believe Henry's balding head and ornery grin won't appear below the surface of this pool.

I can't believe he's gone.

Present Day ~ Clarence read out loud from a yellowed newspaper clipping as Michael backed away from the parking place at Hillcrest Homes. "Says here, 'Famed and notorious professor of agriculture and self-avowed archeologist, Dr. Walter Stevens's assistant drowned yesterday in a freak accident in Osceola, Nebraska.'" He flicked the paper back and forth with his finger. "Seems his assistant, Henry Green, fell into a pool in a cave they were studying near the Gospel Ridge. Wonder where Gospel Ridge is now?"

Michael shrugged. His hand gripped the gearshift on the column, but he was obviously struggling to find first gear. Either the truck was growling, or Michael was. Maybe both.

"Yuck—what a way to go. Listen." Clarence read further. "'He sucked in the putrid waters from the pool as he succumbed to the pool's clutches. When interviewed, Dr. Stevens said he reached for Mr. Green, and had hold of his hand, when Mr. Green pushed away. Dr. Stevens warns all: "Don't go near that pool. You won't come back."'" Ugh."

Clarence folded the clipping. "Wow. Wonder if that pool is still here." He straightened. "We should check it out." Michael wasn't listening. His dark blue shirt appeared even darker at his upper back and underarms. Surely angels didn't sweat.

"What is all that notorious and self-avowed stuff?" Michael finally found first gear. "Where'd you get that clipping?"

"Good shift, Michael. You're getting it. I 'spose angels don't get to drive old trucks too much."

Michael grinned. He was such a muscular stud. For not being able to put in a personal request about what kind of an angel he'd want, Clarence considered himself pretty lucky. God did good. Six weeks ago, he'd never even thought about … having his own angel. Had Michael been with him in prison too?

"Michael—"

The big guy started to shift into second. Grinding. He sighed and shoved the shifter back into neutral. Clutch in. Shifter to second. Sweat dripped from dark ringlets at his temples.

"Just wiggle it. It'll go in."

Grind.

Back to first. Clutch. Speed up. Into second slowly.

Perfect.

Whew.

Michael blew out a breath and flashed a huge grin.

Clarence laughed. "High five, man!" He held his hand high, forgetting Michael's stretch and hit his elbow. Laughed again when Michael adjusted so they could slap hands.

"Hey. Wasn't that the weirdest thing you ever saw, in that guy's room just now?"

"What guy?" Michael must have been concentrating on his driving. Even angels frowned.

"You know. My neighbor at the nursing home."

Michael looked at Clarence out of the corner of his eyes. "Oh. Yeah." Then eyes straight ahead. "What about him?"

"That was just weird. Even scary." Clarence straightened and leaned forward. "I thought you were going to do the angel costume thing in there."

Michael shook his head.

"What? Tell me there wasn't something going on there. Seemed like when he saw you, he started spitting and hissing. How would he know you? He doesn't seem like the angel sort." He hesitated and chuckled. "I know. I'm not the angel sort either."

Michael appeared to be biting his lips. When

Michael decided to clam up, he clammed it up and no amount of pushing would make him talk.

"Okay." Back to the clipping. "I found it in one of my old journals—you know—all those boxes from prison. Yeah, this guy Stevens sounds like a character." Clarence waved the clipping back and forth. "From the University of Nebraska, huh? Sounds more like a movie character." He folded the newspaper clipping. "Can we skip work for a while today and look around? Work on the Town Hall can wait, right? See if we can find what this guy," he opened the clipping, "Dr. Stevens might have found?"

"Sure." Michael's voice boomed, even when he answered softly. "We have time. Some of the wood we ordered for that wall, isn't in yet anyway."

Clarence read the article again. "Gospel Ridge." He rotated in the seat. "That's just North from the park and the nursing home, I think." He craned his neck. "Just up the street. See any street signs?"

Michael shifted into third. The truck lurched.

"Grinding, Michael."

Michael shook his head, muttering.

"What?" Clarence leaned toward him.

"Nothing."

"Did you cuss, Michael?"

"No. I was just telling Father if I was meant to drive a stick shift that He should have built me with a gear shift knob for a hand and a clutch for a foot." His voice trailed off as he turned into the park.

Clarence burst out laughing. "That's okay, Michael." Clarence looked up at the sky, wiping his eyes. "I don't see any lightning coming your way."

Boom!

"What the …"

Michael shook his head and got out. "I … uh, hit the guard rail."

Clarence laughed—a shake your belly kind of laugh. "I thought it was That Old God swinging a two-by-four at you!" He climbed out, wiping his cheeks, and walked to the front of the truck. "It's not too bad." He scanned the rest of the truck. "Looks like it's happened a time or two, right?"

Michael blushed as red as the truck, stepped in front of it and pushed it a couple feet away from the guard rail. Licking his finger, he wiped at the bumper. "A little scrape." He checked the guard rail. "Oh-oh. Red paint." He straightened. "Think they'll arrest me?"

"Did you just push the truck? By yourself?" Clarence shoved against it. "It doesn't even budge when I do that." He straightened, eyeing Michael. "Are all angels that strong? Can you lift the truck?"

"Naw. I mean angels are strong, but I don't want to lift it." He brushed his hands together. "It's dirty."

"You mean you could, but you don't want to."

Clarence chuckled. "You're something else, Michael." He turned toward the park. "Let's explore a little."

He stuffed the newspaper article in his T-shirt pocket. The first thing he saw when he stepped from the parking lot was the huge old playground slide. He shivered. The palms of his hands tingled. He clenched them to make it stop. "I … I, uh." He couldn't finish.

Michael stepped beside him. "Little Bea is alive because of you, Clarence." He reached for Clarence's hands and pried his fingers open. The palms and insides of both arms looked like he wore red braces. Only he didn't. Thick burns ran from his palms to halfway up the inside of his arms.

"Was that only six weeks ago?" Clarence stared at his hands but saw that day. Running till his lungs would burst. Searching to find little Bea and the shock of seeing her at the top of that old slide, hands duct taped to the bars, mouth taped shut. But her eyes. He'd never forget her terrified eyes. "Uh, let's, um … walk to the swimming pool." He wiped his face and took off.

"Nice little playground area." He pointed. "Swimming lessons are on." He glanced at Michael. "You know how to swim?"

Michael blinked.

"Swim. You know." Clarence moved his arms in

his best version of a breaststroke. "Like that. Come on."

Michael followed Clarence on up the hill.

"When I was a kid, the pool was in the same place." He chuckled, rubbing his hands together. "Only we didn't have the huge frog spouting water." He rotated toward the nursing home. "I can see the park from where my rooms are now."

The kids were noisy—singing, yelling, jumping, splashing. A few parents sat visiting or reading. A radio blared from the building speakers. Sun sparkled off the water.

Lifeguards, sitting on their elevated thrones, blew their whistles.

Rest break.

Kids slogged out of the pool at the edges or up the ladders and huddled, wrapped in their towels.

"Look! There's the guy from prison."

"He killed a lady."

"Hey mister! Go back where you belong!"

Clarence swallowed. Nostrils flared. "L-let's look over here, Michael." He tugged on Michael's shirt.

"Look. Look. What's he doing?"

"He's crazy."

"Go away! You need to go away and die!"

The whistles blew again, and the kids forgot all about Clarence and jumped into the pool.

All except two little kids—a dark-haired girl and a freckle-faced boy.

Oh, no.

Clarence wasn't sticking around for more name-calling.

The boy pointed his tiny finger through the chain-link fence. "Look at that big guy." He wiped his face with a green and yellow striped towel. His wet reddish-blond hair plastered against light skin.

"Yeah. He comes into my room at night and sings to me when I'm scared."

"Sometimes he has wings."

"Yeah. He's nice."

No one seemed to hear except Clarence and Michael.

Michael slowly turned, facing them and smiled.

"Hi, Mr. Angel Man." She waved. "Mommy says you dance with me in my dreams." Wide blue eyes pulled them in. Her innocent smile displayed missing teeth.

Michael nodded.

A woman came up behind the two and shushed them, pulling her cover-up together around her shoulders. "Don't talk to strangers, kids. Be nice." She glanced up. "We're praying for you, Sir." She scooted the kids back to the baby pool.

"Bye, Mr. Angel Man. See you tonight in my dreams."

Clarence stumbled almost to his knees. "P-praying for me." He blinked.

Michael reached for him, supporting his weight, one arm around his shoulders. "I got you, Clarence."

"She said she's praying for me." He shook his head. "I don't think I've ever heard anyone say that before." He glanced behind him as they walked away.

The woman was watching them. Smiling and nodding, as she towel-dried her hair.

The little girl waved.

Clarence wiped his face. "I'm okay. I … I just …." Deep breath.

"Where do you want to go now?"

"You sing with those kids at night?" Clarence grinned. "I thought you were with me at night."

"How do you know where I am? You're snoring."

"Got that right." One more glance back. "Well. Here's the old Boy Scout cabin." He stretched his hand. "This was built around the time I was born, if I remember right." He peeked in a window. "Used to have Scout meetings here."

The doorknob rattled.

Clarence looked down to see Michael's hand on it, wiggling it. Clarence peeked in a window, but the Boy Scout flags and tables there didn't bring the expected interest. He scanned the room again. Something …

"Locked." Michael cupped his hands around his eyes, peering through the glass. "Locked up tight. Maybe they don't meet here anymore." He checked the siding. "Pretty dilapidated." He rubbed his hand over it. "We should fix up this building." He picked at peeling brown paint and caulking around the window, then started down the hill, stooped to pick up an empty pop can and hooked a shot into the trash can.

Michael detoured to push kids on the swings. The swings screeched as the children pumped back and forth. Then he jogged to join Clarence on the road that circled the play area.

Clarence sidestepped a pile of dog poop. "Watch out." Weren't there dog laws nowadays? "The clipping said a pool in a cave. Where could a cave be around here?"

"Maybe the city bulldozed it." Michael stepped over the poop. "The city wouldn't just let a cave be open in town. Kids would fall in or get lost, somehow."

"That's how some drowned back then, I guess." Clarence stumbled as he checked the article. "A kid and a woman both drowned sometime before the assistant did." He stopped to read. "Hmm." He pointed to the article, then surveyed his surroundings. "A pool in the park." A foot bridge, below the Scout cabin, crossed the creek to another picnic shed to the right, closer to the railroad tracks. A monstrous cottonwood tree waved its leaves, sparkling in the sunlight, down below to the left edge of the park—right down by the railroad tracks and the creek. And another bridge. "Let's head down there."

Michael followed Clarence to the tree, then the bridge. He ducked under it. "What about here?" He kicked at some footings, and dirt gave way.

Clarence side-stepped down. "I can't believe kids wouldn't explore under here. If I was a kid, I'd be down here every day."

"Me, too. I love to explore." Michael stretched his arms wide. "Father's laboratory for you humans to enjoy."

Clarence skidded on some gravel, almost falling.

"You shouldn't be down here. What if you fall?"

"I'm okay Michael. Besides, I've got you." Clarence grabbed hold of a small tree growing from underneath the bridge as he climbed farther under. "Wouldn't it be something if we found that doctor's cave right here? First time out?"

Michael reached through some brush, yanking it out. A few dead branches trailed along, revealing a small opening.

"Could that be it?"

"Let me see." Michael took a branch, broke it to a foot long and began digging. "Seems pretty soft. Easy to dig."

Chunks of dirt and rocks fell in.

Clarence picked up a stick and helped Michael. The hole expanded to almost three feet across.

"Cool!"

Clarence almost jumped out of his skin and turned around, facing a boy about eight years old. "What do you want, kid?"

"What are you doing here?"

"We are doing a … scientific experiment."

"Cool!"

Damn. Wrong thing to say to a kid to scare him away.

"We are trying not to disturb a thousand-year-old piece of dirt. We are scientists, researchers who are studying … the life cycle of the boring, hard to see carbon … hopper."

"Carbon hopper? Cool."

"No, son." Clarence turned, waving the kid away. "You don't realize what it means. It's dangerous. We can't have anyone else around here, or the c-carbon hopper might run away." He ushered the kid up out of the creek bed and to the playground area. "Stay up here kid, if you know what's good for you."

The kid pointed. "You. You're that man from prison. Aren't you?" He cocked his head and stared Clarence down.

"Well, yes … I am." Clarence put on his mean face and the kid jumped back a few steps. "That's me and don't you ever forget it. Hear?"

The kid ran away, looking back at Michael. He glanced at Clarence only once after Clarence gave him a last growl send off.

"That'll keep him away. I didn't think about kids following us here."

Michael watched the boy run to a house adjacent to the park. "That was mean."

Clarence turned around and faced Michael. "How would you have done it?"

Michael gently picked Clarence up by the collar and lifted him over to the park bench and sat him down. "That's what I would have done."

Clarence gasped and tried to catch his breath, holding his chest, his eyes popping. "Wha? What? What was that?"

"That's how I would have done it. It scares them but doesn't hurt their feelings at all." Michael crossed his arms across his massive chest. "And they think I'm pretty cool after they recover, too."

Clarence growled at him. "You scared the waddin' right out of me. I can hardly breathe." He pounded his chest as his breathing slowly returned to normal. "I might have peed my pants."

There had been many a time in prison …

Michael smiled and hopped into the creek bed.

Clarence followed, a little slower, stepping carefully around rocks and clumps of weeds. Not even a trickle of water flowed through the cattails and grass. Dried hoof prints trailed the creek out of town.

Michael bent down under the bridge and looked into the hole. "We could almost crawl through." He stuck his head in. "Really dark. We'll need some kind of light." He turned to Clarence. "Got a flashlight?"

"No. You?"

"No. They say one should always carry a flashlight in their vehicle. I have one back at the Town Hall for when we work there."

Clarence poked his stick in farther. "Maybe we can just open it up more and that will—"

Michael did the same with another stick, until they had an opening about the size a man could fit through. Or a couple of dare devil kids.

Clarence stood and looked to where he had seen the kid run home. Sure enough, there were two now, standing outside the house watching Clarence and Michael. He slowly put his hand on Michael's arm. "We gotta do this when no one is around."

"What? Why?"

Clarence nodded his head toward the boys.

"Oh-oh."

"We'll have to come back when they are in school." Clarence said. "Wait, it's summer." He wiped his hands on his pants and crawled up the creek bank.

A rumbling of falling rock and dirt stopped him.

He jerked around to see Michael push through the hole and disappear. All that was visible were his shoes.

Clarence climbed back under the bridge and cautiously patted Michael's feet. "Hey buddy. I thought we were coming back when no kids were around. We don't—"

"It's cool in here." Michael's head and face appeared, dirt in his hair and on his cheek. "And I found your pool."

"Wow." Clarence crouched down. "Let me see." He scrambled for a stick to dig with, making the hole larger, but it broke, and he lost his balance. He fell into the hole, tumbling farther in. "Oh. Ow!" He grabbed at a rock. A tree sapling. Tuck and roll, like a football player—an old football player. Except, when he stopped rolling, his foot was wedged, oddly, into some kind of crevice, and his shoulder jammed against rock.

"Clarence! You okay?" Michael's body filled the hole, blocking the light. Sounds of him scrambling against the hard-packed dirt, the old timber support, roots.

For a moment, it was black. Clarence could barely see his hand, then something reflected. Just for a minute. Smelled like a dank basement, only fresher.

Water?

Something sprinkled onto Clarence's skin. Dirt he

guessed. From the fall. Something cracked. Rocks tumbled and hit his feet.

Finally, Michael pushed through the hole and light hit the surface of … a pool.

Clarence's gut lurched. How far down did it go?

Water sparkled when rocks plunked into the water surface. Circles expanded and flowed out to the edges.

Clarence coughed, holding his leg. "Yup. I think we found our pool."

FOUR

June 12, 1937 ~ Journal of Dr. Walter Stevens. Moved camper to Osceola Park, near the pool. Sat in open doorway of camper, drinking coffee, staring at the pool. A dove cooed. Couldn't find it in the huge trees. Pretty little area. Nice slope down to the creek. It'd be prettier if it was green rather than dried up. Nebraska humidity hasn't stifled fresh, clean air yet.

Question: why did water fill the pool, when the creek bed is cracked and flaked?

Question: what was so terrible that Henry was willing to give up life?

I must be tired. Last night, I unrolled my sleeping bag beside the pool. Was hoping … didn't sleep at all. Feeling disjointed. Need to write all this down while it's still clear.

Present Day ~ Michael bent over, bumped his head against the ceiling of the cave, knocking what seemed to be mineral deposits loose onto his shoulders and hair, stinging into his eyes. He brushed his shirt off and blinked. Felt like when he'd gotten sawdust in his eyes at the shop. He wiped the tears as he stepped toward Clarence's voice, feeling his way with his hand against the hard rock wall. When he touched the wall, his fingers stuck, freezing against the cold stone.

Strange. Underground rock wouldn't do that in winter, much less in early summer—especially in a cave. Painful cold. It would take more than blowing hot breath on his fingers to thaw them out. At least for human flesh.

He blew on them anyway. Warmth thawed his hand. White mist flowed and illuminated the space in front of him. The mist froze into slivers that hung in the air, until he swung his arm through them, and they scattered onto the water's surface. This felt suspiciously like—

"Hey Michael. Help an old man up." Clarence's voice reached Michael's ears from somewhere deeper in the cave, layering with an unearthly sound …

Buzzing. Different from the nurses' phones at Hillcrest.

Michael checked behind him, through the hole they had broken open, to the park. Maybe a mower or chainsaw. The truck was where they had left it.

It buzzed again, now more like a hiss. Like a tomcat hissing. Between a hiss and a growl. Like a herd of tomcats hissing and growling.

Time retracted into timelessness.

A brownish murk swirled above the water enveloping more white mist of Michael's breath hitting the cold air.

Strange sensation. The evil presence in the cave grazed Michael's human skin. He shivered as little bumps appeared across his arms, even in the dim light. Same feeling on the back of his neck. Interesting—residing inside two realms: the invisible realm and earthly realm. He knew what to expect in the invisible realm—comrades in the heavenly host, duties in the court of heaven, worship in the throne room. Oh, and demons. But the earthly realm was so unpredictable. He never knew what these humans would do.

"Michael?" Clarence's voice took on a growl, too.

As Michael's eyes became accustomed to the faint light, tiny specks could be seen hovering over the surface of the pool. He stepped toward Clarence.

Must be a breeding pool for mosquitoes. Or some other bugs. Was this earthly or …

Goosebumps again. He touched the wall. Freezing.

Putrid, sulphurous air choked him. He wiped his eyes.

Yup.

Demons. Demons masquerading as pretty fireflies.

They hovered above the surface of the water, like tiny mosquitoes—buzzing. Their minuscule wings reflected the limited light, flitting up and down. They swarmed together, layering with what Michael saw in the spirit realm—sick yellow eyes. They looked like bird swarms that rose and fell, gathering again into bubble shapes, morphing into one giant bird-like creature, hovering over the surface. The longer he studied them, talons became visible and grew, until razor-like edges appeared to cut the thickened air. Then they scattered again, into tiny beings.

Clarence, crumpled against the wall, slapped at one on his arm. "Damn mosquitoes." He flicked it away, wiping a trail of blood from where it had bitten him. He slapped again.

If Clarence only knew what he was hitting. The price of bug spray would be at an all-time high.

Michael slid on some gravel as he worked his way to where Clarence was sitting. "You okay Clarence?" He chuckled. "At least you're not a scaredy-cat." He'd heard that term somewhere—probably from Clarence.

Clarence held out his hand. "Is that a nice way of saying I should look before I leap? Or, am I just plain stupid compulsive?" He groaned as Michael pulled him up.

Michael brushed at Clarence's pants. "Did you hurt yourself? Break anything?"

Clarence slapped his hands away. "I'm okay. Uh … sorry." He toned his voice down. "I'm okay … thanks." He licked his finger and wiped away the blood on his arm. "This is the only blood I see. And it's mine."

Michael wrinkled his face. Maybe not all Clarence's blood—might be other blood mixed in. "Clarence? Maybe we should get out of here." This park and this cave especially, seemed to be a thin place—like a portal that demons and angels accessed. Probably part of the reason he and Clarence had been sent to Osceola. He glanced toward the cave opening. "Might be almost lunch time, you think?"

"A little blood isn't gonna get to me. You queasy, Michael? Do angels get nauseous?"

Michael tamped down the surge of anger. Images looped through his mind—images of bloody sacrifices in the temple, battlefields from the beginning of time, blood streaming down a cross. He closed his eyes, wincing, swallowed and drew in a deep breath.

"Okay. Now that we're down here, what do you want to do?"

"Explore!" Clarence took a step, but instantly his legs buckled, and his hand shot out to the rock wall.

Michael caught him before he fell. "Clarence, you're hurt."

"No. I'm okay." He pushed Michael away and jumped as he touched the rock wall again. "Wow! That's cold!" He turned to Michael. "See? Looks like frost on the walls. But … it's summer." He flapped his arms against his side. "It's really cold in here." As he flapped, demon spirits stirred, swarming in and out through the cave opening, some disappearing into the park.

Good-bye demons. Michael stretched to see the playground equipment just as the swarm enveloped a young mother and two kids. She evidently had seen them coming and had her bug spray out. She jumped up from the park bench and emptied the can into them. She cussed. Sprayed. Then cussed some more.

One by one, tiny creatures fell to the ground like dead flies. A putrid smell way worse than bug spray reached Michael's nose as a dirty orange vapor rose from the ground.

When the haze began to lift, the bug-like demons rolled together into one large demon—each tiny one molding together to form the scales, the extremities, the massive head. It jumped up on its legs, arms out in front, shaking—but plainly not from fear.

It shook its fists at Michael, then at the lady who had sprayed them. Language even Michael couldn't understand spewed from its mouth, along with greenish-brown spit. It shrieked and headed in the direction of the lady and kids.

Michael flinched. "Comrades! Up in arms!" He pointed toward the demon.

Two trees just up from the creek, shuddered. Branches, one on either side of the trunk, grew in girth. Limbs and leaves morphed into feathers on massive wings. A head appeared at the top of the trunk and all in one swoop, two angels charged the demon, swords flashing.

It never saw them coming.

"Michael what on earth are you waving at? More mosquitoes out there?"

Michael nodded. "You could say that." He turned to Clarence. "Ready to explore more of the cave?"

Clarence collapsed to the cave floor, scattering rocks as he landed. He looked up at Michael. "I think I broke my leg."

FIVE

June 12, 1937 ~ Journal of Dr. Walter Stevens ~ Thelma's Diner. I sat alone in a booth at Thelma's Diner, waiting for breakfast. Trying to capture all I can recall from yesterday and last night. And all that happened and was said at the diner earlier. Documenting everything. Just the researcher in me, I guess.

Also eavesdropping. Apparently, Henry's disappearance stirred up ugly memories of that pool.

The town fathers asked me to stay and delve into the pool mystery, but plainly, the townspeople want me gone.

Present Day ~ The backpack was heavier than usual, but not as heavy as Noell's heart. An iron skillet inside her backpack bounced against her in rhythm as she walked. Several copies of an herbal magazine cushioned mismatched dishes. Her face burned as she thought of what Gamma would say if she knew. She had no idea how long it would take to clear out Gamma's house if she packed out say, ten items, each time she left the house. Part of her knew she was stealing from Gamma. But part of her wanted to believe she was helping clear out what the years had dragged in.

The thrift store loved what she donated, and the little ladies there promised to never tell. It was for a good cause—the hospital, right? She was helping Gamma clean, right?

She loved the old smell of the thrift store. Loved digging through the books and even found one or two —usually fantasy or just a good story—a distraction from life.

Every once in a while, she found a treasure like the cup she was going to claim at Gam's. Another find had been a painting of a pool in a secluded area of a forest. Not a picture of water crashing and destroying lives, but of a serene, peaceful little lake. The trees almost hid the tiny pool, branches hanging low, protecting its secrets. She bought it and immediately hung it in her room beside her bed. Just enough below the lamp so it made a small vignette. Nice.

On the way to the thrift store, she passed right by the road's utility building. Huh. Wouldn't hurt to apply there. See what they had available, if anything. Wouldn't hurt. Besides, dirt she could handle—real dirt anyway.

The Roads Department building was pretty plain on the front. The only way you could identify it, was by the hard hat on the pole and the word "Roads." That was it.

She pulled the door open with her hand tucked in her hoodie sleeve. Her thumb slipped out and made contact with the metal handle.

Oh no.

She braced, knowing the chattering would begin.

Millions of voices raced through her mind, layer upon layer, like the season opener of the Husker football team. Deep voices. Women's. A child whimpering.

I hope they can repair that spot in the road. What kind of car is that? I think he likes me. I hate my life. Mommy, Mommy, you're hurting me.

Every conversation, every thought. Every comment, fear, joy, gripe of every person who had grasped that door handle transferred to Noell. Flooded her mind, her emotions.

Not now.

Not here.

Noell backed out of the open door and tore down

the steps. She skirted around the corner of the building and crouched on the ground.

Other people's germs. Gah.

Every person who had touched the door handle left cells or germs or fingerprints. Those zillions of molecules sucked through Noell's skin and traveled to her thoughts.

Faces populated her consciousness before she could grab sanitizer out of her backpack. She even recognized a few: the lady who worked at the drive-inn—the one who always took the money, a guy she had seen driving by Gam's house the other day—why she remembered him, she couldn't guess, a young woman half dragging a tiny whimpering girl. And Gamma? At the Roads Department?

Sanitizer. Sanitizer. She squirted some onto the palm of one hand and rubbed them briskly together. Whew. Voices slowed. Faces blurred and faded.

She still saw Gam.

Okay. Settle down. Go back in there. They might have a job opening for office clerk or something like that. She could run a copy machine.

She sucked in a deep breath and stood, checking the street and drive. She peeked around the corner.

Uh-oh.

Mr. Grimes, a neighbor from two houses down from Gamma's. At the Road's Department? Creepy old man.

Noell could see his kitchen window from her room upstairs at Gamma's. Some nights he would stand at his sink, washing dishes or getting a drink and look out his window at her. She knew he was. She could feel his eyes on her.

He walked stiffly with a walker too, like Gamma. No way she wanted to open the door after him. She knew what he was into.

One day, when she was younger, he had asked her to help with something in his house. "Come on into my house, little one. You can climb to reach something in my kitchen. I'll make it worth your while." He had lifted his walker, pointing it in the direction of his house. "I have ice cream and cookies for your reward." He held the door open, and she walked in past him. She got halfway through his entryway when she smelled it. Barely at first, but with each step, his scent became stronger. Eww! Stinky eggs.

She had spun around and bumped into him. As she scrambled under the walker and between his feet, his shoes gave off a dusty, reddish-brown mist. Gramps had taken Gamma and Noell to Arizona one year and the dirt was that same color.

She pushed off from his shoes and tore out the door. Why she had turned to face him again, she didn't know: maybe to see if he would actually drop his walker and race after her, or maybe to figure out what that red mist was.

Either way, a reddish-brown light began to glow from his body, faint at first, then more visible—just as the stench grew unbearable. An outline of something grew around him, rose above him.

Chills skittered up her arms.

A head formed, then a torso and long arms. Long legs.

She tried to look away as her heart pounded harder. She didn't want to look. She would have more bad dreams. She crouched—tried to look at the floor. Oh, for Gamma's arms around her.

Her feet had grown heavy as if someone was hanging from them. She used to sit on Grampa's foot and wrap her arms and feet around his leg, riding on his foot with each step, until he could no longer move.

Locked down to the spot.

The eyes. Terrifying. Something moved in those yellow eyes.

The being and Mr. Grimes stepped toward her.

Mr. Grimes had forgotten to use his walker when he charged after her. He yelled naughty things, threatened her and Gamma, to make her come back.

The creature stretched its arms after her.

She tried to scream, but only a gasp came out. Something unlocked her feet, and she fled. She made sure she never put her big toe in his yard again.

His scent had made her brain go crazy. It spiked

pictures she didn't want to ever see again. Over the top sensations until she threw up and had to shower to wash it all off.

After Gamma had promised she would kill Mr. Grimes if he ever came after her again, she had wrapped Noell in a big blanket and rocked her until she finally quit shaking and fell asleep.

Creepy old man. Dirty old man.

She turned toward the building entrance. Hurry up, Mr. Grimes.

When she peeked around the corner, he was doing his walker shuffle down the ramp. The last couple feet, he picked up the walker and stepped to his car trunk. He opened it and threw the walker into the trunk, slamming the lid. He hopped into his car and drove off.

Not. Going. In. Especially after him.

She'd rather work at the hospital emptying bedpans than go in after he'd been inside. Well … maybe not.

Maybe they needed help at the thrift store.

She carefully wrapped her sleeve around her hand and opened the door. No voices. No faces. Whew. No bell dinged either. No one was in the office. Smelled like cigarette smoke. Ugh. Maybe this wouldn't work.

"Hello?" she called.

No one came to the counter. Papers fluttered on

the counter, as the door closed behind her. A bulletin board against the rear wall proclaimed safety precautions. Someone's coffee cup had tipped over, draining the residue onto official-looking paperwork. Clear vinyl protected a calendar on the counter in front of her and if she cocked her head just right, she could read day-off requests that had been inked in red. One name was especially repetitive—Rat. What kind of a name was that?

She turned to leave when a truck skidded in and parked in front. A utility truck. Maybe this would work out.

The man walked in, talking on his cell phone. "Yeah, yeah. He escapes from there all the time. They say he grew up around here." He didn't even see her until he got to his desk, sat down, righted his coffee cup—wiping at the mess and happened to look up.

He jumped. "Oh, hello. I'm sorry." To the person on the phone he said, "Hey, I gotta go. There's a young woman … yeah, and I gotta go." He turned away from Noell. "Yeah, that's what I said. Gotta go. I'll call you later."

He tapped it off and stood. "Uh … sorry about that. We don't get many people in here." He gave her a sheepish grin. "May I help you?"

Noell cleared her throat and swallowed. "Yes. I … uh, am here to see about a job. Do you have any openings … for … anything? Outside?" She hesitated. "Even inside?"

"Not at the moment. We did have an opening but filled it last week. It usually takes a day to see if a guy," he cleared his throat, "or gal, will work out. He seems to be good, so far."

"Okay, well if you have anything could you let me know?"

"Why don't you fill out an application, so I have your info and all? Then if we have anything open up, like I said, we just hired a guy, but if anything comes around, we can give you a call." He walked to the desk and rummaged through a drawer, pulled out a sheet of paper and grabbed a pen. "Here you go. Why don't you come around here and sit at the desk and fill it out?"

"Okay. Sure." She followed him to the desk and sat in the office chair, scooting forward. Sliding her backpack off her shoulders, she forgot about the extra weight. It hit the concrete floor harder than planned and something broke. Oh no. Now she felt even worse about stealing Gamma's stuff.

She shook her head and settled in the space. A framed photo of a little old lady was displayed to the right of the coffee mess. Shoulder-length grey hair held back with a pink head band, brown eyes twinkled behind wire rimmed glasses, a joyful smile. Head held high—like a queen.

Noell smiled back.

He stared for a minute, seemed to realize it and went to the other side of the office, found a copy of the Polk County News and unfolded it.

Noell concentrated on the questions in the application. They were the usual: name, address, phone number. She pulled out her phone and tapped to the information she needed.

A question had her stumped. What experience did she have? Roads. She had never … plowed or cleared a road in her life. She mowed. She put that down. And weeded. She kept Gam's yard and flower gardens and vegetable gardens up very well. In fact, the neighbors always commented on how nice they looked, which earned them free flowers and tomatoes.

She filled in the rest of the information with the date she could start being … tomorrow.

"Um, I'm finished. What do you want me to do with it?" She clicked the pen shut.

"I'll take a look and see if I can read it." His eyes twinkled when he smiled. He looked it over, pointing at each answer, reading out loud. "Looks good, Noell. Hey, I'm Mr. Ivertson, but you can call me Steve." He reached out his hand. Thick hand and fingers.

Uh … no.

He waited.

Awkward.

She placed her hand in his. Strong grip. She liked him. Whew.

"Thanks Mr. … Steve. Thanks for your time."

"I'll look things over and if we think we can use you, I'll call."

The radio squawked alive. "Hey, Steve. We have a problem, man. New guy's down. He sprained his foot walking on a sidewalk, the klutz. We're taking him to the hospital now. Wanna get out the paperwork so's we can fill out the report when we get back?"

Steve rushed to the intercom. "Sure thing."

"Hey, we're gonna need to fill that position. This time of year, there's too much outside work for the road crews to do it all and you can't always help, with running the office. Just a thought. Might call the newspaper and put in an ad."

Steve looked over at Noell. "I don't think we need to get in a rush about it. We might have it covered."

"Hey Steve? What about your grandson … Brian? He's a brute."

Steve shook his head. "No. He found a job in Columbus."

"Okay. Well, if you have someone in your back pocket, go for it. But we had to wait long enough for this loser."

"Things have a way of working out, Bud." Steve leaned into the mike again. "Take care of the kid."

He nodded to Noell. "Ready to get to work? You're going to need work clothes, boots. We got the hard hat."

Noell stared. "Yeah. Yes. I'm ready. What time and where?"

He grinned. "Here, at 8 o'clock sharp."

"I'll be here." She started to wave. "Thanks. Bye."

"Thank you." He saluted.

As she closed the door behind her, she paused. He had saluted her. Like Grampa used to.

Later at home, Noell pawed through a pile of boxes on the old back porch. She slid one off the top of the pile and opened it only to find piles of folded fabric—all cotton plaid. She labeled the box: Plaid Farmer Shirt Fabric.

The next box held more of the same. She lifted off another box. A mouse scampered farther under the line of boxes, making her jump. Her skin crawled, fingers trembled. Blowing out a deep breath, she made herself open the next box. T-shirts. Orange. All new, but … old. One after another—all the same shirts. She unfolded the top one. Orange was the right color—but with black lettering: X Marks the Spot. What was Gam doing with a whole box of orange shirts from … X? What was X? Where on earth did she get these? Probably wasn't any use asking Gam because she wouldn't remember.

She pulled three out and held them up to her chest. Big, which was okay. The smell wafting from the one she held reminded her to wash them before she wore them. She tossed four toward the kitchen doorway. Might as well make use of Gam's plethora of supplies.

Another box off the pile. She'd never done this; she'd never gone through any of Gam's stuff. Probably okay to do it now when she needed it for work. Gam always told her to help herself. So, she was. More fabric—all corduroy—all black. Too bad it wasn't Halloween. Bet the school could use this. The magic marker squeaked as she labeled the box: Black Halloween Corduroy for schools. Might as well save time and label it now. You never knew.

The bottom box had printing on it. Men's work boots. Oh, if only.

She ripped it open.

Boots all right. Steel toed. All leather. These had to have been expensive. But the fact that they all had bright pink leather ankle inserts probably explained why they sat in a bottom box in Gam's hoarder house. She pulled out a pair and checked the size. Nine. The next pair was even bigger. Oh, please. The last pair—size eight. Yes!

Shirts. Boots. Now all she needed were jeans. She

pushed at another stack of boxes … annnnd boom! The stack came down around her, contents spilling, a muffled sound of glass breaking.

Oh-oh.

"Hon? You okay out there?" Gam's voice quavered from the living room. "Noell? You okay?"

"Yeah, Gam. Sorry I disturbed you. Just finding things for work and knocked over a stack of boxes." She whispered. "And maybe broke something."

Gam appeared at the door with her walker. She yawned.

"Oh, Gam. I'm sorry. I woke you."

"It's okay, Hon. I needed to wake up." She checked her watch. "Been napping for an hour. If I don't get up, I'll never sleep tonight." She ventured into the porch. "Did you find something you can use?"

Noell held up the boots. "Score!" She showed Gam. "See? These are just my size!"

"Pink, too, I see."

Noell laughed. "Well, I don't really care if they're pink, or purple or brown. But they are free." She glanced up at Gam. "I mean—"

"I have told you that anything in these boxes, or my house for that matter, is yours. I'm just glad you can use them."

Noell grabbed a shirt from the box. "And these shirts are just right."

"Kinda big, aren't they?" Gam tipped her head. "You don't have to look like a boy, do you?"

"They're fine, Gam. Works better for me if I do look like a boy. I'll be working with a bunch of men." She pushed the boxes into the narrow aisle and opened one. "Aww. Cute. Gam look. Little tiny cups and saucers." She held a set up. "What are they for? Tea parties?"

Gam frowned. "I don't remember." She reached for one. "They are cute. Is that what's in the whole box?"

Noell held up boxes of four more sets—all different colors. "Pretty much." One set matched a dish she still had in her backpack. Her face felt hot. Such a turmoil: she was sneaking things to the thrift store, and at the same time, Gamma said she could have anything here. She swallowed and carefully replaced the sets. "I'm glad they didn't break when I knocked everything over. I think something did, but not these."

"It's okay." Gam surveyed the whole porch. "I just don't know how this all happened. I can't remember half—more than half—the stuff in my house." She shrugged and looked up at Noell. "It's a sickness, I'm convinced."

"Maybe." Noell raised her eyebrows in sympathy. "Is it any worse that I am so germaphobic?" She pulled open another box. "Overalls?" She unfolded one and held it up. "Huge." She held another pair in front of her. "It'd be too weird if you had my size in here." She dug deeper, piling them on the floor. "Yeah! Here's one." She tugged it from the box. "And another."

"Throw 'em here and we can wash them."

Noell tossed them to land on Gam's walker.

"Nice shot," Gamma said.

"Is it okay if I—"

"You can have anything here you want. Make use of it." Gamma shrugged. "I keep saying it needs to be cleaned out. Maybe this is what will get me going on it." She sighed. "I don't know when all this happened. Your Grampa loved auctions, couldn't resist a sale." She dipped her head. "And then after he died, I guess I kept right on buying." She folded the overalls over the walker bar. "An auction here. Hardware store downtown had a going-out-of-business sale, and I'd go." She looked around the porch. "It's all useful … or … it was. To somebody."

Noell stepped over the piles and hugged Gam. "It's okay Gam. Look how it's helping me." She glanced over her shoulder. "I don't need the extra-large ones, but this is really saving me money." She hugged her again. "Thanks Gam. I'll help too. Okay? We'll do this together."

"Maybe guys at your work could use some of this."

Noell looked at the box of pink boots. "Well … some of it." She laughed. "We could start a new fad with those boots." She pulled at another box and laughed. "Gam, did you know I would work for the roads department?" She held up an orange work vest with stripes of reflective tape running up and down the vest. "Gam? A boxful!"

"I didn't know." She shook her head, a smug look on her face. "Maybe."

SIX

June 12, 1937 ~ Journal of Dr. Walter Stevens ~ Thelma's Diner. The doorbell—literally a bell— keeps ringing, as people keep coming in. A man across the aisle keeps repeating that the pool was of the devil. Over and over. Each time, someone shushes him. But he says it again. "The city needs to fill in that pool."

I'm not sure dirt will keep demons in.

A young boy, who appears to be about eight, in the next booth, keeps staring.

Terrifying.

The kid never blinks.

Present Day ~ Clarence leaned against the nursing home wall in the reception area, letting one crutch rest against his body. "I don't know how I get myself into these predicaments." Tears threatened but he wiped his whole face.

Deep breath. Push on.

Michael came in the door, carrying the hospital release bag of orders and meds.

Lisha walked up beside Clarence. "You want a wheelchair, Mr. Clarence?" She pointed down the hall. "Issa long way to your room."

"Naw. Naw. I got this." It was a long hall.

Something bumped behind his knees.

Carol. Wheelchair.

He sat. Never thought a wheelchair would feel so good.

Lisha propped his leg on the footrest, picked up his crutches and joined Michael, grabbing the bag. "This all they sent, Mr. Michael? No ropes to tie him in his bed? Keep him out of caves 'n stuff."

"Lisha!" Carol shook her head. "Give him some sympathy."

"Well, iss true. Need to lash him to his bed or his chair. Then he won't—"

"Enough!" Carol patted Clarence's shoulder.

"She's right." Clarence's chin jutted and his eyes burned. "Stupid old man. Stupid ideas."

"Aw, Clarence." Lisha stepped alongside the

wheelchair. "I didn't mean nothin' by it. Just kidding."

He worked his jaw side-to-side. "No. You're right. Stupid to think I can go into pools and caves. I just need to stay in my room and die." He stared straight ahead, nostrils flaring, eyes burning. He was barely able to lock in emotions.

An elderly, blue-haired woman squealed from her room. "Oh, Mr. Timmelsen! What did you do?"

Damn! He covered his eyes. If only he could disappear. Where was that time-travel stuff when a guy needed it? He motioned to Carol to keep moving, but she stopped.

He pulled himself up in the chair and gave a half-smile. "Hello Mrs. Martin." He patted his leg. "It's not broken. It's nothing serious. Just a splint." Damn it hurt. Sedative from the procedure must be wearing off. He wanted to kick himself. "I'll be all right."

Mrs. Martin mouthed an O in sympathy, as Carol pushed the wheelchair on by. "Uh, I'll tell Mrs. Hatly." She waved her frail hand. "She'll want to know."

Clarence ducked down. The gossip had begun.

He counted the rooms as they flew past, until his own. Mr. Wainwright's door was closed. Good. Good riddance.

At his room, someone had taped a "Get Well Soon" sign to his door. He grabbed at it but missed as they turned into his room. Balloons hung from his mirror, and a lone cupcake sat on a Happy Birthday party plate. No candle. No party.

As they crossed the threshold, a strange foreboding invaded Clarence. He had partly been kidding about wanting to die—just wanted sympathy. But … something felt off in his room. A darkness settled over him, fear maybe, or maybe his leg hurt, but his rooms felt different. He hadn't even been gone a day.

"Looks like someone set up a welcome home party." Carol parked the wheelchair next to the bed and locked the brakes. "Staff must have closed up your room when they cleaned this morning." She opened the blinds and the window. "Needs some fresh air and sunlight."

Sunlight helped brighten the room up a bit, but still, there was something wrong in Hillcrest room 204.

Carol leaned in. "And you aren't going to die. It's not even that bad of an injury, as injuries go." She checked his pulse and blood pressure. "Good as new." She brushed his shirt off and checked his arms. "I want you to take a shower."

Clarence Timmelsen burst out laughing. "You want me to what? I just get back from the emergency room and you say I need a shower? They washed my face and my leg in the hospital." Clarence slumped. "I'm gonna die, anyway. I won't need a shower when they shove me in the ground."

Carol backed out the door.

"No. No!" Clarence fumbled with the wheelchair. "Damn! Damn, damn." He stretched his hand to Carol. "Don't leave me with her!"

"Oh, wah." Lisha Hall crossed her arms across her ample chest, a glint in her dark brown eyes. Her ever-moving hips circled to the tune of "I'm in charge here, and I don't care what you have to say about it!"

He found the wheelchair brakes and released one. "I don't need a bath. Go get Mr. … uh, who was the guy that was shitting in my toilet when I first got here? Go get him. He probably still stinks."

"He died last week." She reached up and yanked at his hair, grown longer over the month. "Hair's greasy. An, watch your mouth! This ain't no prison!" She pinched a brown nose with her fingers, her pinkie waving. "There is a smell in here that is worse than your favorite cheese."

He glanced at a table in the corner of the room and scrunched his face. The paper plate of leftover cheese and crackers had only been sitting out for a few days. "It's the cheese, I swear. Michael didn't finish it up."

"That cheese don't smell like BO!" She shook her head. "You gettin' baptized! I get to legally drown you!" She pointed toward the door. "You're comin' with me!"

"Isn't there some kind of nursing home policy that states that this is my home, and I don't have to do anything I damn well don't want to?" He stuck his face in hers.

Her mouth twitched back and forth. "Yaa know, you don't look like you're eighty, but I could hep you get there." Dreadlocks tied at the back of her head, shook like a limp Raggedy Ann doll.

He twisted his lips to the side. Not gonna laugh. Not gonna. Tears threatened as he eyed her size twenty-something aide uniform, pink elephants frolicking all over it as she bumped her other hip up for emphasis.

"Dontchu laugh, Mr. Clarence."

He snorted.

"Dontchu even. I'll have to wrap my stethoscope around your neck and tie it tight."

He covered his mouth. Oh, he loved this goofy woman. But if she ever found out, he was dead, like in stink dead.

He turned to look one more time—maybe she'd quietly left the room. She stuck her tongue out and grinned that toothy big-mouth grin. He lost it. "I'll go. Just gather my stuff, okay?" He poked his finger at her. "When I get back, you can help me put my journals and stuff away." He glanced at the stack of boxes.

She looked at his leg. "I'll help. Now, let's go!"

She gathered soap and towel and washcloth from the bathroom, clean underwear, and socks from his chest of drawers and dumped it all on his lap.

She steered him into the hall and almost ran into Harold Dexter. She grabbed him just in time, before he toppled over his walker.

"How are you doing, ole buddy? She round you up for a shower, too?" His hair dripped onto the shoulders of his plaid shirt; his little up-side-down American flag pin sparkled. He sniffed the air. "You don't stink. Much." He raised his hand high in the air. "Hey, sorry to hear about your leg."

Clarence slapped Harold's hand above his head as he passed him. "It's okay. Hey. Come over later."

"I can do that." Harold fumbled with the flag. "Maybe then we can shoot a round of pool?"

Clarence glanced at his leg. "Sure. We'll see how it goes."

Lisha prodded Clarence from behind. "No pool for you if you don't get a shower."

Harold pushed his walker ahead. "She gonna drown you, Clarence?"

"She thinks she is. She doesn't know it, but when I get in there, I turn the faucet on and just sit on the stool and watch the water run down the drain. Then I splash a little on me." He grinned. "She never knows."

Harold laughed. "You slick dude, you. Then rub in some soap behind your ears and you're good."

Clarence high-fived Harold again. "You got it buddy. That's my cologne."

Lisha sniffed the air. "Huh. Must be why Harold here, always smells better than you do with his aftershave. What's it called Mr. Harold? Wet Dog? Cain't 'member."

"Ouch! I'll remember you when it's time for Christmas gifts."

"You'll forget all about it come Christmas. With your mind, the way it's goin'."

Lisha opened the door to the shower and pulled a trash bag out of her pocket. "Git your pants off and I'll wrap your leg. Gotta keep it dry." She turned her back and counted, "One-Mississippi, two-Mississippi. Ya done yet?"

He stripped and wrapped a towel around himself. "I'm done. Let's get this over with."

She wrapped the plastic over the bandage and taped it.

Just before he closed the door, he stuck his tongue out at her. Then he closed it and locked it.

The doorknob rattled.

"I can get a key, Mr. Clarence. You old …"

He started the shower. Ahh, quiet. She could yell but not loud enough to be heard over the running water. He started to push out of the chair, then remembered the brakes. He pulled himself up by the grab bars and stood under the hot water. He was dirty. This was so much better than those open showers at the prison. You could never relax there. You never knew who was going to sneak up and ….

He worked his jaw back and forth, teeth grinding. His stomach clenched.

He gripped the bar of soap so hard it slipped out of his hand and hit the shower wall.

Slow down, Clarence. Breathe. You're not in prison anymore.

He held onto the grip bar, picked up the soap in the washcloth and got wet. It hadn't been so bad toward the end, but when he first got to prison—the memories almost brought him to his knees—even now, sixty years later. God, he shouldn't be alive today.

That was when he had learned to keep to himself. Never trust anyone. Even the guards. Well, some guards. Lester had been the one guard who would somehow always show up when Clarence was in trouble.

Clarence would find himself surrounded by huge, evil inmates.

Threatened.

Terrified.

And Lester would appear, beat stick in hand, eyes darting from face to face.

Clarence could never quite figure out why the inmates backed off. Lester was stocky but a full head shorter than most.

If they didn't back off right away, Lester would side-step the biggest inmate to the nearest wall and press the beat stick against the man's neck until he relinquished. Pipsqueak, the squealer of the gang, would always scream in a high-pitched voice, "Call off your angels, Lester. They be choking me!"

Angels? Michael was an angel, but … Clarence had never seen him do the stuff Pipsqueak had screamed about.

He lathered up. White soapsuds slid away from the palms of his hands, revealing ropy scars. He'd been burned bad twice. Once right after his mom had died. Then again just a few weeks ago. They were still tender.

Strange. He'd been so completely focused on saving little Bea he had hardly felt the slide poles burning his hands. Seemed like a lifetime ago. That little girl and her mommy had claimed a huge piece of his heart.

He turned off the water and toweled dry. Patted his belly as he dressed. He needed to get a treadmill. Or walk more. He looked at his plastic-wrapped leg —when it was better. They'd never had desserts at prison like they did here. Brownies. Angel food cake with glaze. Apple crisp—his favorite.

How could Pipsqueak see Lester's angels? Why could Clarence see Michael? Not everyone could. Well, the nurses and women sometimes seemed to—called him irresistible.

Little Bea could see him—angel costume and all. She was just sweet. That had to be why.

But Pipsqueak? He was not.

Michael half-smiled.

Clarence had no clue.

Michael had parked the truck and taken him into Hillcrest. Poor guy. Michael had never broken or sprained legs, arms, anything as a human, but from what he could see, it hurt. Clarence was in pain. He never even noticed when Michael left.

Of course, that was no fault of Clarence's. Most people never thought about the supernatural, or the invisible realm.

Maybe someday, he'd let him in on the … secret. He chuckled to himself.

No secret, except to those who didn't believe.

The one's who did wouldn't be surprised. Well, maybe some would be and maybe a little.

Free of that grinding little vehicle. He didn't want to complain, but he wasn't used to limitations or re-strictions on his movement.

The only restriction he relished in was following the Father's love. Wherever Father moved, he would go too.

He stood a minute, closing his eyes.

Yeshua. Firstborn of all creation. Prince of Peace. Creator of mankind.

He lingered, wings unfurling, soaking in the Father's wealth of love. His spirit soared, lifting him into the atmosphere. The rush of exhilaration caught him off guard today. Probably because he had been in human form almost past his tolerance. Just about outside of his province of Father's protection.

Deep sigh.

He floated back to the ground, and his wings faded.

A wide-eyed kid stared as he walked by, following a woman. She stopped at a doorway, and he bumped into her. Michael chuckled at the stories he would tell his mom. Poor kid.

It happened a lot. Some kids were still so pure that the other realm was very visible to them. They hadn't been abused or so affected by the world—yet.

Michael connected on a regular basis with a couple of kids. Their sweet spirit was refreshing and a joy.

He laughed just thinking about one little girl who, whenever she saw him, broke out in dance. Swirling and kicking and jumping. Sometimes she got into trouble, because of course Mommy or Daddy didn't see him. Or it happened in a place where she shouldn't be dancing, according to the rules.

Time was short. People didn't know.

But she did. She knew to dance while dancing was still allowed.

Michael didn't know the future—it wasn't for angels to know.

But.

He could see that the earth was becoming more evil. Every day it grew darker and darker. People became more corrupt. Cruelty abounded.

Just thinking about what he saw people do to each other, no matter what culture, nationality, or faith, made Michael cringe and tear up.

Nation against nation. Father against son. Son against father. Neighbor against neighbor and friend against friend.

How Father's heart grieved.

SEVEN

June 12, 1937 ~ Dr. Steven's Journal ~ Breakfast at Thelma's Diner. Every seat is occupied. Overalls and jeans. Suits. House dresses. Every walk of life. All seated in protest to my presence. I came unglued. "What are you looking at?" I startled even myself. I leaned over my plate of eggs and bacon, poured syrup over all of it, making a lake to dip my toast in.

At that point I'd had enough of the stares and whispers. Felt like I was back in the classroom when students were thinking about the weekend binge and their college plunderings, instead of the lecture I'd worked hard to prepare.

My stomach growled and so did I. I cut my eggs, dipped the bite in syrup and just about got it to my mouth. But the staring and loudly whispered comments pressed at me. I dropped the fork on my plate. The clatter brought everyone to attention.

Huh. I should use that in the classroom. Drop a fork on a plate.

"Okay." Really loud. Louder than in a lecture.

A woman somewhere shushed me.

"These people don't care if I yell." I stood up and walked the aisle between my booth table and the counter. "You people are nosy and want to know what I am finding, so I'll tell you."

Present Day ~ Noell opened a couple cans of vegetable beef soup, dumped the contents into a sauce pan and turned up the heat under the pan. Had she eaten lunch?

Gams sat at the kitchen table, flitting through grocery ads. "Man, the cost of bottled water has gone up. I might have to start filling my own."

Noell rolled her eyes. "Gam—"

"Now don't start. I know it costs less if I fill my own."

"You can just drink out of a glass."

"Listen to you, Miss Picky Face."

Noell looked down at her new white slippers.

Gam cleared her throat and flipped pages.

Noell glanced around the kitchen. Coupon boxes were piled next to the stove. They didn't hold coupons, they held money. Cookbooks were stacked floor to ceiling—all along the outside wall—not just one stack but lining the whole wall. Gam said it added insulation. She said she'd get around to reading them … someday.

She and Gramps had had a good time going through them and trying recipes. Probably that was the main reason she hoarded them—because she couldn't have him.

There were days when those walls pushed in on Noell.

Today was one.

Gotta get her own place.

And not argue with Gamma.

She sprinkled salt and pepper over the soup in the pan and added a handful of shredded cheese to melt as she stirred. She opened the cupboard door and chose two bowls. Funny, the insides of the cupboards were clean and orderly. "Oh, I saw Mr. Grimes at the Roads Department. He is so creepy."

Gam stirred. "He didn't come on to you or anything, did he?"

"I didn't even talk to him. I hid when I saw him and didn't go in until he left, but—"

"If he ever touches you, I'll kill him." She

pointed to the 22 rifle propped in the corner behind the back door.

"Gam, you—"

Gam looked at Noell, a determined look on her face. "I'm serious. I can shoot that thing. At least I used to. I used to be a crack shot. Just ask your grandpa …"

"Oh, Gam." Noell hugged her and kissed her forehead. "You still miss him."

"Terribly. Seems like yesterday he … we were cooking. Laughing." She sighed and turned the page on the flyer she was reading. "When he was here, we did everything together." A tear slipped down her cheek. "I hope and pray you find a man just like Grandpa."

Noell smiled and stirred the soup. "Me too."

"Say, could you hand me that list above you there? The one with the pink hippo on it?"

Noell reached above the stove and picked through the papers, coupons, and general clutter on a small shelf. Old mail, used stamps, old lists. "Where? I don't see a hippo on anything." As she moved things on the shelf, she knocked an old pencil stub into the soup pan. "Argh. No! That's nasty."

"Honey, just fish it out and it'll be fine. We can still eat the soup."

She removed it with a slotted spoon. "No. I'll have to start over. That's nasty."

"It's okay. Just turn up the burner. The heat will burn out the … germs."

Noell shuddered. "Seriously?" She choked, dropped the spoon. Ran into the bathroom and slammed the door. She knew she was loud, and Gamma heard, but she couldn't handle the fact that she might be ingesting germs and eraser crumbs. You couldn't wash that off—or out. The thought made her retch even more. Her eyes watered, her mouth watered. She grabbed a clean washcloth from the linen closet, rinsed it in warm water and wiped her eyes, her face. She breathed deeply as she looked at herself in the mirror above the sink. Busy geometric wallpaper surrounding the mirror made her dizzy. Her eyes crossed and she gasped as her legs crumpled. She fell to the floor, knowing she was going down, arms flailing to prevent a fall against the hard porcelain toilet, sink or bathtub.

"Noell? Noell honey? Are you okay?"

Gram's voice became fainter, then louder.

She opened her eyes and saw huge beings behind Gam—all smiling down at her, long flowing hair, so she almost couldn't see their features, their eyes gleaming.

She wanted to dance as she looked at them, but she blinked and they were gone. "Gam, did I hit my head?"

"No dear, thank God." She patted her chest. "You could have so easily, in that tiny bathroom."

Noell looked around her. She sat on Gam's favorite furniture—the Italian leather sofa. "How did I get in here?" She tried to sit up, but Gam pushed her down. "Did you carry me all the way in here? Gam?"

Gam laughed. "Oh, my sakes no. The paper boy came by just at the right time. He heard me scream and ran in. He carried you in here. He's," she turned in her chair, "where did you go, son? Well, for Pete's sake, where did he go?"

A guy peeked into the living room from the front porch. "Uh … here Ma'am. Didn't want to interrupt."

"Come on in, and you're not interrupting anything." Gam ushered him in with her arm. "Meet my granddaughter. She's awake and can't believe you carried her in here."

Noell lifted her head slightly. "Hi. Thanks for helping me. I'm surprised you could," she really looked at him—trim, fit, muscled out, "lift … me. You're a paper boy? You look more like …" She checked Gam. "Well, thanks."

He was blushing. "Glad to help. Just happened along at the right time, I guess."

"Would you like something to drink … or …" She sat up, making both him and Gam jump.

"Don't you think you should rest, honey? Just lay

back and rest while we get you something to drink." Gam pushed out of her chair and sank back down. Second try, she stood and was able to stay standing, arranging her jeans and shirt. "What can I get you?"

"Water would be fine, Gam." She rushed ahead. "But, could it be—"

"I know. One of my store-bought water bottles. Sure baby." She sat her walker down in the direction of the kitchen. "Anything for you, sir?"

He shrugged. "Sure. I'll take a water. Please."

Gam shuffled out to the kitchen.

Noell glanced at him.

He cleared his throat. "My name is Fletch, Fletch Anderson. What's yours?"

"Noell Carpenter. Nice to meet you."

His eyes flitted about the room, bouncing on every pile, each stack of boxes. They rushed back to hers like a scared puppy first meeting the neighbor's Rottweiler.

Her neck was on fire. Her stomach clenched. "I'm sorry … for this …" She swallowed. "It's … well … it's kinda messy."

He waved the apology away. "It's okay. It's easy to see that your grandma can't do it all herself. It's a lot to take care of, a house is."

She gathered her courage. "Where do you live? Close by?"

"I do. I live on the other side of Mr. Grimes." He smiled.

Cute. Blond hair trimmed up front and sides, longer in the back. Filled out his T-shirt.

"The old house with the black front brick. Black brick is kinda unusual, so you probably remember seeing it." He blushed again.

Even cuter.

"I do remember it. Nice old house."

He nodded. "I like it. Uh—"

"Here we are. Sorry it took so long, but I remembered the cookies I baked." Gam pushed the walker ahead. A bag dangled from it that held the water bottles. She offered one to Noell and one to Fletch.

"Thank you, Mrs. … Um, I'm sorry Ma'am. I didn't get your name."

"Oh, people just call me Gam." She sat down with a grunt. "I'm Gwendolyn Randolph Carpenter." She wrinkled her nose. "Gam is just fine." She jumped. "Oh, the cookies." She reached into the walker basket, retrieved a plastic lidded container, and opened it.

"I'm hungry." Noell jumped. "Gam! The stove! The soup!"

Fletch waved her back down. "It's okay. I turned it off. Nothing burned."

"Whew! Thank you, Fletch." She hesitated. "You

want to stay for supper? We're having … soup." She eyed Gamma. "Maybe."

He smiled. "I really should be getting back to my paper route. People get mad if their paper isn't on time." He stood and held up the water bottle. "Thanks for the water."

"Wait! Here're some cookies for the road!" Gam held out the container.

He grabbed a couple. "Thanks. Gotta run." He held the container for Noell to reach into, and hesitated. "Sometime maybe we could … go for a walk or take in a movie … sometime."

Noell took a cookie and tapped it against the container. "Sure. Sometime. A walk would be fun … fine … sometime."

Fletch smiled and took a bite. He looked for a place to set the container down, then handed it to Gamma. "See ya then." To Gam. "Thanks for the cookies." He mumbled through crumbs. "They're great. We don't … bake … cookies." He held the water bottle high. "And the water."

"You're sure welcome. Come back anytime— even when you don't have to deliver papers."

"Thanks. I will." He left by way of the front porch and stumbled into a stack of cardboard boxes.

"He's nice. A nice young man. And he rescued you." Gam raised her eyebrows.

"Shhh. Gam, he can hear you." She half stood, stretched. "He isn't even out the door yet."

The front door squeaked as it closed.

Noell blew out a breath. She'd hardly talked to guys she knew in school, much less a total stranger. "Can we just have cookies for supper? I feel like the whole day is upside down now. How can everything go crazy all of a sudden?"

EIGHT

June 12, 1937 ~ Dr. Steven's Journal ~ Thelma's. Stood up for myself. Made a woman cry. Never a good day when you make a woman cry.

I turned to the packed diner, hands on my hips. "I was just traveling through town with my assistant—with Henry. We were exploring your little demonic cave when he drowned there. I have no idea what is in your pool that would make three people disappear. I'd like to know, too."

I brushed crumbs out of my beard. "What your town fathers failed to research was that the one they now called on to check this all out—me—is in fact, just a professor of agriculture at the University of Nebraska in Lincoln." I growled again—felt good. "I'm not even a hydrologist. He studies water." I pounded my chest—a little dramatic, I admit. "I study ... dirt!"

One man snickered.

I pointed directly at the man. "Exactly. I study dirt and how to make things grow." I took my wallet from my back pocket and slipped a card out. "Here are my credentials." I even waved the card in front of Snicker man's face and a few others, including the waitress as she poured coffee. "See? What's it say on this University Staff card?"

The waitress leaned in to read the card, dripping steaming coffee onto a huge man in open-air overalls; the sides flapped open to reveal his fat belly. "Professor of Agriculture," she said.

"Hey! That's hot!" The man rubbed his hand. "Watch it!"

Either she was oblivious to burning a customer or didn't care. She nodded to the people in the diner. "That's what it says, all right."

"So, in your estimation, does a Professor of Agriculture—meaning a guy who teaches about dirt and seeds?" I hesitated and thought a minute. "Crops and growing things." I took a breath, hoping to gain the sympathy of a few farmers. "Does what I do have anything to do with a pool that magically swallows people and doesn't let us find them to bury them?"

"Yes. Yes, it does." A woman, sharing a booth with a simply dressed man, spoke up. "It does." She swallowed, never made eye contact, and never stopped stirring her coffee. "We have enough goin' on here with farmin' so bad." She looked around the diner, then her eyes pierced mine. "Have you ever been in a dust storm, Mr. Professor? You ever been in dust so thick you can't breathe?" Her eyes welled up. "And Mr. Professor … why, with this drought, would a pool be filled with water?" She jumped from the booth and pushed past me, her hands covering her mouth. Sobbing.

Present Day ~ Michael hovered between Clarence in the shower and Mr. Wainwright's room.

The demon in Mr. Wainwright was stirring. It must sense that the body it inhabited was not the best choice for taking over Hillcrest … or the world, if it got that far. The old, wrinkled and badly aged body was close to shutting down. And look out Hillcrest when that happened.

That was a tough moment for an angel.

If humans only knew.

Clarence turned off the water in the shower, unaware of Michael's presence.

Michael chuckled as Clarence spewed a few choice words. Must be tough to dry off, dress, and stay standing—all with an injured leg. Clarence was very sturdy, normally, and had kept strong and active in prison, shaming younger men when he ran on the treadmill or outside in the enclosed courtyard.

Lisha stopped by the door and listened. She shook her head and chuckled when Clarence erupted with a few more words. "Musta dropped his sock." She tried the doorknob, then knocked. "You okay in there, Mr. Clarence?"

"How the hell do you think I am? My leg hurts. I'm in a nursing home." Pause. "And I dropped my sock in the water."

Michael smiled. Goofy man. Goofy, goofy man. Been through some stuff, that's for sure. Only Father knew the outcome of this man's life.

Michael always had known kids and animals could see him. But why Clarence? This guy was not pure in heart. Not anymore.

"Well, pick up your sock then, Mr. Clarence." Lisha faked a sob and rattled the doorknob. "I can't hep you if you don't unlock this door."

"You don't care," Clarence said. "I just hurt my leg."

She patted her hefty chest. "Oh, be still my heart. I'm cryin' for you. It's not broken—you're just saying that to get sym-path-y." She pounded on the door. "Now open this door, or I can't hep you!" She reached in her pocket and drew out a key just as the door opened.

Clarence stood in the doorway, hair plastered

against his head, his favorite Led Zeppelin T-shirt on backwards. The plastic bag from his leg was on the wet floor beside the wheelchair.

A young high school med aide, Tandy, walked by carrying a glass of juice.

"If that's fo Mr. Wainwright, you're gonna need a straw." Lisha took the damp towels from Clarence.

Tandy smirked and drew a straw from her pocket. "Oh. One of these?"

Lisha squinted. "Little Miss Smarty Pants."

"Well, at least I'm little." Tandy bumped up her hip in imitation of Lisha.

Clarence chuckled. "Wonder where she learned that." He bumped up his hip, holding onto the grab bar to keep his balance.

Lisha backed up. Her eyes popped so big there was white all around the iris.

Clarence sat in his wheelchair. "Michael. Here it comes." He covered his face. "Thar she blows!"

Michael couldn't help himself. Laughter bubbled up from his gut and burst out his mouth.

"I've never heard you laugh before, Michael." Clarence chuckled. "You should do it more often."

Michael laughed again. "I'd just get you in trouble."

"Who's Michael?" Tandy swiveled on her heel. "Who laughed just now?" Goosebumps dotted her arms. The straw sailed to the floor.

"Aw. Are you scared Little Miss Smarty Pants?" Lisha patted her back with an extra push toward Mr. Wainwright's room.

Tandy stumbled but righted herself. "I'm going to report you, Lisha. You'll be sorry you pushed me." She picked up the straw.

"Oh, I'm scared o you." She turned to Clarence. "Come on Mr. Clarence. Let's get you to your room, so's you can lay down."

Michael stood in the hall between Clarence's door and Mr. Wainwright's. He watched Lisha help Clarence to his bed and at the same time he could see Tandy drop the straw into the juice and hold it to Mr. Wainwright's mouth.

Keys jingled from down the hall. The maintenance guy stopped and checked his clipboard. He circled something on the paper and entered Mr. Wainwright's room. "Here to check the blinds."

Tandy glanced up and grinned. "Really? He has been complaining that they're broken."

The maintenance guy shook his head. "Ha. Ha."

She focused on Mr. Wainwright. "Here Mr. Wainwright. Take a sip of juice." She sighed. "So sad." She dripped some onto his lips. "Bet he can't even taste this."

"Bet he can't even hear you." The maintenance guy tapped the window, pulled the blinds up and down. "Seem okay to me." He checked it off his list. "You're Tandy, aren't you?"

"That's what the name tag says." She stuck her tongue out. She read his, wrinkling her nose. "Carl. Somebody must have hated you to name you Carl."

"Hey! I like my name." He checked the chest of drawers and pulled the top drawer open, digging through the contents with his pen. He hooked a gold pocket watch and pulled it out, the chain entangling with a string. "Jackpot." He slipped it into his pocket.

Mr. Wainwright's eyes moved as Michael drew near the door to his room. He began gurgling and spitting the instant he saw Michael.

Carl pulled the watch out. "Think he knows?"

Tandy shook her head. "Naw. He'll never know. He's almost dead anyway. I heard the nurses talking about him. They can't figure out what's keeping him alive."

Carl dropped the watch back into his pocket and fished around in the drawer again.

Michael entered the room.

Carl looked up. "You feel something? Something just changed in here."

"Well yeah, stupid." Tandy wiped her hand on a tissue. "I just felt something. He just spit on my hand."

"What's going on with that guy?" Carl tried to follow where Mr. Wainwright's eyes went. "It's like he can see something." He flopped the clipboard against his hip. "There's nothing there."

Michael stood next to the bed.

The demon rose up from the upper part of the body and glared at Michael. "You leave them alone. They're my new recruits and you can't have them. They have a flair for the boss's ways."

Michael stood his ground. "Father has a claim on them and no matter what you do, they are His."

Tandy froze. "What did you say?" She stepped away from the bed.

"Nothing. I didn't say anything." Carl patted his shirt pocket.

"They are mine!" The demon roared. Mr. Wainwright's body heaved several inches off the bed with the force.

Michael slowly shook his head.

"Mine!"

Carl shuddered. "What? What's going on here?"

Tandy shivered and dropped the juice. "Did … did you see that?" The glass bounced off the vinyl flooring, and juice splattered against the wall. She ran from the room.

Carl followed her.

Lisha rushed to the hall. "What's going on here? What's all the ruckus?"

"He's … he's possessed." Tandy threw the straw and ran.

Michael calmly walked from the room and stood beside Lisha.

She took a deep breath and entered Clarence's room, hung up the towel and checked her list. "I don't know why, Mr. Clarence, but when I'm with you I want to smack you on the forehead, but then I want to hug you."

"Don't you smack me. I'll smack you right back." He glanced at Michael. "Besides, Michael is here, and he'll get you if you hurt me. Right Michael?" Clarence crossed his arms.

"Oh, really. Well, you tell your Michael that I'll smack whoever I wanna smack." She poked the air, unknowingly stabbing Michael in the ribs.

"Tell him yourself. You're tickling him right now," Clarence said.

She poked Michael again. "Ha. Ha."

Michael laughed.

Taking a step back, Lisha's eyes grew huge. "You weren't laughing." She checked the room, patting her chest. "And I wasn't, either." Poking Michael again. "Then who was? There's nobody here but you and me."

Michael patted her shoulder. "You're doing a great job, Lisha, taking care of these people. Especially Mr. Clarence."

Lisha teared up and listened. "Did you …?" She sucked in a ragged breath. "Right now, I feel like I did when my big brother was alive and he told me I was bein' a good girl. Atta girl time. How?"

Clarence glanced from Lisha to Michael.

Michael nodded.

Back to Lisha. "Well. Maybe you did get an atta girl. But from M-Michael."

NINE

June 12, 1937 ~ Dr. Steven's Journal ~ I watched the woman through the window as she ran to a pickup truck. She hopped inside and slammed the door.

Oh no.

"Was that? Was she family of one of the …?"

The man who had been sitting with her slowly stood and turned to face me. He towered over me and I'm very tall and lanky. He walked right up to me and stopped, his chin at the top of my head.

"Our son drowned in that pool." His Adam's apple bobbed up and down. His jaw flexed. He stabbed me in the chest with his skinny finger.

I stepped back with each stab, until I was backed into a table.

"And I don't care if you deliver babies, I want you to find my boy … er … find out what happened to him down there." His feet were planted at fighting stance as he talked. His fists clenched. Then he pointed to the truck outside. The woman must have been hiding on the seat, but she could still be heard.

I swallowed and straightened—pulled myself up to as much height as I could muster—still only eyeball to buttons on the man's shirt. I glanced at the truck, then up at the man in front of me.

One-by-one, I met eyes with each person now standing, surrounding the man. Every eye was upon me. This was one community I didn't want to disappoint. The atmosphere was sparking. Emotions stabbed little arrows toward me from each person in the diner, making goosebumps rise on my skin.

I couldn't blame them.

I grabbed my straw hat from the bench seat. "I'll try to find the boy. But just so we're clear on one thing—I don't know anything about doing this and I can't promise anything. I can't promise I'll find his … him. I can't promise anything." I adjusted the toothpick in my hat band. "Are we clear?"

The man relaxed and lowered his fists, nodding. "Clear."

The people gathering behind him all nodded.

"Clear."

"Agreed."

A small-boned woman waved her hand from in

back of the crowd. They parted. She was standing on a bench seat. "Just one thing, sir. If I may."

I nodded. "Yes, Ma'am."

She stepped onto the floor and walked toward me. "My sister drowned in that pool, too." She blinked away tears. "Could you find her too?"

I blew out a breath and stared at her, then glanced outside toward the truck. I slowly nodded with each word. "I'll do my best." I breathed deeply. "I just may die trying, but I'll … I'll do … we'll do what we can."

Present Day ~ Clarence woke. Prison didn't allow naps unless an inmate was sick. He was in trouble … but wait. This wasn't prison. This was the old people's home. There was his calendar proclaiming Hillcrest Homes. Must have been sleeping hard because he felt like he was trapped inside a prison cell. Time to get … he groaned. Leg. Ow.

Stupid to hurt it. Stupid to go in that cave. What had he been thinking? He was not a sixty-year-old man anymore.

He would stay in his room. Stay in bed.

Die.

He slowly rolled over, away from the wall, pulling on the restraining bars. "I hope this heals fast.

They should have cut off the damn leg." He rubbed his eyes.

"Hello, Clarence." A raspy voice greeted him from across the room.

Clarence's eyes popped open. Heat burned up his torso. He shuddered as every nerve in his body screamed "run."

Mr. Wainwright stared back at him from the love seat. Grinning. Black eyes snapping. He tossed out a candy bar. "Three Musketeer? It'll help get your mind off your poor leg. Sorry you hurt it, but you need to learn to keep your nose … and your leg … out of other people's business."

"C-Carol?" Clarence raised up and tried to swing his leg around to the floor but got nowhere. "Ow! Carol!" He focused on the man dressed in all black across from him. "Get out! Get out of my room!"

Carol rushed in. "What? What on earth is the matter? Why are you yelling?"

"Get this bastard out of my …" Only Mr. Wainwright wasn't there. "He's … Mr. Wainwright was just here. Check the bathroom. Probably shitting in my … or my closet."

"Clarence, you've been through a trauma and you're getting all mixed up."

"I am not! Look. Look! He left a candy bar. Three Musketeers. He asked if I wanted one. And he threw it at me."

Carol teased him. "Mr. Wainwright can't blink an eye by himself, so how could he come into your room and leave you a candy bar?"

He tried to sit up. "Oh. Ow."

She helped him roll to a sitting position. "I've got a pain pill for you."

"No. I don't want one." He rubbed his head, his fingers through his hair. "I swear he was here. Just like before." He looked her in the eye. "You don't believe me, do you."

She chuckled. "Well. It's hard when he is right in the next room, pretty much comatose. He hasn't spoken or moved on his own since he was admitted."

"He moved his eyes and spit at Michael."

"He did spit … at Michael. He got his pink Tylenol all over my hand. I give you that." She eased onto the love seat. "But Clarence, it's impossible for him to be in your room."

"He sat, right where you are right now." Clarence searched the bed for the candy. "Here." He held up the candy bar. "Here we go. Evidence that he was here. Where would I get a candy bar?"

"The candy machine down at the nurses station." Carol shook her head. "Clarence." She frowned. "Ever since you were admitted, I knew we would be friends. Do I like all the residents? Of course. Some … more than others. But I knew you and I would be friends."

"We are friends." Clarence flipped the candy over and over. "And I know this is weird. Crazy. But … why would I make this up?"

Silence.

She pressed her lips together. "I don't know." Shook her head. "I don't know. Let's just go on from here. Deal with what's in front of us." She pointed. "Like your leg. I was on my way with a pain pill, when I heard you yell my name."

"I don't want any pills."

"It'll help you this first few days so you can relax instead of tensing up. It hurts more when you're tense." She dumped a pill into the palm of his hand. "Hey. The burn scars on your hands aren't as red. Getting better."

He tossed the pill in his mouth and gulped down water. "No more after this. I'll see how I am without it."

"You're just like Joe. He never wanted to take any meds. This is just to get you through the next few days." She nodded. "Okay?"

"Just a couple days." He dropped the candy bar onto the bedside table. "How is husband Joe doing?"

"Same. The same." She fiddled with the paper med cup in her hand, then looked up at Clarence.

"Rough, huh." He nodded.

Her eyes welled up and she nodded.

She perked up. "Remember when the hawk broke

into your room?" She looked out the window. "You were holing up then, too. I don't think you're supposed to stay in your room. You need to get out of here every day, or hawks … and neighbors break in." She smiled.

He chuckled and nodded. "That was some big bird. Wish we could have kept him."

Mrs. Hatly toddled by the open doorway with her walker and winked. Oh, she's cute. A sparkly pin accented her white blouse and a pink ribbon headband, matching her sweater, held back her shoulder-length gray hair. But her brown eyes. Always twinkly. "Is this a good time to visit?"

Carol jumped up. "Of course it is."

Lisha followed Mrs. Hatly carrying a tray of cookies and coffee. She placed it on the side table and pulled it closer to the bed. She pulled up a straight chair for Mrs. Hatly.

Oh-oh. He'd been railroaded. By three ladies. What a way to go.

Carol excused herself and Lisha served them with finesse, her little brown pinkie at attention.

Mrs. Hatly giggled when Lisha handed her a cup of coffee.

Clarence's face burned. He picked up a cookie and nibbled it.

Mrs. Hatly broke hers and ate the bite.

He stole a look at her.

She giggled and closed her eyes.

She was a much better guest than Mr. Wainwright. She made him feel all gooey inside, but Mr. Wainwright made him downright terrified.

Clarence didn't say a word—just ate his cookies and dipped into his coffee. And peeked at her.

Every time he looked at her, she had her eyes closed and was smiling. Every once-in-a-while, she moved her lips, then took a bite of cookie.

Prettiest lady on the planet.

Later, Lisha peeked in. "Uh, sorry to break this up but time to get ready for bed." She helped Mrs. Hatly stand and gathered their dishes.

"Thank you, Lisha, for the coffee and cookies. Delicious."

"You're welcome, Mrs. Hatly. Want help going back to your room?"

"I can make it."

Clarence perked up. "I'd help you, but …"

"That's okay. I hope your leg gets better. You have a good night, Clarence. God willing, I'll see you in the morning."

"What do you mean, God willing?" He tossed the candy bar to the trash.

"Good shot." She pushed back her head band. "Well, some night one of us might slip into heaven." She pushed up her sleeves and started out the door. "Good night, Mr. Timmelsen."

He sat up straight. "Good night, Mrs. Hatly. I hope to see you tomorrow."

And she left.

What if she died over night?

That would break his heart.

TEN

June 15, 1937 ~ Dr. Steven's Journal ~ Poolside samples of water and soil. I dipped the glass test tube in the pool and waited for water to bubble in. This would be the sixth sample. Before I carefully placed it in the holder with the other five test tubes, I tapped it with a fingernail. There was something different about this water—almost luminescent. Beautiful rainbow of blues and greens. I glanced back at the pool.

Incredibly clear.

Present Day ~ Katty Randolph hit enter. Her fingers fumbled at the computer. How long would it take before she didn't want a fix?

She shivered. Would she ever?

Coffee didn't help. She was addicted to that, too.

Cartoons blasted from the TV.

"Bea! Turn that down!"

She stood too fast, and her chair caught on the torn vinyl. Crappy trailer house. The chair landed hard behind her, making her jump. Every cell shattered. Her skin crawled.

Bea didn't even hear it.

Katty stomped to the TV and turned it off. "You have been in front of this TV for hours. Go outside and play." Too loud. Louder than she meant.

Oh God.

Clarence had said this would be tougher than getting Bea away from her rotten dad.

"Mommy."

"I can do this. I can do this." Katty turned away and wiped her eyes.

"Are you crying, Mommy?" Bea's tiny fingers caressed Katty's leg—made her skin crawl.

The month in rehab had been terrible. No Bea. No drugs. No booze. But this: back to life, going to school, helping Clarence set up his legal firm.

God.

The trailer was a disaster. Toys. Too many toys.

She picked up a broken Barbie. Pieces of the latest fast food toy giveaway scattered under the sofa.

Torn books. Food bits from when the neighbor kid—The Terror—had been over.

Trying to be the model mom. Play dates. Healthy treats. Not too much TV.

She flopped onto the couch, and odors of too many spilled drinks floated to her nostrils. Juice. Booze.

The couch wasn't the only thing that stunk.

Her life stunk.

How had she let Clarence talk her into this? Be his legal assistant?

Little fingers folded between her own. Dirty fingernails. Tiny fingers rubbed hers. Big brown eyes searched her own.

Precious. Precious.

Katty had never loved Bea more than when the effects of the drugs mostly wore off. For the first time she really saw her little girl. How could she have done all … treated her like …

She choked and drew Bea to her, onto her lap and breathed. This little piece of her. Yeah, of nasty Phil, too. Conceived in abuse and birthed alone.

But now Katty could see. Turn that horrible beginning for this child into something real and … meaningful.

God help me give her the love she deserves.

A tiny tear dropped onto their entwined fingers.

Bea looked up. "Mommy, you're crying again."

"I just love you so much." Katty wiped her face and snuggled deeper into Bea. "We're gonna make it. We're gonna be okay."

Bea gasped. "Mommy, the lights."

Katty raised her head. Tiny lights floated around them, dancing between them, on Bea's head.

Bea giggled. "There's one on your head. Two. Three. One's on your nose." She leaned away, staring into Katty's eyes. "They're in your eyes. Sparkles in your eyes."

Katty blinked. Don't move. Don't miss this. Were they … Clarence called them angels … had they been here all along? Had she just been too drunk to see?

Oh, precious, precious.

Bea snuggled into her and held out her hand. A bigger one lit there, shining, sparkling, soothing.

"Oh, God. Dear God. These lights are too beautiful to be from anywhere but You. I don't get it. I don't know if I'm going crazy …" She brushed back Bea's tangled hair. "But if you can see them, Baby Bea, then it's not a flashback or … withdrawal."

She leaned into the sofa and pulled the tattered quilt around them. "Homework can wait. That para-crap will wait."

"Mommy. Where's Clarence?" Bea pulled the quilt up under her chin.

"I don't know, Baby." She sighed. "At the nursing

home, I guess. He doesn't run away from there so much anymore."

"We need to go see him."

"What? Right now?"

Bea looked out the window. "Yeah. Right now."

Katty snuggled Bea close. "Baby Bea. He's busy. We'll go tomorrow." She pulled the quilt up under Bea's chin. "Why? What are you … thinking?"

The tiny lights reflected in Bea's deep brown eyes, flitting, stirring all around her head. She seemed unaware of their presence right now.

"Mommy. I see water. Clarence in water." She looked into Katty's eyes. "Is he swimming?"

ELEVEN

June 16, 1937 ~ Dr. Steven's Journal ~ The cave wasn't the most convenient place to complete my research, so I picked up the pan and climbed up the hill to the campsite. I had spent yesterday setting up a table, chair, and journals right outside the camper. Didn't have to worry about rain. I made my own equipment to suit my use and the test tube holder is one of many. A round pan with a flat lid was just deep enough to cover the test tubes in a wire rack. Just right for when I do field work.

Like at the devil pool.

Present day ~ Stop sign.
Oh. No.

Michael downshifted. Why could he not anticipate these stops until he was almost too late?

He came to a full stop and shifted down again. He should ask Father or another angel about stick shift trucks. He never could get the sequencing down. Clutch in. Brake on. Then shift. Oh wait. Wasn't it shift, then clutch?

Guess not.

Grinding.

Sigh. He was going to ruin this truck.

It wouldn't be so bad, except Clarence snickered every time he would grind the gears.

Like now.

Clarence had his hand over his mouth, but Michael knew he was laughing.

"Did you ever drive a stick shift?"

Silence.

"Well, did you?"

"I'm not saying." Clarence reached over and patted Michael's shoulder. "You're doing a great job grinding them gears … for an angel." Clarence turned toward him. "Hey, isn't there some kind of magic you could use to help you find the gears?"

He had his hand over his mouth, but Michael could see him grinning. Good to get Clarence out again and see him laughing, even if it was at Michael's expense. Clarence tended to get depressed and shut everyone out, so when Michael had suggested they take a drive, using the excuse to look for pools, Clarence was ready to go.

Clarence wiped it away. "I mean. Well, not magic, that would be … well, what if you prayed?"

Michael stuck his tongue out. Why humans? Why not dogs or cats. Or rabbits. Why humans?

Clutch.

Shift into second.

"Smooth." Clarence applauded. "That was smooth."

Face was getting hot. In the human world, that meant he was blushing. His face must be red. He glanced in the rear view mirror.

Yup.

Wait.

He looked in the mirror again.

Angels. A whole host of them.

One sitting between them.

What was that low rumble?

Michael sought Father.

The angel put out his hand and sword to stop.

Michael slowed and stopped.

Killed it.

"What?" Clarence straightened. "Why are we stopping in the middle of the road?" He had his finger following along each mile line on the map. "Why did you stop?"

Michael ignored Clarence as he let himself seek Father's face.

Stop. Don't go any farther. Get out of the truck and back the way you came.

Michael opened his door. "Get out. Go back the way we came."

"Well, I don't see—"

"Now!" Michael stepped out. The angels surrounded him as he stepped backwards away from the truck. He looked over at Clarence, who was just getting out.

An angel swooped in beside Clarence, grabbed him and sent him flying past the truck's tail end, cane nowhere in sight. At the same instant, the front of the truck jerked down and forward, the ground sucking it down. Clarence screamed. Guess he'd never flown with angels before.

Michael scanned the area.

Tiny mice scattered in terror. One ran under the truck. Another skittered toward the hole. Wrong way.

Angels already on it.

A farmer sat on a tractor to the right of the road, just over the fence. It looked like he was backing to a long trailer stacked with irrigation pipe.

Michael had been so involved with grinding the gears, he had lost connection with the invisible world.

Always stay focused. He wanted to kick himself.

Too late now.

The truck shuddered as the ground opened in front of it.

An angel grabbed Clarence again and flew him farther back on the road. Clarence was screaming above the roar of the shifting ground.

Angels escorted Michael to the same place.

Dust settled and debris clattered to the ground. It seemed like hours, then it was quiet.

Clarence stopped coughing and pounded his chest.

Michael reached over to pat his back.

That wasn't Clarence.

Michael looked up to see a large man right beside him. Red in the face, sweat poured from under his ball hat, which read "If You Ate breakfast, Thank a Farmer."

The man hadn't seen Michael or Clarence. His eyes were glued to a spot just ahead, to the right of the truck.

Michael followed the man's gaze and gasped.

The tractor's exhaust pipe was sticking out above the surface of the ground. Nothing else was visible. No engine. No big tires. Just the exhaust pipe.

"Look at that." Clarence limped toward it.

Michael grabbed his arm. "Clarence, listen."

He stopped. "What is that? That rumble?"

The farmer's hand flew to his mouth. "My tractor!"

The ground roared and shook.

The tractor shifted. The exhaust pipe disappeared.

The farmer screamed. "My tractor! I just got it yesterday." He sobbed and shuddered. He started toward the hole.

Michael tackled him. "Sir, you could have been down that hole with it. You are alive."

Clarence was trembling. "Right. You could be dead! You can get another tractor."

"A hole swallowed it." He moaned. "I don't have insurance for a hole! For some monster that swallows tractors!"

Both Clarence and Michael patted his huge shoulders. "Sir, you are going to be okay."

The man's stomach growled. "My lunch! My lunch was in that tractor. My lunch was eaten by a hole!" He fell down in a fit. He pounded the ground.

Michael watched as his own truck shook and shuddered. In a way, he wouldn't mind if …

Silence.

Pop!

The whole section of ground gave way, sending his truck to the same grave as the tractor. Right under his own sinking feet—

Angels swooped in, scooped up the farmer and Clarence.

Michael jumped into one angel's arms, grinning. They landed on level ground. Michael's angel dusted him off, making a show of it. "You okay, Sir? You shouldn't get dirty." Hard slap on the back.

Michael coughed and leaned over, hands on his knees.

"You okay, Michael?" Clarence hollered.

Michael waved. "Yeah. I'm fine." Head back down and speaking so only the angel could hear. "I just need to wrestle down a pig-headed angel, that's all." He kicked behind him, tripping the angel, who flew out of the earth's atmosphere.

Another angel butted him from behind, sending Michael headlong into the dirt.

"Michael!" Clarence started up the incline. "You okay? Did you hit your head?"

Michael wiped the grin off his face. "Naw. I'm fine. I'll be right there."

As soon as Clarence limped over and peered in the hole, Michael turned and slammed his fist into another angel's chest, sending him flying into the physical realm, visible to anyone human. His laughter echoed between the hills.

Clarence turned again. "Was that you laughing?"

Michael started toward him. "Naw. I think it was a bird or something. Some scared animal. Must have been startled by the sink hole."

The angel rushed Michael from behind and

pinned his arms across his chest, so it looked like Michael was just standing, his arms crossed. He was able to hold his ground, tottering to a standstill.

"Hey, sorry about your truck, Michael." Clarence glanced behind him at the hole.

"It's okay. It might be okay if we can just get it out somehow." Michael broke free, sending another angel tumbling through the atmosphere. His deep laugh rumbled across both dimensions.

Clarence jumped and grabbed the farmer's shoulder for balance. "Whoa! Watch out. Here comes another landslide!"

An alert resounded through the invisible realm, and the host of angels saluted Michael. "Got to go. Good to rumble with you Brother. God keep you." The angel sped off, along with others. A trail of lightning sparks followed them.

"Michael, did you hear that?" Clarence shielded his eyes from the sun. "Such a strange day. Thunder. And not a cloud in the sky. Weird stuff."

Michael picked his way to where Clarence and the farmer stood. "Yeah. Was that lightning just now? Maybe the sink holes are caused by lightning strikes. Or thunder. I didn't hear any, though." He patted the farmer's back. "Sorry about your tractor, Mr. ..."

The farmer seemed in a daze. "Mr. ... Gustafson. Merle Gustafson." He fished his cell phone out of his pocket and stepped away. "Hello, Mabel? Call our insurance …"

An angel flew over, slowed and gently placed Clarence's cane on the ground in front of him.

"Michael!" Clarence pointed at it. "Did you see that? My cane just appeared."

Michael grinned as he bent to pick it up. "Well, miracles do happen."

Clarence took the cane, examined it. "I got my cane back, but I'm afraid your truck is a goner. It bashed into the tractor." Clarence shook his head. "I'm not sure what kind of a crane could ever pull them out." He patted Michael. "Sorry."

Michael tried to feel disappointed. "Well, I'll just have to start looking for another one, I guess." He nodded at the farmer.

This time it would be an automatic.

TWELVE

June 17, 1937—The Osceola Times: "Famed and notorious Archeologist and Professor of Agriculture, Dr. Walter Stevens' assistant drowned June 11th, in a freak accident. It seems his assistant Henry Green, fell into a pool in a cave they were studying near the Gospel Ridge Road. He sucked in the putrid waters from the pool as he succumbed to the pool's clutches. Upon interviewing Dr. Stevens, he said he reached for Mr. Green, and had hold of his hand, when Mr. Green pushed away. Dr. Stevens warns all, "Don't go near that pool. You won't come back." Mr. Green's head went under again and Dr. Stevens grabbed for his hair and his ear. According to Dr. Stevens, "It was the strangest thing. I had hold of him. But he pushed my hand away. Maybe it was just a fish." Since there is no body to bury, members of the community will hold a bar-side service next Thursday, the 24th of June, for Mr. Henry Green at 6 p.m., giving all attendees time to celebrate his life thereafter."

I let the article flutter to the table and shook my head. My stomach growled, reminding me I hadn't eaten in two days. How can someone forget to eat?

Back to the article. Nice of the community. Seemed a nice reason to throw a drinking binge. Henry would have liked that.

I wanted to run, or drive, as far away from Osceola as I could get, but I knew I couldn't. Either I find Henry or the secret to this pool.

Or both.

Present Day ~ Noell clicked her nails on the washer as water poured down on her new clothes. That was always funny to her: they had to be years old, not just months, but had never been worn. New. Old.

She chuckled as she slammed the lid and checked the settings. They were just overalls and T-shirts, so normal setting should work.

She glanced at the boots sitting on the side chair. Pink. That made her chuckle. Oh, she'd get teased. She didn't even know the other employees, but she had a feeling they'd laugh.

She examined one. They were well-made boots.

Worth a couple of hundred dollars, at least. Smelled new—a musty sort of new. Stitching was perfect. The sole had never touched ground. No dirt. No dust. No dog poop!

No skin cells from someone else's foot to make her go crazy with voices and pictures of that person's demented life. It had taken repeated sprays with cleanser and rubbing with a towel to clean the boots she wore now. The only voice she heard when she put them on was hers. Which wasn't all that great either.

She shook off her slipper and gingerly pushed her foot inside the boot. Felt okay. She wiggled her toes. Plenty of room, even if she had on thicker socks for winter.

Huh. She started to flip off her other slipper when Gamma cried out from the porch.

Crash!

"Gam?"

She stopped and listened.

Louder this time. "Gamma?"

She dropped the other boot and ran. Clunk in the boot. Slide in the slipper.

Clunk. Slide.

She pushed open the porch door.

"Gamma! Gam? Where are you?"

Boxes were scattered all over one end of the room, in the aisle. Everything was in a shambles. The only thing she could see of Gamma was her walker and it was up-side-down.

"Gam!" Noel screamed and tried to dig herself toward the walker. One box fell on top of her and broke open, puking out fabrics in a rainbow of pastel colors. She tried to push it to the side but there was no place to put it.

"Gam?" Noell dug deeper. "Gam, are you okay?" She reached between two boxes, trying to fish for Gam's hair, her sweatshirt.

Hair. Gam's hair. Soft hair.

Noell was weeping now. "Gam? Answer if you can."

She somehow found the strength to leverage between two boxes and push one off, then lift the other.

She knelt. "Gam. I'm here."

She watched her chest.

"But you're not." Sob. "You're already gone."

Gamma's glasses were askew—half on and half off.

Noell took them and wiped the lenses on her T-shirt. Then eased them onto Gamma's face, careful around her ears and nose. She stroked Gam's cheek. A tear was there.

She checked Gam's chest again.

Gone.

Wiping her own face, she scanned the boxes

broken open around them, until she saw fabric in Gamma's hand.

She gently pulled it from her fingers—still watching for signs of life.

None.

What was this fabric from? It was a dress. Just about her size now. She tried to see what box it had come from. They were all too tossed around. She smelled the dress.

Oh God! Shouldn't have done that! No. She had to stay with Gam.

No!

Gam's smells first. There was love, joy, then fear and grief. Oh, Gam. What was this dress from? The smells took her deeper.

Deeper.

No.

The dream.

Mommy.

Mommy's hand reached out to her from the water. The dress fabric floated and billowed around Mommy's body.

Her eyes gleamed with a love that Noell had never seen in previous dreams.

Then Mommy drifted away. Her eyes never closed. Her hand always reached toward Noell.

"Mommy." Noell stretched her hand out. "Mommy, don't leave me."

Sobbing, Noell felt hands lift her from the water.

She turned to see Grampa, his eyes full of tears. "Grampa. Mommy."

She looked down at Mommy, only it was Gamma.

She looked up at Grampa.

But it was Fletch. He had tears in his eyes, too.

His hands gripped her arms, pulling her from the mess.

She stared into his wide eyes, until …

"Gam." She broke. "Gam's dead."

THIRTEEN

June 19, 1937 ~ Dr. Steven's Journal ~ The Pool. Good thing it was summer because it was still chilly in the cave.

My heart was pounding. I am a good swimmer, but so was Henry. And maybe the woman who drowned was a swimmer also.

I sit and start to untie my leather boots.

I checked the knots in the heavy rope tied around my waist and followed it to where it stopped in the hands of the heavy-set man wearing the open-air overalls. The man nodded.

He had just shown up with the rope draped over his arms.

I nodded back and sucked in a deep breath. And blew it out. Sucked in another. And out. One more look at the man and I drew in a breath and stepped into the pool. There was no choice but to go in.

———

Present Day ~ Noell hesitated at the door.

Hillcrest Homes. Room number 204. That was the correct number. The name was right.

She glanced at the page from the phone book. The right address. A nursing home?

She glanced back down the hall. Wheelchairs. People snoozing. Walkers. Nurses.

A dark-skinned aide passed her. "Hey suga." She stopped. "You need somebody?" She checked the door. "Oh, you muss be at the wrong place." She turned full-on.

There was a lot of her.

"Um." Noell held up the page and pointed to the entry. "Clarence Timmelsen? A lawyer?" She shoved it into her purse and started down the hall. "I must be really messed up."

"No. That's him." The aide knocked on the door. "You might a messed up, but this is where he lives and laws." She pushed at the door. "Mr. Clarence. Someone to see you."

Only no one was in the room.

The woman knocked again. "Mr. Clarence? Where

you at?" She checked the rooms. "Nobody home. Huh." She dropped her pen and notepad into her pocket. "I'll go chase him down. Be right back." She waved Noell into the room. "Jus go on in and sit a spell."

"It's okay?"

The woman's dreads bounced as she walked. "Sure. Go on in and sit down."

Noell almost chuckled. This woman chasing anybody down would be almost funny. She bit her lips so as not to laugh out loud as the woman barreled down the hall.

"Clarence?" The woman peeked into every room as she passed them. "You hiding, Mr. Clarence?"

Noell could still hear her, as she stepped into the room. It looked like an office. She turned and compared it with the bedroom across the hall. Definitely a bedroom. Back to his rooms—definitely an office with framed documents adding the credibility she needed to see. Probably could fake those, too.

Cute little girl in the balloon photo. The woman with her looked familiar. Must have seen her around town.

A yellowed newspaper clipping had been slipped in along the edge of the frame of one of the documents. She slung her backpack over her shoulder and skimmed the article. Huh.

Noell read it in a whisper. "It seems his assistant Henry Green, fell into a pool in a cave they were studying near the Gospel Ridge Road." A pool in Osceola? Who was Henry Green? Dr. Stevens seemed famous—for back then. 1937?

Katty gathered Bea into her arms. "I don't know if Clarence even knows how to swim." She breathed in Bea. So sweet. Even if she did need a bath. Something so fresh about her. "Shall we go see him? I'm sick of studying."

"I'm sick of studying too, Mommy. Let's go!" Bea jumped down and found her shoes. "Put my shoes on, Mommy."

Katty laughed. "Uh-uh. You can do it." She slipped on her sandals and grabbed her purse. She checked her face in the mirror. Fine wrinkles around her eyes and mouth—she was only twenty-four. Oh well. No make-up—they were just going to the nursing home. Most people there couldn't see.

Bea pulled on one boot and then the other.

Wrong feet.

"Do you really think you need boots Bea? It's summer." She pulled them off and found Bea's sandals and strapped them on. "Ready?"

Bea raced to the door, then back to her drawings. "I need to take this to Clarence. He needs a new drawing."

Katty smiled. "He sure does." There were only five hanging on his wall, right now.

She closed the door and locked it. Felt so secure with the new lock. Clarence had made sure it was safe. The new deck looked good, too. The planter dressed it up even more. She'd never had flowers before. She'd never had the money ... before. Gulp. It had always gone for booze or cigarettes or ... drugs.

"Mommy, come on. Clarence needs us."

Katty bent to pick a leaf of lavender. She pinched it and breathed it in. Best smell ever. She tucked the leaf into her pocket.

Bea jumped up the steps. "Mommy. I want one."

"Don't pull the plant out. Just take your thumbnail and cut one leaf off ... like this." She showed Bea how.

Bea walked to the car sniffing it.

Noell read more of the article, until a man cleared his throat from the hall.

His loud voice made her jump. "Lisha, that you? Who wants to see me? I have an appointment ... now."

The woman lumbered back to the doorway. "Where you been? I've been looking all over for you." She pointed to Noell. "Your appointment is here, and I ain't yo sec-re-tary."

"I was outside having a smoke."

Noell raised her eyebrows. This might not work.

The woman flicked his ear. "You don smoke, 'member?"

The door opened all the way, and a tall, rough-looking man stood before Noell in jeans and a black T-shirt with a yellow-plaid necktie, a splint on his leg. Greying hair slicked behind his ears and curled to his shoulders. A full beard was clipped close to his face. Bushy eyebrows arched above clear blue eyes. His skin wasn't even all that wrinkled.

"Are you Noell?" He held out his hand.

"Uh, yes." She dropped her sweater.

He limped and stooped to pick it up.

She reached for it, but he swung it into the room in welcome.

"Well," said the aide, "ya found Mr. Lawyer Man, and I have to give somebody a bath."

Noell hesitated.

"He's okay. He just looks scary. He's really a pussycat—right Mr. Clarence?" The aide chuckled and patted Noell on the shoulder.

Sanitizer. Sanitizer.

She held her breath.

The aide must have just washed her hands. Sometimes the vibes didn't flow through clothes. Whew.

"If he gets scary, or sum-thin, I'll be down the hall."

"Thanks … uh, Lisha." She automatically read the upside-down name tag. Gamma always thought that was astounding.

Before Noell caught herself, she righted it.

She braced herself for voices or trembling.

Nothing. Huh.

"Oh, yeah. I caught it on a bed when I was tuckin' in the sheets." Lisha patted her chest. "Thanks."

"Come on in and …" Again, he waved her sweater into the room. "It's nothing fancy, but it's my little office. Sorry to make you wait."

She stared at the shirt and the tie. Then at him. Was she still in the wrong place?

His eyes followed hers to his tie. "Oh. Pardon me. A friend and I were just teasing about the fact that I should dress more professionally." He pulled the tie from his neck and wound it around the door-knob. "May I help you?"

She stared at his shirt. Led Zeppelin? "Are you Mr. Timmelsen? Clarence Timmelsen?" She glanced at the wall again. All the certificates proclaimed "Clarence Timmelsen," so he had to be legitimate.

The sun was shining. Birds were pooping on Katty's car, so she guessed the bird kingdom was okay. The wind wasn't even blowing today. Beautiful day.

She buckled Bea into the car seat Clarence had bought for them. He really felt like a grandfather. She didn't even want to know if she had a real one or not. He'd probably be mean, just like her mom and dad had been. Why hadn't she seen before, how precious this little one was and that she was following exactly in the same path as her parents had—cruelty, abuse, addictions, rape, incest? She blinked back tears so Bea wouldn't see. The drugs and alcohol had masked her wounded soul. Now, though it was painful, she was determined to bust through and face it all. No masks.

Even Clarence was gruff sometimes because of what he had been through, but he melted when Bea walked into his rooms.

The parking lot at Hillcrest was full. She had to park farther away. Sometimes resident families needed to be closer to the door. There had been a day that she wouldn't have thought about that. About what other people needed.

So much had changed since she had become sober.

What hadn't changed was that Bea could un-buckle her car seat in two seconds flat. She always beat. Car seats were supposed to be child-proof. Little Houdini.

"Bea. Wait! Don't get out. You are so short, other people can't see you and if you run out—"

She ran out.

"Bea! Stop!"

Bea finally did stop but not before a small pickup had to slam on the brakes to avoid hitting her.

"Bea!" Katty grabbed her hand and yanked her back. "You almost got hit!" Her hand was at Bea's backside, ready to …

Bea's face crumpled and she shrank from Katty. "I'm sorry, Mommy. I just want to see Clarence."

"I know. But you wouldn't see him if you were dead, right?" Some days with this child about did her in. It didn't help that today of all days, she woke with a splitting headache. When would this be better? She wanted a fix so bad. Just one drink.

A med aide walked past on her way to her car. "Gonna have to tie that kid up. She's always running ahead, huh."

Bea clung to Katty.

"No, not tie her up. Just make her mind." Katty picked up Bea and marched across the parking lot to the entrance and put her down. "I won't tie you up, but I will make sure you mind. You are so fast! That truck could have hit you!"

Bea snuggled into Katty's neck. "I'm sorry Mommy." She placed her little hands against Katty's cheeks and turned her head. Face to face. Nose to nose. "I'm sorry Mommy." She looked deep into Katty's eyes.

They forgot about the world or anyone else around them and connected. Katty had never let anyone look into her soul that deeply. But here was her own four-year-old daughter doing just that. Deep sigh.

"Excuse me." A lady toting two beautiful bouquets pressed the automatic door plate with her elbow.

Katty jumped and stepped aside. "Oh, sorry. We were just … I'm sorry."

"Don't stop that huggy-huggy stuff for me." She grinned at them on the other side of the now-closed-door and made a face at Bea—her eyes crossed and mouth wide.

"Yes. Please come in." Clarence pulled a chair closer to the desk and sat in the other one, propping his leg up on an open desk drawer. "Have a seat. Um, would you like something to drink? We have pop, coffee—"

Noell wasn't buying. "No thanks." The seat appeared worn, but not dirty. She sat, hugging the folder to her chest. What was she doing here? She should have gone downtown to another law office. She didn't have a clue. That's what yellow pages were for.

He sat back in his chair. "You were reading my wall of frames. I hope it all looks satisfactory to you."

Noell looked at the wall again. "Yes, it does. Cute little girl." The newspaper clipping fanned in the airflow, catching her eye again. "Interesting article."

His eyes roamed over the frames. "Article?" Found it. "Oh, yes. Quite a perplexing thing. Poor Henry Green. I wish we had more information, but I'm just beginning to search it out." He patted his leg. "That's how I hurt my leg."

She cringed. "Is it going to be okay?"

"Oh, sure. It's better every day." He folded his hands in his lap. "Well, what brings you here today, Noell?"

Tears threatened again. No. He'd offer some old dirty handkerchief, or Kleenex from a dusty box. She couldn't cry here. She swallowed. "My name is Noell Carpenter."

He held out his hand. Thick fingers. Spiky white hairs grew from between each knuckle. Long fingernails. Like Grampa's.

Gah. Her insides turned to jelly.

She stared, then slowly placed hers in his.

Breathe.

Her vision exploded with pictures of hammers, saws, and sawdust. Old cars drove on somewhat familiar streets. Signs on buildings looked like ones from the antique shop. A younger version of the man before her embracing a beautiful young woman. An awful car crash. Pictures of a prison—lines of inmates dressed alike in orange and a terrified Mr. Timmelsen backed against a wall. She cringed, and just as she was about to run out the door, she saw him walk into the town as it was now.

She jerked her hand from his and scooted away.

"Are you okay? You look like you just saw a ghost. I know I'm old and scary, but usually people just want to slap me or kick me, not shy away."

Words wouldn't come out. She started to stand to leave but saw her sweater hanging on the back of his chair. "It's just me. I … uh …"

"It's okay. Is there something I can help you with?"

Lisha barged into the room. "You can hep me with this plate o cookies and milk, thas what. And I want to slap you almost every day." She balanced a tray with a plate of cookies and two tall glasses of milk. "Sometimes every minute." She stopped. "Lookit your messy desk. Now, how am I s'posed to set this down?"

Clarence pushed the boxes to the opposite edge

of the desk. He brushed what appeared to be crumbs to the floor.

"Thas better." Lisha carefully placed the tray and gave Noell a napkin, patting it onto her lap, then offered the cookies.

Her stomach began to churn. "Um, no thank you."

"What?" Lisha stepped away, her hand on her hip. "What? You don't like cookies?" She looked down her nose at Clarence. "What is wrong with this gal, Mr. Clarence?" She carefully picked one up, holding her pinkie in a salute, and placed it on the napkin on Noell's lap. "There. And here's your milk, so's you can reach it, in case you're a dipper." She backed away, hands on both hips.

Clarence held out a hand.

"Oh, you can git your own." She sauntered out the door.

"See how she is?" Clarence reached for the napkins and a cookie. He dipped his in a glass of milk and slurped a bite down. "Mm." He looked over at Noell. "Aren't you going to eat yours? She'll be back and will make sure you do, so you might as well do it in peace."

Lisha's voice rang from the hallway. "I heard dat." A cart rattled past the open door.

He stood, limped to the door, using the wall for balance, and shut it. "There."

Noell stared at the glass of milk, then the cookie still on her lap.

Clarence licked a drip of milk from his finger.

She picked up her cookie and licked sweat from her upper lip.

He seemed to be taking a long time eating his.

She finally stowed her file behind her on the chair, scooted closer to the desk and picked up the glass. The cookie just fit. She dipped and took a nibble. Not bad. Another tiny bite. Chocolate chip. Her favorite. Gam's too.

A tear escaped her eye. She knew he was watching her. No pressure.

At the last bite, she almost regretted it was gone. She drank the cold milk, even sucked up cookie chunks and set the glass back on the desk, licking her lips. She folded the napkin and wiped her mouth.

"Better?"

She shrugged and half-smiled. Nodded. "Thanks."

Bea giggled as Katty set her down.

"Push the button, Bea." Katty made sure she had hold of Bea's other hand, before she ran into the building, possibly knocking a resident over. "Let's go see Clarence."

They pushed the automatic door button, Katty's mind still on the visual of that pickup almost hitting Bea. "Just remember. You are gonna stay in the car seat until I get you out from now on. No running ahead. Got it?"

Bea was distracted by the ice cream machine. "Mommy. Can I have some ice cream?"

Katty bent down to Bea, eye-to-eye. "Did you hear me? You have to stay buckled in until I un-buckle you. And no running ahead." Katty turned Bea's face toward hers. "Got it?"

"Got it." Bea danced beside the counter, almost bumping into Mrs. Hatley with her walker.

"Bea! Look out. You're going to knock her over."

Mrs. Hatley wasn't much bigger than Bea. She almost didn't need to bend to talk to Bea. "How are you sweetheart?" She touched Bea's cheek with her withered hand.

"Good." Bea's eyes never left the ice cream machine.

Mrs. Hatly giggled. "She wants ice cream." She looked up at Katty. "Can she?"

Katty shrugged. "I guess. She lives for it."

"Me too. You'd think I'd be tired of it." Mrs. Hatly reached for a cone with a white wrapper and filled it expertly. "Here you go Little Bea."

Bea said thank you at the same time Katty said, "What do you say, Bea?"

"Are you having one Mrs. Hatly?" Katty took hers and licked.

"I've had mine for today. Goes great with break-fast." She patted Bea's head. "Heading to see Clarence?"

Bea started to dance. "Mommy can I go?"

Katty took her arm. "Slow down or you'll spill your ice cream cone. And walk." Down the hall were several residents in wheelchairs and walkers. Using canes or holding onto the railing. "No running. Got it?"

"Got it." Bea skipped until Katty caught up with her. She stopped and jumped up and rotated. "Bye, Mrs. Hatly. Thanks for the ice cream."

Mrs. Hatly laughed and waved. "Bye, Dear."

Bea stuck her head in Harold's door and ran to him, almost dumping the ice cream cone down his shirt.

"Whoa Little Bea!" He hugged her. "Can I have a lick?"

She held it to his mouth. "Sure. Here."

He laughed. "No. I just had one. You eat it. I was just kidding." He set her on the floor again. "Beside I can have one anytime I want." He patted his gut. "And I don't really need anymore."

Katty rounded up Bea. "See ya Harold."

He waved. "Bye, you two."

"By Harad." Bea blew him a kiss.

He caught it with his hand and blew her one back.

Katty sighed. People here had Bea so spoiled. Guess it wasn't a bad thing. She looked down the hall behind them. Every person who could see her, were all watching Bea. And every one of them had a huge grin on their face.

She looked ahead of her at Bea, skipping and dripping ice cream on the newly replaced carpet. Touching everyone. She was chatting with one woman who had no idea who anyone was, much less this tiny munchkin, who made even her smile a toothless grin.

Something so rich came over Katty at that moment.

What if Clarence hadn't shown up in the park that day? What if his big hands hadn't picked Bea up and away from Katty? Katty had already scratched and clawed Bea by then. What if he hadn't intervened and sat Katty down on that park bench and firmly gotten in her face about her addictions and parenting habits?

Her eyes filled with tears as she watched Bea jabber to the staff.

***

"So, tell me why you're here, Noell." He took out a small yellow legal pad and clicked his pen open.

She sat, drew in a deep breath, and opened the

file. "This is my grandma's." She hesitated. Sobs threatened. Another tear slid down her cheek.

A Kleenex box slid into view under her chin. There was Grandpa's hand again, only attached to Clarence's arm instead. She followed the hand up the arm and the arm to the face.

There was gentleness there. And heart. For her.

He might be rough looking, but …

The tears gushed. Sobs. She pulled one Kleenex after another, until the sobs dwindled and there was a pile of smashed, balled-up tissues on the floor.

"Oh, I'm sorry. I'll get—"

He already had the trash can in front of her, picking the mess up.

"Oh, God. Let me. That's nasty." Sobs erupted again. "I'm so sorry."

He tucked the Kleenex box beside her on the chair and positioned the trash can beside her.

"You-you picked up my snotty …" Hiccup.

He looked at his hands and nodded.

Ropy scars lined the insides of both hands.

"Your hands." Before she thought, she gently touched them. "Oh my." Aware of how close she was to him, she pulled back. But not before he clasped her hand in his.

Flashes of a tiny girl. He was holding a tiny girl in his arms with such love and completeness.

Oh, this was not going to work. This was too

much. How could she sit here and every other minute want to burst into tears?

He held out his other hand for the file and released her hand.

Biting her lips together, she handed it over.

He opened the file, flipped through the contents —death certificate, funeral cost estimates, the deed to the house. Thank God for that lock-box—Gamma had kept everything she might ever need in a heartbeat, in there. She hoped it was all there, because going through the whole house to find one small document would take at least three years.

"So, this was your grandma, Gwendolyn Randolph Carpenter?"

Noell nodded. "Excuse me." She skirted into the bathroom with the Kleenex box under her arm and blew her nose. Yuck. She washed her hands and sat back down. "Yes."

"And she just passed away I see … two days ago. You've had the service?"

She shook her head. "Tomorrow." People talked about closure when they had a service for their loved ones. There would be no closure. Some lady she didn't know would sing a song. A preacher would preach about someone he had never known. They'd had to put it off till now to give her a chance to find all the right documents.

"What was the cause of death? Says here on the coroner's report she fell?"

Noell fidgeted with the box of tissues. Deep breath. "She did, but she was knocked down by falling boxes." She looked up at Clarence. "Lots of boxes. That's why if there is something else you need, I might never find it."

He shot her a rueful smile. "Kind of a hoarder, was she?"

"Yes. Not kind-of."

"I see." He clicked on his computer and started a search. "Looks like she owned the house and property free and clear. I'll need to go to the courthouse and take care of all the proceedings, but I think it looks pretty easy to transfer it all to you. Do you have an ID with you?"

Noell fished it out of her purse.

"Looks good. It all looks good, Noell. I think it should be pretty easy. There are no other siblings or relatives that would have a right to this property?"

"None that I know of."

"Okay, well, I'll get on it. I'm assuming you just want to put the property into your name so you can live there and assume rightful ownership?"

"I guess. I'm not sure I want to live there, though." Actually, she wasn't sure she could bear it at all. "It's ... well, pretty full of stuff." Including memories—thousands per square inch.

"Maybe at a certain point you might want to have a sale."

She cocked her head. "Maybe. I just don't know yet. I don't know how to do this."

He turned to her. "You need to give yourself some time to figure things out. Don't jump into anything too fast. You need to let yourself … grieve, too." He seemed to drift away when he said that. "We all need to let things take their course in these matters."

"Okay."

Clarence closed the file and tapped it on the desk. "Do you want to check back in a day or two and I can let you know what I've come up with? Do you need any help at the house? I have a very large friend who is as trustworthy as God, who could help."

"Trustworthy as God?"

Clarence grinned. "Yes. As God. His name is Michael." He hesitated. "But some days, he seems … to be busy, so we can't find him."

Odd. "Well, I guess I'm going to need the help if he isn't too expensive. And what does this cost?" She waved her hand over the file.

"Nothing."

She started to open her mouth but closed it. She shook her head. "Grandpa always said if it's free there's something wrong with it. Or something like that."

"I know. There's a saying like that." He leaned his elbows on his knees. "I'm just going to be honest with you." He glanced up at her then back to the floor. "I spent some time in prison. No, I spent sixty years in prison."

Bea laid her ice cream cone on a nearby counter. She hesitated beside a reclining wheelchair where a woman, sound asleep, snored with her mouth open.

Katty jumped. She could almost read Bea's mind. That stinker was going to climb on. She was torn between rescuing the poor woman or wiping up the ice cream—until a nurse held up her just-a-minute finger.

"She's okay. Let her be." The nurse watched from a foot or more away as Bea slowly climbed on up.

Bea kept a constant soft-voiced chatter to the woman as she settled on her lap. "It's okay, lady. I won't hurt you. You are okay. I only kill bad guys. I don't kill ladies. I'm a lady too, so I don't kill ladies." She sat ever so gently on the woman's lap.

The woman's eyes fluttered open and the first thing she saw was Bea's precious face.

Katty held her breath and stepped closer. Bea's face glowed. Her eyes were round and soft as she looked at the woman. Her hair curled around her head like a halo. Bea's whole head glowed.

Katty rotated. Where was that light coming from? There wasn't even a skylight above. She cupped her hand over her mouth.

The nurse still motioned for Katty not to interrupt, wiping her own eyes.

The old woman raised a fluttering hand and caressed Bea's cheek.

Bea leaned into it, placing her own hand against the woman's. "It's okay, lady. You're gonna see Jesus soon."

The woman's eyes grew large. A tear slipped down her cheek. She started babbling to Bea.

"I know. I know." Bea gently touched the woman's cheek with her other hand. "He's coming for you." She looked down at the wheelchair. "You won't need this in heaven." Bea's head popped up. "Can I have it? This looks like fun."

The woman bubbled with giggles. Spittle drooled out one corner of her mouth.

The nurse jumped to wipe it away, but Bea beat her to it and wiped her hand on her shorts.

The woman cooed. In her own world she seemed to made sense.

Made sense to Bea too. Because Bea answered back in the same language.

By this time, two other staff members had gathered beside the nurse.

One was weeping.

The other took her phone out of her pocket and took a picture.

Holy moment.

Katty sighed. Oh, if only Bea had that with Katty's own parents. She didn't even know where they were and that was fine. This was much better. This was pure.

And miraculous.

"What is going on here? Why is that child on my mother's lap?"

A stern, loud voice made them all jump.

A slender woman stomped up to the nurse. "What is she doing to her?" The woman was dressed in designer jeans and a soft black leather jacket, a leather purse slung over one shoulder.

The nurse jumped and gently lifted Bea off the woman.

The old woman protested. "No. No. No. NO!" She reached for Bea with her good arm. Her wrinkled face contorted in anguish. "No. No!"

"She shouldn't have been on her at all!" The woman started to slap Bea.

Katty jumped but the nurse moved faster.

The nurse lifted Bea to the other side of the

woman's wheelchair, away from the daughter and let Bea kiss the old woman.

The woman hugged her, patted her back and kissed her. A toothless kiss was never so pure and lovely.

Bea patted her and spoke back to the woman, soothing her.

The woman babbled back, softer now.

Katty stepped beside the nurse and lifted Bea from her, careful to avoid the daughter.

The daughter seethed. "Children should never be allowed in here in the first place. Same thing for hospitals. No children allowed." She roughly caressed her mother's hand, avoiding her face. "That little girl needs a spanking."

"No. She deserves a medal. An award for reaching your mother when none of us could ever get her to respond. She deserves a hug at least." The nurse stepped to Katty and hugged little Bea. "Thanks little one." She tucked a finger under Bea's chin. "You can come here anytime." She looked at the daughter. "Kids are welcome here."

A cat strolled up and rubbed against the daughter's leg and meowed.

Bea scrambled from Katty's arms to pet it.

The daughter kicked at it—missed and got Bea.

"Ow! She kicked me!" Bea bounced to the carpet, rubbed her arm and wailed.

The cat hissed and bit the daughter.

"Ow!" The daughter kicked at it again.

The nurse had anticipated the second kick and picked up the kitty, handing it to the aide next to her. She grabbed Bea and handed her to Katty. "Are you okay, sweetheart?"

"I'm going to talk to the board about this!" The woman turned the wheelchair around. "Maybe this nursing home doesn't need my dollars anymore." She stormed down the hall.

The old lady continued babbling and stretching to see Bea.

Bea started to cry as she was wheeled away.

"Stop!" The nurse grabbed Bea and caught up with the daughter. "Stop."

The old woman calmed down.

Bea stopped crying.

The nurse leaned Bea over so she could lay her head on the old woman's chest.

The old woman patted Bea's head, babbling and sobbing. "Love. Love. You."

Bea lifted her head. "I love you, too."

The daughter snarled. "Well, I never got that from her."

"Hmph." The nurse started back to Katty, Bea still in her arms. "Makes sense." She stood in front of Katty and started to hand over Bea.

Bea clung to her neck, hugging the nurse.

The nurse patted her back and kissed her cheek. "Thank you, Little Bea. You made Old Gloria's day. You made her life, just now." She set her down in front of Katty. "And you can come here anytime." She kissed her again.

Katty scooped up Bea and hugged her. "Baby Bea, I've never seen you do that before."

"It's because of Jesus and the little lights."

Noell froze. Sixty years in prison. The pictures in her mind had been right. She shivered. Except for Mr. Grimes, it was the first time her visions had been confirmed.

Clarence checked her face. "I know. You're wondering if you should even be here in this room with me right now. Am I right?"

She couldn't move.

"Yup. Prison." He sat back. "And if I … well, things happened there." He swallowed. "Bad things. I was just a kid when I went in." He seemed to forget about her and disappeared into his memories. "Fights broke out." He jingled change in his pocket. "I killed a man."

She hugged her backpack on her lap. Held her breath.

"They kicked me out of prison to this nursing

home. I was … no I still am, angry. At what life stole from me. Ask Sheriff Dennison—he'll tell you I was innocent." He rubbed his beard and clasped his hands together. "But since coming here, I have met some of the greatest people in the whole world. I haven't told anyone else this, but I know I'm here for a reason."

He shook his head. "I'm not religious, but there's something going on here and I have to do everything I can to find out what it is." He turned to her. "Make sense?"

She bit her lips again. And slowly shook her head.

He chuckled. "I know. It doesn't make sense. But even that black lady that brought us the cookies and milk?" He shook his head. "Ornery as she is, I know even she is helping me replace what I lost all those years. I'm not your regular lawyer either." He spread his hands across the front of his T-shirt. "Led Zeppelin."

Something like happiness connected her heart with her lips. He was kind of likable. In a weathered, hard sort-of-way.

"So … free." He tipped his head and faced her. "I don't know how long I have left on this earth, but there are things I still want to do. And one is help other people. No, keep others from having to go through what I went through. You're young. You have your whole life ahead of you. If I can somehow help you get where you need to be in life, even if it's just helping you with your grandma's estate, then why not?"

She locked eyes with him. Sincerity? Honesty? "Okay. Thanks. Thank you."

He stood and proceeded to wrap the rest of the cookies in a napkin. "You'd better take these, so Lisha doesn't hang us both for not eating them. Okay?" He held them out to her.

"They were really good."

"Especially in cold milk."

She nodded as she stuffed them in her purse, just as a knock came at the door.

Lisha popped in. "You two done wit my tray? You ate them all?"

"Yup! Thanks Lisha." Clarence held out his arm to Noell. "This is Noell and she will be coming here once in a while."

"Hi." Noell half-nodded.

Lisha laughed. "Yeah, I know I'm scary." She pointed at Clarence. "But he's the scary one. Never, I say, never take him seriously. He's all hot air."

Clarence shoved her out the door. "And to think I thought she was the enemy when I first moved here. I was right."

From the hall: "I heard that."

Noell picked up her purse. She hesitated. "Um … who is the little girl?"

"Little girl?" He squinted.

Noell had never, ever pursued her visions, her pictures that opened when people touched her, or when she touched a doorknob or their belongings. Ever.

Until now.

"When you shook my hand … before. When you touched mine, I saw … or I got a picture of a little girl in your arms. She had big brown eyes and kind of thin hair." Deep breath. She blinked. "She must love you very much, because she snuggled into your arms."

To her surprise, he teared up too. He shook his head, chin quivering. "That's my Little One. My Bea." He stepped to the wall with rows of frames and photographs. "Here she is with her mommy, Katty."

Noell stepped closer. Sweet. "She's so tiny. Really pretty. So's her mom. Where are they? Do they live here?"

"They do. Katty is in fact, going to school to be a paralegal, to work here with me." He grinned.

For the first time ever, she was glad she hadn't run out. "Wow. I hope I get to meet them someday."

"I'm sure you will, Noell."

Katty walked down the hall to Clarence's room, Bea's arms tight around her neck. "What? I can kind of understand Jesus. But the little lights?"

"Clarence!" Bea struggled to get down and ran to Clarence.

"Little One!" His deep voice rumbled as he reached out his arms and gathered her close. He smothered her in kisses, breathing deeply. "Oh, I've missed you!"

"We were just here yesterday!"

"Oh, I know, but I need you every day!" He held her away to look at her. "I need my Bea fix every day! Did you grow?"

Bea giggled and went for the tape dispenser on his desk.

Katty shifted. "I need a fix every day, but it's not exactly ..."

He tilted his head and looked at her. "Tough day, Katty?"

"Every day is tough." She shook her head. "Does it get any easier?"

"I admit I haven't had withdrawals, but I experienced them first-hand with many cell-mates over the years." He stood in front of her. Slowly he pulled her close, her head at his chest.

His after shave smelled like outside in the morning—fresh and restoring. She shuddered as she breathed him in. Her arms found their way around him, holding on tight. Before Clarence, she'd never had a hug that didn't require something in return.

"It's gonna be okay, Katty. You'll see. It always works out."

She nodded into his neck. Another deep breath. And another.

He slowly released her and held her at arm's length.

Those eyes. So blue. The sky was the same color through the window behind him. She wiped her tears from his neck.

A young blond woman was standing behind the door.

Katty jumped. "Oh! I'm sorry. I didn't see you there. Sorry Clarence, we butted in on an appointment. I-I'll be all right."

"I know you will. But I needed that hug just as much as you did." He laughed. "Maybe more." He turned to the young woman and held his arm wide. "This is Noell. We've just been talking about what to do with her Gamma's things and how to settle her estate."

He put his arm around Katty's shoulders and faced Noell. "And this is Katty, my … assistant, my friend, my … daughter? Granddaughter?" He chuckled and reached for Bea. "And this is Bea, my little," he looked at Katty. "My little great-granddaughter." He put his arm around Katty. "This is my new family."

Wow.

Bea hugged him then stopped. "Were you in water? Did you take a bath?"

He chuckled. "Well, I took a shower." He sniffed his armpits. "Why, do I stink?"

"She came to me a little while ago and said you were swimming. Talked about water." Katty raised her eyebrows. "Demanded to come see you."

Clarence looked Bea in the eyes. "Hmm. Well, I don't know. Was it a shower or a pool you saw me in, Little One?"

Bea put her hands on each side of his face. "You were underwater. There wasn't any ladder to get out. You were swimming underwater and couldn't get out."

Clarence looked at Katty, his eyebrows raised.

Katty shrugged her shoulders and looked back at him. "Maybe it was the Frosted Flakes she had for breakfast?"

Bea pointed to Noell. "You were there, too."

Clarence turned to Noell. "Noell. Are you all right?"

Noell still stood behind the door. Her face had turned pale. Her eyes were wide.

"Maybe Noell knows what it means." Katty pointed at her.

They all turned to Noell.

"Are you okay, Noell? You look terrified." Clarence put Bea down.

Noell turned. "I-I need to go." She had gathered her things.

Clarence held out his arms to her.

Noell blinked her eyes. Her cheeks were wet. "I'm sorry." And she ran.

"Noell, don't go." Katty stepped to the hall, then back to Clarence. "We ran her off. I'm sorry."

Noell rushed down the hall, past the nurse's station, and disappeared around the corner.

Clarence hobbled to the door. "No. We were done, but her Gamma just died, and she is pretty tender."

"She's really pretty." The memory of her own reflection in the mirror earlier—fine lines and all—flashed in her mind.

Clarence patted her shoulder and hugged her. "And so are you." He turned into the room. "And so are you, Bea." He choked on his words.

Bea had taped her drawings to the wall below Clarence's framed certificates, but the tape was stuck in her hair and on her shirt and to one picture. She looked up, grinning as Clarence pulled it off her shirt.

"What happened?" Katty followed him.

"Look." He laughed. "We might need to buy more tape."

FOURTEEN

June 19, 1937 ~ Dr. Steven's Journal ~ Today is the day. The pool beckons. I have never been so terrified. I stand by my outdoor lab, arms crossed over my chest, staring into it. Mumbling.

I know I need to go in. There is no way I'll ever find out what's in that pool if I don't.

I wiggled my toes in the dirt beside the pool. I don't know how Henry did it—how he jumped in. What had he been thinking? I knew what I was thinking—that this was the last place I wanted to be. The water was cool and refreshing as I stepped in, but one moment I was just up to my knees and the next, I was underwater. I glimpsed the Open-Air Overalls Man before I plunged in—he saluted. Not a good sign.

Present Day ~ Michael sighed. There were days when people saw Michael and things of the Kingdom, and then there were days when they were so engrossed with phones, business, life, that they didn't see what was right in front of them.

Today was one of those days.

He walked down the hall in Hillcrest, passed several residents and staff and was only greeted by one angel—Chrioni, who had a long-time assignment over Mrs. Hatly. Lucky angel.

Michael passed her, smiled, and waved. She always saw him. He always felt her prayers.

He passed by Mr. Wainwright's room on the way to Clarence's. The man, or rather, the demon, hissed and gurgled through its host, Mr. Wainwright.

Michael shook his head.

Sad.

Mr. Wainwright's body didn't stand a chance of survival with a demon of that rank trying to operate through him.

As Michael stood at the doorway, Mr. Wainwright shuddered. His eyes bulged and his upper body left the bed as he pushed a hand at Michael.

The man began to shriek, drawing Lisha, then Carol. They tried to restrain him, but the demon was strong, and the body of Mr. Wainwright was not.

Mr. Wainwright shuddered again and dropped back on his bed.

A fragile voice behind Michael spoke, "God help that man. Don't let him die without You."

Mrs. Hatly shook her fist and Chrioni grinned behind her.

Michael turned in time to see Carol close Mr. Wainwright's eyes.

There was a pause.

A life was gone from the earth, but a much more sinister being was released to roam.

Mr. Wainwright's body shuddered. The first thing the demon saw as it slithered out of Mr. Wainwright was Michael.

Chrioni and Michael joined swords above Mrs. Hatly as the demon rushed from the room.

Michael followed the demon on down the hall. It must be looking for another host. They were always wild-eyed when they came out of a body, but this one was unusual. It was a higher rank than most because the other demons growled and grudgingly bowed as it passed them. It was not the biggest Michael had seen, but something about this creature was different.

It flitted down the hall, in and out of rooms, until it entered the reception area and bumped into a man entering the building.

The guy had a black suit on, black-rimmed glasses and pure white hair.

The receptionist stood and held out her hand. "Mr. Zee?"

The man shook her hand, looking her up and down. "Yes, I am. Are you the greeter for my new kingdom?"

She half-smiled. "My name is Loretta. I'm the Office Manager here at Hillcrest. I could give you the penny tour."

He nodded. "I'd like that."

Michael edged around the man and so did the demon. It must smell something—an attractive aroma —to hover like it was. Or it sensed an assignment. Either way, Michael was on alert. He couldn't do anything unless the receptionist took authority with her words.

As she showed Mr. Zee around, the demon followed, seemed to be listening. Noting possibilities.

When Loretta entered the administrator's office, Mr. Zee slapped the nameplate on the door and informed her that the first job she needed to complete was correcting it to Mr. Zee, Administrator, not Miss Henningway.

He strutted around the desk to the chair and settled in.

Michael realized that the demon recognized Pride and Arrogance in the man. It took seconds for it to make itself at home in Mr. Zee.

The body that the demon now inhabited was

strong and fit, unlike Mr. Wainwright. The demon had chosen well. Very strategic and cunning.

This demon. Michael had seen it before but not for a long time. It was the same one to inhabit Henry Green—hence the candy bars from its host. Good thing Clarence had thrown that one away. The demon could have owned the town by now if Henry hadn't given up.

Mr. Zee's eyes fluttered—a download.

Michael couldn't read his mind or the mind of the demon, but he could guess at the assignment: conquer the receptionist, then Hillcrest Homes.

Then the town of Osceola. It'd try to get back what could have been his through Henry, long ago.

A shaky voice penetrated Michael's thoughts. "Father, keep us safe. Protect us and our angels. Shed Your Light … give us wisdom."

Mrs. Hatly.

Michael soared. An answer. A Hider. The demon was a Hider and that meant that Michael would have to be extra diligent and gather in more of the host, for a Hider could go undetected for centuries, just as this one had—at least since Henry. It was a high-ranking demon—a principality.

Thanks to Mrs. Hatly's prayer, Michael had the answer to centuries of questions.

FIFTEEN

June 22, 1937 ~ Dr. Steven's Journal ~ The Pool. I'd heard of people seeing their lives pass before them like cinema as they drowned. I'd rather have Les Misérables play in my mind than my past. Back up for air. Overall Man was still there. Still saluting.

Under water. Beautiful water. Instead of reflecting light, it seemed to be light somehow. Not like a flashlight beam, but it radiated light, like a warm brick gives off heat. I adjusted my goggles—there seemed to be shadows of fish? Too big.

Present Day ~ Clarence buttoned his suit jacket around his Led Zeppelin T-shirt.

Well, it wasn't his suit jacket. He'd borrowed the

jacket from Harold. It was a little snug. He tapped the American flag pin to make sure it was upright.

He leaned against Michael's truck. "Nice service, huh Michael?" Probably should have used his crutches—his leg was starting to throb.

The church was the usual white churchy building with a tall steeple. Steps led up to the sanctuary where they had just come from. He guessed that for a church it was okay.

Michael seemed distracted. They had been inside listening to the preacher drone on about the Bible, kind of. At least he was speaking eloquently about God stuff. And about Noell's grandma without even knowing her.

The angel should have felt right at home.

"Um, Michael, you okay?"

No answer.

Clarence gave him a shove.

"What?" Michael pulled out of his stupor and looked down at Clarence.

"I just made a comment and you ignored me. I said, nice service."

Michael barely nodded, glanced back to the church building, then at Clarence. Then at the church roof. His eyes were focused, his body tense. He seemed to grow taller, more filled out. His fists clenched, but Clarence couldn't see why. A couple of birds flew off, but that was all.

Angels were really strange sometimes.

One old man appeared from inside the church and started down the steps, followed by an elderly lady dressed to the nines. It was summer, but she even had a fur stole on. Her hair was done up in a swirl or a bun or some such style. Heels. Oh my. Kind of pretty for an old lady.

Mrs. Hatly had her beat, though.

Where was Noell?

There she came—

No, it was the preacher. He turned and held out his arm to someone behind him.

Clarence counted up: the soloist, preacher, four servers, organist. There had been more people helping with the service than attendees. Oh, and the little boy helping the preacher.

And Noell. Here she came.

Clarence buttoned his suit jacket and stood tall when she stepped outside, but unbuttoned the jacket right away, to breathe. He needed to get his own suit if he was going to lawyer in this town. More funerals —maybe weddings. The Led Zeppelin shirt would stay, somehow.

Noell shook the preacher's hand and made her way down the steps. Her long blond hair was tied back with a white ribbon. She'd honored her Gamma by wearing a white summer dress.

"She's a really pretty young woman, huh, Michael."

No reply.

"Michael!" Clarence jabbed Michael in the arm.

He was still watching the roof. Maybe Clarence needed to get his eyes checked, but he didn't see a thing. A loose shingle or two. But nothing that would distract him to that extent.

She reached the bottom of the steps and stopped, looking lonely and abandoned. The expression on her face broke Clarence's heart. She looked like she wanted to … well, her Gamma had just died, and from her story the other day, she was completely alone.

Huh. Just like him.

He looked up at the giant next to him. Well, at least blood ties were all gone.

She slowly walked in their direction. Her eyes were swollen and red. She clutched a couple of programs to her chest. The closer she got, the more her chin quivered.

Clarence opened his arms. What was it about these nice young women? He was an ex-con, but somehow, they were drawn to him. It wasn't even creepy, just … nice. He used to be nice before prison, but now, most of the ladies at Hillcrest thought he was a bastard. Called him names to his face. Sometimes he probably deserved it.

But Katty and little Bea and now Noell seemed to be drawn to him. He guessed he had something they needed. Felt good to be needed.

And they … they reminded him of Annie. His Dearly Beloved, even after all these years. He'd never forget her. Her love. The way she had looked at him, as if he was the only man on this earth.

Noell hesitated, then took a step closer. Then another. And soon she walked into his hug.

The tears poured out. Sobbed. She was just a kid. All alone.

Clarence felt Michael stiffen beside him. He looked above Noell's head.

The preacher walked toward them.

Weren't angels supposed to like preachers?

He held out his hand to Clarence, ignoring Michael.

"Hello." Clarence extended his hand too.

Noell started and turned around, leaning into Clarence when she saw who it was. She tried to smile.

Clarence shook his hand and released. "Nice service, Rev."

"Uh, thank you." He turned to Noell and handed her a paper. "I forgot to give this to you." He smiled a suggestive smile. "I hope you'll call me if there is ever anything I can help you with."

What did he mean by that?

She nodded, taking the paper, tucking into Clarence even more.

She opened it as the man walked up the steps to the church.

He turned at the door and saluted them.

Noell gasped. "This is his bill."

"For services rendered?"

Michael jabbed him.

"Sorry. That just came out." He cleared his throat. "He could have waited and sent it next week."

She scanned the bill and wiped her eyes. Hiccuped.

"It's okay, Noell. From what I saw yesterday in your grandma's file, she left you with more than enough to live on, plus take care of this."

She looked to where the pastor had rushed to and shook her head. "He did the job, but I'm not sure Gamma would have liked him. He was creepy." She looked up at Michael. "Sorry."

Michael smiled at her and took her hand. He bowed deeply.

She blushed.

Clarence stared at Noell when she shook Michael's hand and blinked when Michael kissed hers. "Noell! You can see Michael?" The preacher obviously hadn't seen Michael, but Noell could. A nice warning about the preacher.

She chuckled. "Of course I can see him. Why wouldn't I?" Her eyes flitted between them.

Clarence slumped. "Well, most people …" He looked up at Michael and sighed.

Noell wiped her face and yawned. "I better get to work."

"Looks like you better take a nap first." Clarence touched her shoulder. "I'm sure the Roads Department could do without you for one day." He straightened. "We should go have lunch at the Tasty View." He checked with Michael. "Right?"

No response.

Back to Noell. "My treat," Clarence said. "Besides, don't churches usually have a lunch after a funeral?"

Noell shrugged. "The preacher told me that since it would be such a small service, it would be too expensive to feed just a few." She shrugged. "I guess he's right."

Clarence stared at the door where he'd last seen the preacher. "Damn bast …" He shook his head. "Sorry."

A wind began to stir up leaves and twigs in a small whirlwind in the street right next to them. Each leaf and piece of trash collected into a vortex and rose up in a pillar. Taller and taller.

Chirping and screeching of birds became louder as they gathered, making conversation difficult.

There couldn't be that many birds in this small town. There appeared to be hundreds—maybe thousands—rolling and swarming, up and around and heading right for Clarence, Noell and Michael.

Michael pushed into Clarence and Noell. "Run, humans." He herded them toward the huge church sign and hid them behind it.

Leaves and birds splattered against the big sign.

Clarence crouched against Noell.

Michael seemed to grow again, rising tall, hovering over them.

Debris hit Noell's legs making her flinch.

"Watch out. Here it comes again!" Michael ducked into Noell and Clarence, his huge arms around them. He seemed to stretch, covering them with his body, like a spiritual tent.

Michael moved. He shifted. Tensed.

Clarence looked up to see Michael pointing into the wind. Plainly, Michael was tall enough—or could stretch enough—to see over the sign. Clarence scrunched under Michael and tried to look around him, but he couldn't see anything other than leaves and trash slapping against the sign and Michael.

He seemed to be directing something. Or commanding … that was it.

Who was this guy, anyway?

Michael could see something that Clarence couldn't. Or was there a layer of this human world under a layer of Michael's angel world. Like two different realms superimposed over each other.

Michael released them and backed away; his eyes still intense. His body still engaged.

Clarence backed up. "Noell, we're crushing you. Are you okay?"

Her hair had come undone, the ribbon on the ground. She covered her mouth with both hands and collapsed at their feet.

"Noell. It's okay. It's over now." Clarence looked up at Michael. "Right, Michael? It's gone, right?" He helped her stand, picking leaves from her hair. "What was that?" Clarence put his arm around Noell's shoulders. "What can you see that I can't—we can't see? Were those demons and not just birds?"

Noell began to tremble. "No, wait. Demons?" She stared at Clarence, then Michael.

Clarence let go of Noell and pressed closer to Michael. "Michael." He lowered his voice. "Michael. Y-you've told me you can … you know, really … with your eyes." He stretched his arms wide. "That there is activity here, things going on that we normally aren't aware of, right? Sounds we can't hear, either. Right?"

Michael visibly sighed. He stared at the church building. Seemed to be thinking.

"Yes. There is a realm." He scanned the church yard. "A realm where … angels and demons operate.

And there is something," he cleared his throat. "Something is brewing."

Clarence shook his head. "I thought the invisible realm was like when computers send messages. Like radio waves. The computer makes a little airplane message and flies it to another computer. Right?"

Michael chuckled. "Kind of."

Clarence stomped his foot. "Don't humor me, Michael." Clarence scanned the property. "In prison, I could feel it, almost sense something. A wave or," he searched his memory, "a presence? I'd be in my cell, and something would pass through me. I couldn't see anything, but it gave me chills."

"I can feel something right now." Noell nodded and wiped her face. "My skin is crawling. My head wants to explode."

Clarence looked up at Michael. "How can she feel it and I can't?" He pointed at Michael. "And how can she see you?"

"Wait a minute." She touched Michael's arm. "Why wouldn't I see you?"

Michael leaned down to her. "You have a pure heart. You're not without troubles or problems, but your heart remains with Him."

She frowned, shaking her head. "But ... I don't go to church."

"That's not it. A good church is great, although

…" He paused. "It's about Him." Michael pointed to the sky.

Clarence jingled the change in his pocket. "You mean, God?"

Noell blew out a breath. "Wait? Are you an angel?" Shaking her head, she began to weep.

Michael smiled.

Clarence stood as tall as he could. "Yup. He's an angel."

SIXTEEN

June 23, 1937 ~ Dr. Steven's Journal ~ The Pool. I held my hands together in the form of praying hands and stopped, still holding my breath. Prayer. Yes Lord. I get so busy. I ask for your protection for us all —especially the man who is holding the other end of this rope.

Up for air. Back down. As I pushed my hands together the water became thick. Or some sort of pressure pushed my hands apart. The more I am in this water, the more it baffles me. It's beautiful, but mysterious. I studied slide after slide under the microscope and saw the same bacteria, algae, and amoeba.

Nothing dangerous here.

Present Day ~ Noell knew she was as conspicuous as a purple lion in the jungles of Africa, this first day at the Roads Department. Or as a white woman in an all-Spanish church.

Pink work boots. Orange shirt. The blue overalls weren't bad. Just baggy. No skinny jeans for this job. A new-old lunchbox that touted Mickey Rooney from Gam's stash. She should take it to the antique store and see if she could sell it. Mickey Rooney was from like in the fifties, wasn't he? Wonder what it was like to be famous on a lunch box.

Most people wanted fame and fortune. He got a lunch box. Who was this Mickey Rooney, anyway? Bet Gam would know.

Wait. Gam. Tears threatened. Not here.

Maybe the lady that ran the antique store would know.

Whew. Her jacket was too warm, but she wanted it along. Her always-present backpack hung from one shoulder, complete with a red bandana that Gam had tied there.

Did everything have to make her think of Gamma?

Getting a lawyer to help her take care of Gam's stuff, like her will and the house? God, that had been hard. It had been tough enough to call the funeral home, much less the lawyer.

The Roads building was in sight, a couple blocks

away. Oatmeal she'd eaten for breakfast felt like a brick now.

This was a job she'd never done.

But she was excited, too. She was ready. Would she be driving one of the rocking trucks that she saw around town? Or doing office work? It'd be terrible if she got there today, and they stuck her on the copy machine—1000 copies an hour. Ugh.

Would she be raking leaves? Driving one of those huge maintainers? She hadn't even thought of that until now. How did you drive one of those things?

Or would she be mowing the sides of the roads, the ditches? She'd seen a woman doing that in another county. So much to think about, and she hadn't even started.

She reached the building. It was a typical roads building, made of red concrete blocks and metal siding. A sloped roof with plenty of wires going in and out. She'd heard that they broadcast road conditions to places like the sheriff's department and the schools. Five or six towers reached for heaven from the roof and around the building, making her look up too. As she opened the entrance door, a whoosh of air followed her. Leaves fluttered inside with her.

That would probably be her first job here. Sweeping up those leaves.

She walked to the counter. No one was here. The

clock on the wall said 7:52, so she was a little early, but the place was unlocked.

She should have eaten something different. Her stomach had to be filled with those little fruit flies fluttering around inside. The ones that hovered over the bowl of too-ripe peaches. She wished she could swat at the ones in her stomach.

Steve Ivertson was the office guy's name. Or the manager. Or the boss. He had seemed nice when he hired her. Hopefully he was always nice.

A truck drove up behind the building. Half a minute later, the back door of the building opened, and Steve popped in. "I knew you'd be on time. You hit me as the kind of person that would either be early or right on time."

She waved shyly. "Hi."

He motioned her on back to the break room. "Hey. Sorry about your grandma." He cleared his throat. "Thanks for letting me know. I saw her name on the Funeral Home sign—Gwendolyn Randolph Carpenter? I'm really sorry Noell. Do you need more time off?"

She fidgeted with her backpack strap, head bowed. "That was Gamma." Her chin wouldn't stop quivering. "But I'm all right. There's stuff to do at home, but I needed to—"

"Get away? I know. I'm not very good at that

kind of stuff." He nodded, lifted his hard hat, and scratched his head. "But if you need—"

"No, I'm okay. I need the money. A funeral costs …"

Silence.

"Uh, yeah. Tough for a young girl your age to deal with. If there's anything I can do …"

Awkward silence.

"Well, come on in and I'll show you around." He pointed to lockers along one wall. "Here's where you can stash your stuff." He looked over at Noell. "You travel light for a girl. My wife would have brought a suitcase to stay all day."

She smiled. Lockers would be nice. "Can we lock our locker?"

"Sure. We even have some combo locks, so just let me know if you want one." He waved toward the restrooms. "There're the bathrooms. We have a men's and women's, so's you have one all to yourself. The guys all have to share, and you will be liking not having to share with them. Us." He chuckled, pointed to himself.

"Here's all kinds of vending machines. The last boss loved candy, so he installed three snack machines and two drink machines. Kinda nice. I'm not sure we'd get the city to do that now." He opened a refrigerator door and showed her a space for her food. "Everybody is pretty respectful of each other's food."

He opened the microwave door and closed it fast. "Gross. It's a full kitchen. Microwave, stove, cupboards. You can claim a cupboard if you like. It comes in handy if we are here overnight." He looked at Noell. "That doesn't happen very often, but when it does, like in an ice storm, or disaster, or snowstorm, it's nice to have a place to warm up some soup."

He reached into a cupboard drawer and handed Noell a combination lock. "You okay with remembering numbers and stuff? Like your own combination?"

She nodded.

"Some of the guys aren't … well, every once in a while, somebody has to hack a lock because they can't remember the combination numbers."

"No, I can remember stuff like that."

Steve stepped back and surveyed Noell. "I'll bet you're a pretty smart girl. We can sure use somebody like you here."

She smiled. "Hope it works out." She was beginning to sound like Steve. Which wasn't a bad thing. She was gonna like this guy.

The entrance door slammed.

"Hey, I found it first."

"Naw, it's my pop. Hands off!"

Voices got louder the closer they got.

"You are not my boss. And I found it first!"

"Well," Steve said, "the kids—er the others are here. Let's go meet them. It's as good a time as any. I'll show you what I want you to do in a bit."

She stashed her lunch box in her locker along with her jacket and backpack and locked it. She yanked on it. Seemed secure. She ripped off the tape with the combination written on it and pressed it on the inside of her hard hat.

Deep breath. Meet the guys. She was no more eager or good at meeting new people than she was eating someone else's cooking.

She turned to go into the next room when she heard one of the guys. "Really? A girl? To replace Ned. You are kidding, right?"

Another voice. "A girl can't do what he did."

"Besides, he's coming back sometime."

"Guys, she is in the next room. And we need the help now. I'm sure she will fit in fine. She seems to have a lot more on the ball than you did, Ken. We had to teach you how to run the coffee maker. Remember?"

Noell slipped into the main room, wishing she was invisible.

"Here she is." Steve swept his arm toward Noell in the main room of the Roads Department. "Here's our new hire."

Noell wanted to slink past them all and slide out the entrance door, like an invisible ninja. Instead, she nodded at the row of guys and swallowed. Her face and neck burned. She'd never measure up to these guys—to this job.

There was a line of five guys, including Steve. All were of the male gender, but as one or two ogled her, their place on the status quo slipped to bottom feeders. She may be a hard core germaphobe, but she also had built-in radar where men were concerned. She was proud of it. She lived by it.

Steve introduced them all. One man seemed older —his name was Bill. Gray and brown hair barely visible under the hard hat. Lines around his dark eyes and mouth— bet he smiled a lot. He tipped his hard hat at her.

She tipped her head.

Another had unruly curly hair stuffed under his hard hat, but a nice smile. He also filled out his work shirt the best of them all. "Hi." His name was Rat, for whatever reason. This must be the guy who had all the requests for days off.

She turned to the last two. One seemed Spanish descent, but sometimes it was hard to tell until they talked. His name was Miguel. The other guy, Ken, was maybe nearer her age and well … cute by a high school girl's standards, but Noell could see right through him. He wouldn't look at her though. At least the Spanish guy smiled a friendly smile, even though he looked tired this early in the morning.

Steve held out his hand. "Guys, this is Noell Carpenter. Ned's replacement."

Someone, Noell couldn't detect who, snickered.

"You mean Ned's temp replacement."

"Remember." Steve commanded respect. "We all started as novices when we got here. Well, except for Miguel here." Steve scratched the stubble on his chin. "I think today, since we are starting over kind of, with Ned gone and Noell new, we should start with the typical shove-it."

Groans all around.

Noell looked at each man, then Steve.

Steve grinned at her. "It'll be a good way for us all to get to know you and learn to work together. I'll show you where you need to be and help you today. We are all helping each other."

Ken blew out an exasperated breath. "I feel like I'm in Kindergarten."

"Huh. You act like it too." Rat shoved him to the door.

They filed out to the trucks. Rat walked beside Noell. "Nice boots. Where'd you get the pink?"

She smiled. "My Gam ... er, Grandma had them. Thanks." She got in the truck up front with Steve, avoiding the men in the other truck for now. They slammed doors, and Steve revved the truck. "The shove-it," he explained, "is filling potholes. It's a fill-the-day-up task but has to be done in a rotation because the roads get so much traffic these days." He nodded her direction. "You'll direct traffic around where we are filling holes. Your sign has STOP on one side and SLOW on the other. Just watch the traffic and let them flow as we work. We don't work in a long stretch of road when we do this, like in big time construction, so if you run into trouble, I'm right there. It helps us to get to know each other and you. Okay?"

She nodded. "Okay."

They drove about five miles outside of town and all got out. It was a long stretch of asphalt road, but she could see places that needed to be filled. The guys in the other truck were unloading equipment, tar, and buckets.

Steve showed Noell her sign and where to stand. He turned it one way, then the other. That was it. Pretty easy. STOP. SLOW.

The guys got set up on the road, and Noell took her place. Just her and the sign. She looked both ways. And again. No cars. No trucks. Not even a bicycle. This could get boring. She thought back to the hospital and bedpans. Hands down. This was better.

She could smell the fresh air, even though it was laced with tar. She could see and hear birds chirping. Way better than ... well, what bedpans had in them.

Wait. A car. Or a truck. Hard to see from this distance.

It turned off before it got to where they were working.

After a while, the guys started bickering about something. They had to clean out the hole, blow away any debris, and fill it with hot smelly tar. Yuck. Rat and Miguel were the only two who seemed to know what they were doing. Ken didn't know didly; she didn't know didly but could tell already Ken knew nothing about the job. Or didn't care. Both. Rat was right in there as was Miguel. Steve, as foreman, had to stand and watch and make sure it was done right. And Bill seemed to be able to do anything because he probably cared.

Oh, another car. Or truck. Too far to see again.

As it drove closer, she saw it was a newer red pickup truck. Two men were in it. She looked behind her at the gang, to see if the truck needed to stop or slow. She caught Steve's eye. He shrugged. He was no help.

She turned to the pickup and checked the road both ways and how much space they were taking up.

Ken's leg was over the line.

She turned the sign to STOP and held it up for the pickup to see. It was still far away, so she had time to change it, but she felt they should stop. Out of the corner of her eye, she saw Steve nod. Whew.

This couldn't be hard, but it was her first day, her first time doing this. And for the safety of the guys, she had to do it right. Plus, she wanted to keep this job. For some reason, she felt this was falling into some sort of a plan. Maybe. She had never dreamed of working construction.

She truly wanted to make a difference, but how?

Today? She could make a difference for the men in the red truck driving toward her, to keep them safe, no matter how they felt about her making them stop.

Today. She could make a difference in the Roads guys' lives by keeping traffic away, so they wouldn't get hurt.

The red pickup stopped. She glanced down at the work in progress and at Steve, who had become very interested in making sure Ken cleaned the debris out of the hole. She glanced behind her. A car was coming up fast from the other direction. She had to make the pickup stay put. Dust and the glare made it hard to see if the occupants were paying attention. She tapped the pole onto the asphalt—STOP!

The other side of her sign read SLOW, but if the car was doing anything, it was speeding up.

"Steve?" she shouted.

Steve stepped beside her on the center line, a kind of shield from the dust and dirt but also the car.

The car came up on them quickly, but at the moment it might have passed them and possibly hurt

Steve, it came to a halt, sending gravel and dust flying. The driver at the wheel lurched forward in his seat. Not hurt, but startled. Had he even seen them until now?

"Woah! That driver is crazy." Rat growled as he tamped tar down with his shovel. "What was he thinking?"

The guy looked as baffled as she felt. She turned around to make sure the pickup was still stopped, and it was. They were put. They were not edging forward. Just waiting.

Steve pointed to the sign. SLOW. And motioned for the car to go. The guy must have been very startled by stopping so fast, because he just inched by as he drove around them.

"Did you see that guy?" Rat stood behind her. "He was terrified for some reason."

"Well, he stopped crazy fast, but didn't hit the windshield. Just shook him up, that's all." Ken bounced the shovel on the surface of the road. "I've stopped fast before and didn't know how I did it. We may never know," he finished in a soft, sing-song voice.

The guys laughed—all except Steve. "Okay. He's around. You can … you know what to do, Noell." He nodded. "Good job."

Good job? She grinned, teeth and all. She never

smiled that big. But she never heard "good job" from anyone but Gam.

She flipped the sign to SLOW and nodded to the men in the red pickup.

They started up and drove around them and stopped beside Noell. "Hey. What's a road crew doing out here?"

Noell smiled and showed them the holes. "Just fixing the road."

The old man leaned over the younger one. "It's a great day to be out here, huh. Beautiful sunshine, birds twittering."

"Hey!" She pointed. "Mr. Timmelsen! Right?" Those blue eyes. She'd know them anywhere. "And Michael! Hi!"

Clarence squinted and held up his hand to block the glare.

She lifted her hard hat.

"Noell? What are you doing out here?" Clarence chuckled. "Well, dumb question on my part. You're working for the Roads Department. Good job!"

She grinned again.

"And, yes, it is a beautiful day!" She checked the road, both directions.

"Say, have any of you guys," Clarence shook his head, "and Noell. Have you seen any caves around here? You're out and about, working the roads all over. Have you seen any caves?"

Noell looked at Steve and back to Clarence. "I haven't, but … I just started working on the Roads crew today." She motioned for Steve to join her. "Steve? Mr. Timmelsen, here, wants to know about caves."

Since the whole crew heard the question, they all stood up like she had addressed all of them, instead of just Steve.

Steve walked over to the red pickup. "Nice truck. What year is this?" He surveyed the back bed of the truck and walked around to the front.

Noell froze. Could Steve see an angel? How could some people see Michael sometimes and other times, not? Did the angel get to choose? Angels could have some fun with that—a red truck without a driver.

Michael cleared his throat. "Uh … it's a 19. Well, I'm not sure. I'm not really—"

Clarence leaned over again. "It's a 2006 Ford." He nodded. "A Ranger, right, Michael? Pretty neat, huh. He just got it, right, Michael?" He looked over at Michael. "Where did you get this anyway?"

The big man blushed. "Well, … uh … Father gave it to me. I didn't get to pick it out, but I love it. It runs good and gets me—us—where we need to go."

Clarence looked at Michael. "You got it from …

your father? Woah." He patted the dash in front of him. "Takes this little truck up a whole new level."

Noell raised her eyebrows and blew out a breath. "Your Father?"

Michael gripped the steering wheel and peered up at her, a half-smile on his lips. His eyes twinkled, challenging her—no daring her, to believe.

She, in her hard hat, dusty in her orange X shirt, hesitated, but rose to the dare and smiled. Full teeth grin. Inside her, something solidified. Something went down so deep in her that she knew. She just knew.

Michael patted the steering wheel. "It's an automatic." He grinned.

Clarence sputtered and raised his eyebrows. "Uh, yeah. Back to the caves. Are there any around here? Seems like this area is pretty flat and wouldn't be prone to caves."

Steve looked back at the crew. "Hey guys. You can still work while we talk, okay?"

Noell checked for cars both ways. Nothing.

Steve tapped his hard hat. "You know, just the other day—"

"Hey Steve." Rat moved the bucket. "Want to check this?"

Steve nodded and turned to Bill. "Bill. You remember anything about a cave or an underground spring? You've been on the crew longer. Anything?" He walked over to the crew.

Bill pushed his hard hat off his forehead and scratched. "You know, I do remember something. It was a while ago, though." He put the hat back on. "It might have been on the old Gustafson place—you know—about a mile," he turned around in a circle, "south from here. That way." He pointed in the direction the red truck was headed. He looked over his shoulder. "But that might have been dug up and leveled years ago. You know how they change the lay of the land for their pivots. Gustafson sure rings a bell though."

Clarence and Michael exchanged a look.

Steve perked up. "Yeah. Just the other day—"

"We." Clarence paused. "We know where that's at, huh Michael."

Michael's eyes widened and nodded.

Noell checked for cars again. "What-what happened?"

Michael began tapping the steering wheel. "My other truck, the grinding truck, fell down a sink-hole at Merle Gustafson's place."

Noell leaned down.

Clarence's eyes were wide too.

Steve slapped his hard hat. "That was you guys?" He looked back at Bill. "His other truck is the one at Merle Gustafson's farm." His hand made a dive motion as he whistled. "Along with Merle's new tractor."

The whole crew stopped working and chatter began.

"We heard about that."

"Can you get it out?"

Miguel leaned on his shovel. "Insurance pay for that?"

Clarence glanced at Michael. "Well, we don't think so ... we don't know yet, right Michael?"

Michael shrugged.

"Well, we better be off. Thanks." Clarence leaned over and reached out his hand. "Clarence Timmelsen. I live at Hillcrest Homes. This here's Michael, my ... right hand man." He looked at Michael. "Or am I your right-hand man?" He laughed. "Anyway, get in touch with us if you think of anything or find any caves around here."

Noell checked the road and flipped her sign to SLOW.

Steve turned back to the crew. "We'll keep you in mind if we find anything."

"Okay. Thanks!"

The red truck drove off, leaving them in its dust. Even though it drove off slowly, there was an awful lot of dust. They all stood coughing until Noell realized that a big semi had pulled up beside them. She hadn't even had time to switch the sign to STOP. The dust had prevented her from seeing it.

A big man with hairy arms leaned out the driver's side window. A dog barked on the passenger seat. "You want me to stop or slow? You decide, because you're the one with the sign, little lady."

Her face burned. She looked over at the gang. "I guess you can go." She tapped the sign on the road.

The driver shifted and drove forward, shifting the whole way down the road, until she couldn't see the truck anymore.

Bill's head popped up. "Hey, you know? There used to be a cave in town."

"In town?" Steve pointed to another car coming close in. "A cave in town? That's crazy. I think your rememberer is done remembering."

"No. Really. Something about … drownings, too." He lifted his hardhat and scratched. Wiped his face. "Seems like it was close to where the nursing home was built."

Noell flipped her sign. "Hillcrest Homes?"

"Yeah. Maybe I should give that guy a call, huh?"

"Okay, guys. I think we're done here. Looks good." Steve picked up a shovel. "We'll go back to town and break for lunch. Then we'll have a go at the downtown curb access. We still need to break down the last one on the East side. Main and Hawkeye.

That's where we left off." He patted Bill on the shoulder. "Remember that corner, Bill?"

Bill pulled his hardhat down over his face. "Main and Hawkeye," he mumbled into the hat. "It's because I drove the truck into the street signs, and they will be forever in my line of vision."

Rat laughed. "You drove the truck into the sign?" He picked up a bucket and walked to the truck. "Knock it over did ya?"

Bill dropped his chin to his chest and followed the guys, dragging his shovel on the dirt.

They slammed the truck doors closed on the rest of the conversation.

Noell picked up her sign and walked it to the truck. What an easy morning. Other than meeting the guys and dealing with people who don't follow the signs, it was an easy morning. And she got paid for it.

The moment with Michael. Worth it all.

Never had she dreamed she would be comfortable with five guys on a dirt road. Huh.

Steve pounded on the outside of the door. "Okay. Let's go."

Noell smiled to herself. She was going to like this job. She might even let herself like Rat. He needed to change his name though—gave her the creeps.

SEVENTEEN

June 24, 1937 ~ Dr. Steven's Journal ~ Bar-side Service. Three people attended. I was one. Plus the guy sitting at the bar.

"Let us pray."

I removed my straw hat and bowed my head when the Reverend began to pray. First time attending a funeral service inside a bar. A distinct odor of alcohol could be perceived with each word that was prayed.

Never mind. It didn't matter.

Henry's own brother hadn't even shown up. His own brother.

I guess that didn't matter either. I just hope Henry is in a better place—heaven.

The preacher cleared his throat.

The man next to me removed his hat.

Preacher cleared his throat again and the men placed their beers on the table.

"We are all gathered here to remember … what was his name?"

Where had they found this guy? I need to write as much as I can remember—no one would ever believe this funeral. "Henry. Henry Green."

"Yeah. He lived a long life and will be remembered. Amen."

"Amen!" The others raised their beers. "To Henry Green!"

Henry deserved better.

Present Day ~ New day. Clarence dressed and shuffled to the window in his bedroom. Looked like a beautiful day. The park had just been mowed. He could smell it even through the glass. Trees swayed with the breeze, like ballet dancers with their branches held high in graceful form. If he leaned to his left, he could see the bridge where the pool was from his window.

He hobbled to his office. Four walls. A hurt leg. Even though he had been out with Michael, he couldn't shake feeling trapped. When he first moved in, he escaped regularly. Explored the town. Now, when he couldn't, he needed to.

At least he had two rooms. Clarence Timmelsen, Law Office. Rooms 202 and 204, Hillcrest Homes in Osceola, Nebraska—a nursing home.

At first when Carol had broached the idea to him, he balked. Would anyone hire a lawyer in a nursing home? Plenty had hired him when his shingle hung in prison. Inmates thinking he could get them free—when they were guilty.

He had no idea who would hire him here, but now that he was getting organized, it made sense. He counted on his fingers—Carol had asked for help for her husband Joe, Mrs. Hatly's insurance company had been skipping out on payments, and now Noell with her Gamma's estate. Sweet girl.

He glanced out the office window. He didn't have to mow. He didn't have to plan dinner and definitely didn't need to cook or clean up, although he was friends with the guy who did. Nice guy.

He didn't even have to clean his room, although he did once in a while to help out.

Living in a nursing home made perfect sense to an eighty-year-old man who had spent the last sixty years in prison. He hadn't always felt that way. Six weeks ago, he had either wanted to die or go back to prison.

When he let himself be honest, getting shipped

back to the town where it all started was the best thing that could have happened—most days.

Carol knocked. "Clarence, you need anything?" She nodded toward his leg. "How's the pain?"

He shook his head. "It's a low roar."

"If it's roaring, then you need something." She opened the chart in her hand, flipping pages.

"No." He shook his head. "Not."

She pursed her lips. "You sure?"

"Yup."

She wrote in his chart, reading it out loud, "Resident refuses pain meds," and stuck her tongue out at him. Putting the file in the cart, she mumbled something about him being a stubborn man.

He smiled as she left and scanned his rooms. The boxes loaded with books could wait. He closed the cardboard flaps.

He peeked into another box close by. Old law books. It had taken him a long time to even decide to be a lawyer. He had done it for the wrong reason —revenge.

He kicked at a box. That hurt—still couldn't get used to the pain in his leg. He could go through the rest tomorrow.

Right now? Coffee with Mrs. Hatly, the cutest lady and his best friend in all of Hillcrest Homes. Maybe the world. Next to Carol and Harold, his detective buddy.

Somebody kicked his door open, banging it into the shelving unit behind.

"You Clarence Timmelsen?"

"Yeah. Who wants to know?"

In stumbled a beautiful young woman. Well, she looked young in comparison to the residents. A kid with braces and pimples followed her in, like a toddler chasing candy, tongue practically drooling. They each lugged heavy cardboard boxes.

She slammed hers down on the desk and stood, straightening her gapping blouse. Too short a skirt. Spike heels.

"How do you even walk in those things? They look dangerous." Clarence followed her to the desk and lifted the flaps of the box. "What's all this? What'd you say your name was?"

"I didn't." She caught her breath. "I'm Pete's secretary." When she didn't get a response from Clarence, she continued. "Pete Malovitch? Remember him? You killed him if I remember right?"

Clarence froze and shoved his hands at her. "I had nothing to do with that. Sheriff shot him." Pieces of the Pete puzzle began to fit together. This woman and Pete …. He checked her left hand. They were—

She slapped a document down on the desk. "Sign here for boxes delivered. I don't want the likes of you coming after me, saying I didn't deliver your stuff."

"My stuff? Why would Pete have had my stuff?"

He flipped the box flap open again. "This isn't mine, it's …." The top document. Dad's name. "Dawes Timmelsen?" He tensed and coughed, choked. "How'd you get my dad's stuff?"

"Pete had it in his old building next to ours … uh, his." She sniffed. "He bought the building from the Clynder family." She pointed a long red fingernail at the space on the release form. "Sign." She grabbed a pen from his desk and shoved it at him. "I've been left with clearing out the buildings, so I'm clearing this out to you. If you don't want it, throw it out. Burn it. I don't care, but don't you ever give it back to me. Hear?"

"I hear." Clarence signed her release, then opened the flaps, taking the top documents out. "Thanks, I think."

She stomped out, bumping into the kid. "Drop it down anywhere. And make it fast. We have lots left to do."

The kid dropped his box next to the desk, and ran smack-dab into Carol, knocking her against the wall.

"Excuse me." Carol pulled her white nursing jacket closer to her body, flapping one front over the other.

The kid skirted around her and followed the woman.

Carol leaned into Clarence, whispering. "Who was that?"

"You don't know? It's Pete Malovitch's bi … uh, secretary." He pointed to the boxes. "She was neighborly enough to drop these off. And I have no idea whose they are, except this top paper has my dad's name on it." He sighed and rubbed his neck, tossed the papers back into the box.

"And the kid?"

"No idea! Her love puppy?"

"Clarence!" She popped him on the shoulder. Turning into the room, she scanned the framed certificates on the wall. "I haven't had time to look at these."

He checked the wall too, a half-smile on his lips. Never got to hang those in prison. "Like it?"

"Yes. Very impressive. Looks like a law office." She inspected Annie's picture and the one of Bea and Katty. "Annie was a very pretty woman. Little Bea could be her child."

Clarence looked closer. "You're right. Something about the eyes." He crossed his arms, lingering at the photographs. "Sweet kid, that's all I know. We were drawn together by serendipity or whatever."

Carol laughed. "Maybe God?"

That God stuff. He shook his head. "Maybe not?"

She punched him again. "What if I were to tell you that I believe that Joe and I were drawn together by God? Joe believed it too."

Oh-oh. She was setting him up again.

He removed some papers from one of the boxes and pretended to read one. "Well, if that's what you and Joe want to believe. That's your business." He checked her expression. "How is old Joe, anyway? Doing better?"

"Well." She swallowed. "That's really why I came in." She glanced at the hall. "Could we—"

"Shut the door?" He shoved it closed. "Let me get all official here." He pushed the box to the other side of the desk and offered her a side chair. "Welcome to my law office." He waved at the wall full of frames. "I'm open for business, thanks to this real kind … and cute lady who works here."

She blushed.

He took a seat. "How can I help you, Ma'am?"

She half-smiled. She bit her lips into her mouth and sat. Took a deep breath.

He reached for her hand and squeezed it. "What is it? Joe?"

She nodded.

"Is he worse?"

She nodded again. A tear slipped down one cheek.

His own eyes burned. He had grown to love Carol in these short weeks since arriving at the nursing home. She had such a big heart. She had almost let him keep the hawk.

Carol swallowed again and took a deep breath.

"He's worse, and the doctor is counseling me to take him off all support. He said last night that I need a lawyer." She crumpled. "And you're the only one I know." She wiped her face. "Will you help me?"

"Of course I'll help you." He softened his voice. "You let me know what specifically you need, and I'll—"

"Medical power of attorney. That's what the doctor said." She searched his face. "Am I giving up if I do this?"

He shook his head and patted her hand. "No, Carol. You are planning for whatever happens. What if he lives? What if he ... this is just a protection for you and him."

"And if he dies? What does it do?"

He pointed toward her. "It gives you direction—the doctor direction. You don't have to think about what to do. It's already set forth. As long as we are assured that Joe understands—that he can sign ... even if he can only sign an X." He cocked his head. "Make sense?"

She nodded. "Okay. Well. Let's do this." She looked down at her lanyard, fingered the keys together. "I know he would want me to do the right thing." She stood and opened the door, deep breath. "The other thing?" She bowed her head. "I feel God telling me to forgive Joe."

"What?" Clarence shook his head. "Forgive Joe? For what?"

She held up her hands. "I know. It's not his fault, but I might be holding this illness and what it's done to our life, against him. Kinda. It is the right thing, isn't it?"

He walked around the desk and hugged her. "When Annie died, there were a lot of stupid things going on—like her dad, the judge. The town." He jutted his chin out, tears welled in his eyes. It still got to him. "Well … I knew after a while that I had to move on. That's when I got the idea to be a lawyer. At first, I wanted to take Judge Green down for putting me away, so I figured I could get back at him somehow if I was a lawyer. But after a while, people started coming to me—even guards—for help." He shrugged. "I kind of felt Annie giving me that, so I could make something good out of my life—even there in prison."

She took a deep breath.

He hugged her again. "And you will too … make something good out of this."

She let out a sob but swallowed it. Deep sigh again. She peeked up at him. "Thanks Clarence." She hugged him back. "I'm so glad you moved here."

He laughed. "I didn't have much to say about it." He had wanted to kill that old bastard judge—he still wanted to kill him. Judge Green was the reason he was in this nursing home. His blood began to boil, but he squelched it. Stuff it down. Deep breath. "But." He glanced out the window, then back at her. "I'm glad too." He paused. "Maybe. Just maybe that was your God getting me out of prison and … here."

What a precious lady Carol was.

Michael leaned against the wall of the office as Carol and Clarence talked.

Neither seemed to see him.

It didn't matter. He must be available. Be ready for a time when the humans rose to who they could be.

So, he was patient.

Of the people he had served throughout time, most didn't understand that.

One elderly lady had understood. Harriet. She had taught a Bible study in another town. Before Clarence was born, she had been Michael's charge. Angels had swarmed around her when she yelled out Scripture, and then they flew out on assignment. She had it figured out.

When the Word had gone forth from her mouth, angels had dropped jewels from heaven onto her lap. She'd ask Father where they were needed, and He'd point out the person.

Probably helped the popularity of her Bible study. But, once people—mostly women—heard her teach, they were hooked by her words from Father's heart, more than seeking any gems.

Harriet had seen him every time. From the time she was a tiny girl, she had been able to see him. She never forgot how.

She was one of few.

He hoped that someday Clarence would be able to see him all the time.

The woman with a youth carrying boxes had just left.

An angel had followed each one and they had bowed in greeting—the woman's angel carrying an open book and pen, scribbling what she said as he walked. He barely had time to acknowledge Michael.

Michael had some humans like that. Constantly talking.

The woman had slammed her box down on the desk, her face red and flushed. Her black eyes darted from Clarence to the boxes and around the room. What she didn't realize was a demon about the size of a moth perched on top of her head, grinning at Michael. It had seemed to hold two strands of her hair like reins, turning her head this way and that.

From where Michael stood, she had appeared terrified. Whatever was in her heart must be painful.

Clarence had stopped short when she accused

him of killing Pete. A dark thread had flown around Clarence's neck, and a spider-like demon crawled up his right shoulder. It cinched the thread up tight, making it harder for Clarence to breathe, much less swallow. Fear choked out any truth that Clarence might have spoken.

Another spirit had climbed out of her blouse, which was already stretching at the buttons, revealing black lace.

The poor kid with her.

Michael had to restrain himself. Unless the kid told her she needed to fix her blouse, or something like that, Michael couldn't interfere.

When Clarence had scanned the top document, the demon pulled the thread tighter.

A mist rose up from behind the woman—above her, gathering into the shape of a brown-skinned creature that hovered above her. It reeked, and pus oozed from sores on its skin. Probably what stunk.

The woman's voice had gotten louder. "I don't care, but don't you ever give it back to me! Hear?" The big demon crossed its arms across a bulbous chest. It had glared condescendingly at the angels— until it spied Michael. Then it shivered and more sores broke out, the mist becoming thicker.

When she had stomped out and Carol came in, the whole atmosphere changed. Her angel, Jehoel, had bowed low, one shoulder down—football offense style—to Michael and grinned.

No time for a wrestling match.

Michael had skimmed his hand along the thread that by now had made a deep, dark crease along Clarence's neck. When he had released it, it fluttered to the floor.

Clarence let go of a deep breath and swallowed. Rubbed his neck.

Jehoel edged closer. He was a seasoned warrior, like Carol. They made a good pair. He swiftly rotated, sword instantly out.

Something had hissed from the direction of the hallway.

Carol visibly shivered.

Mr. Wainwright's demon had drawn in more spirits. More hissing. Stronger. Louder.

Growling. Deep guttural noises.

Michael bowed his head as she and Clarence hugged.

Jehoel did too.

Precious friendships among humans. Almost like angels.

Jehoel's presence grew stronger, his glow brighter. "Rise up, Michael." He drew his sword. "Incoming!"

Michael drew his and they crossed them over Carol and Clarence.

Two demons slammed into the swords and vanished. A putrid brown mist curled around them, hanging in the air.

Carol had peeked up at Clarence. "Thanks Clarence." She had hugged him back. "I'm so glad you moved here."

Clarence had talked about the Lord—Michael held his hand high.

Jehoel clasped Michael's hand. "Lord rules!"

"Always!"

Michael still gripped Jehoel's hand high above his head and prayed. "Father, help us hear your heartbeat. Help us do Your will. Keep us strong."

"I'm glad your charge moved here, Bro. It's been a long time since you and I have been together on assignment."

"Agreed."

More growls.

"I hope you enjoyed your last vacation, Jehoel, because this run is going to tax you plenty. Stay alert. This demon is full of surprises."

"Vacation? That family had numerous children and several grandparents still living. That's a vacation?"

Michael smiled. "The destiny of those children is powerful in the Kingdom."

Little Bea, too.

Carol waved at Clarence as she left the room.

Jehoel saluted Michael and stayed at Carol's side.

Clarence sat at his desk and scanned the paper in front of him. "Dawes Timmelsen. Huh."

Michael leaned against the wall, his head above the roofline, scanning the realm around Hillcrest—watching, waiting.

EIGHTEEN

June 25, 1937 ~ Dr. Steven's Journal ~ The Pool.
Open-Air Overalls Man introduced himself today—
his name is Paul. Named after the Apostle Paul, he
said. "That is the only resemblance." He brought his
grandson, who wears overalls too—open air. His
name is Ralph. Spitting image of his grandad. Can't
wait to meet the rest of the family.

Back in the pool today. I have tested the water at
length. Jars line up on shelves and wooden boxes I
built against the camper. Each jar holds two inches of
pool water and has been tested for buoyancy, by
putting a different object into it—a ball, leaf, pen,
pebble. Interesting thing—doesn't matter how heavy
or light an object is, everything sinks. A leaf sinks. A
rock sinks. The pool pulls it under. Is there an under-
tow? Is there another pool deeper that draws objects

deeper? Why would gravity work only on the objects and not the water? Why did it seem that it was the water with the force of gravity? At the deepest the rope would allow me to go, I felt like I would turn inside out. I don't know how else to describe it, but almost like when a person hits a cold spot in a lake or river, I hit a place where I could almost see inside myself. I feel less and less a researcher/scientist and more a guinea pig, but who is doing the research on me?

Present Day ~ Noell stood at the copy machine. Fifty copies of this. Fifty copies of that.

She looked around the Roads Department office. How did she go from mowing for Gam, to a flag girl? And now inside making copies.

She really did do a great job as sign girl. Steve even said so the day before yesterday. When she checked the calendar on the counter, she had already been a week on the job. Almost payday!

She tapped the copies on the counter and counted piles. One. Two. Three. Ten piles of fifty copies each. She felt like she was doing stuff that didn't need to be done. Like busy work just to keep her … busy. A waste of her time. A waste of company money.

She looked at the clock. Lunch. She didn't know

where the guys were, but it was noon, and she was going to have lunch.

She gathered up all the copies and put them in their slots, like Steve had asked her to. There had been no phone calls, so no phone messages. No deliveries. No one had stopped in for anything. Gah. Boring morning.

She walked into the break room, opened her locker, and took out her backpack. Her stomach growled as she fished out her lunch and water bottle. She started to set it on the table, but someone had spilled soda or something again. It was sticky—made her cringe. She had washed off the table earlier, just like she always did because the guys came in every day and slammed their junk on the table. They always left it with dirt and crumbs. She was sure they liked having a maid to clean up after them.

The radio sputtered to life. "Hey Noell, we need you out here. Steve just cut himself bad."

It had been quiet all morning, so this made her jump. She ran for the radio. "Hey Ken. What do you want me to do?" She looked out the window at the company truck.

"Get the first aid kit and drive it out here. We are three miles south on the Stovepipe Road."

"St-stovepipe Road?"

"The black top that connects with the street you are on. Just get the kit and jump in the truck. Then drive straight south three miles. You can't miss us. We have the crane."

"Okay. I'll be right out." She grabbed her sandwiches and drink and put them away. She gathered up bottled water too, just in case, and ran for the door. "Got keys. The first aid kit."

She slammed the door but came back in right away. "Do I lock the door? I don't have a key, so I guess not." She went back outside. "But I can't leave it unlocked. They have cash in here. There is equipment in here—"

The radio buzzed from inside. "Hey, Noell, if you're still there, just slam the door. It usually is hard to open so people just think it's locked. Steve has the key in case you did lock it. Come on! We need that kit."

Did they have cameras over the door? She slammed the door so hard she felt like the glass would break. Note to self. See that all vehicles have first aid kits. Not that she wasn't glad to help, but what if it was bad and she didn't get there in time? That made her kick it in gear. She jumped into the truck, tossing the water bottles on the seat. Ahh. Stick shift. Bill had taught her how, but never by herself.

She started it up and killed it right off. Okay. Clutch. Brake. Start it and let the clutch off slowly. Killed it.

She tried again. It roared to life. Yay. She backed out and killed it again. Started it again. Forward.

Three miles. Two. One. She saw the crane up ahead. What were they doing with a crane?

She pulled into a farm drive off the road, close to where the guys were, and killed the engine. Dang! Humbling. Embarrassing.

She shifted into park and got out, retrieved the emergency kit and the water, and ran to the group. Steve was down on the ground, groaning. She couldn't see what had happened. But once she saw his hand she understood. He had told her almost every day, even when she was working inside, to never hang onto a cable or it would cut your hand. Oh my.

"I just ... I just," Steve looked down at the loader.

It sat at an unusual angle in a deep hole. If a feather landed on it, it would slide down deeper.

A bird lit on the seat.

A low growl became a roar. Noell jumped and shielded Steve as the loader slid deeper into the hole. Dust and mud splattered them all. A terrible choking, flushing sound could be heard from the depths of the hole, taking the loader deeper until only the shovel could be seen above ground.

"I was on that. I was sitting right there. It started to slide, and I grabbed the closest thing."

Noell cringed. "A guide wire?"

He nodded and wiped his face. He looked a lot older than he was, lying there with a bloody hand. She had never noticed the gray in his hair, until now.

Bill knelt beside Steve. "You could have been in that hole with the loader if you hadn't 'a grabbed the wire."

The three of them stared toward the hole.

Noell came to first. "Okay. We have to get your hand fixed up." She knelt beside him and opened the emergency kit. "Anybody know first aid?"

Everybody backed away.

"Big help you guys are." She fished into the kit and found bandages and tape and set to work. "Anybody have any honey in their lunch box?"

"Honey? Are you crazy?" Ken said.

Bill leaned in. "No, I think she's onto something here." He held out his hand to them all. "Anybody?"

Miguel fished in his lunch box and pulled out three little samples. "Si?"

"Bueno, buddy." Bill patted him on the shoulder and gathered them for Noell.

She squeezed one out over Steve's hand and immediately wrapped it in a bandage and taped it up to keep it clean and to keep the honey in place on the wound. "Okay. Let's get him to the hospital."

Steve jumped. "No. No hospital. The last time I was there—"

"Take him to the hospital." Noell replaced the bandages in the kit. "There are pieces of the metal in his flesh, and he has to get them taken out. Now."

They all jumped.

Noell didn't know where that came from, but they figured out real fast she meant business.

Steve was still whining about going to the hospital as they helped him to his feet. Finally, Rat and Bill, one on either side, lifted him off his feet and got him into the truck. They drove away.

Noell cleaned up the emergency kit and put it away. Ken started to sit down and take out a smoke. Miguel stood, a confused look on his face. He looked at the cable and the crane, like he should be doing something. He kept stepping away from the hole, toward the other truck.

"Well, what were you doing?" Noell asked. "We should just keep working so Steve can relax. You know once he's bandaged up, he'll come right back out here."

Ken piped up from the ground. "Aww, he won't come back. They'll put him on some kind of antibiotics and pain meds, and he'll have to sleep it off." He threw his cigarette on the ground.

Noell walked over and stomped the cigarette butt out. "We are going back to work." She looked at Miguel. "Okay?"

He nodded. "Si." He walked to the crane and

started it up. He pointed to where he needed Ken. Noell followed to see if she could help. They were clearing the way to put a new culvert in, hence the crane. And now, they needed to fish the loader out. That might have to wait.

She put her safety glasses and her hard hat on. Luckily hers were still in the truck. Gloves on. Glad she hadn't dressed just for office work today, like she had wanted to.

Ken walked over to the hole, but not as close as the others had been. "Why would that happen? What would make that fall down in there?" He pointed. "It's a sink hole thing."

Noell crossed her arms over her chest. "Seems to be happening a lot. The Gustafson place, too." Interesting.

She became the gopher as they continued to work. Moved rocks away, handed them a tool, ran to the truck to retrieve something. She gave them all water, even gave lazy Ken a bottle.

When Steve got back, they were done with the job, with Ken looking like he'd worked all afternoon. They'd even managed to hook the loader and pull it out. The crane was handy to have around.

The hospital had saved Steve's hand and commented on Noell's honey dressing. It had acted as an antibiotic, reducing the chance of infection.

They cleaned up and went back to the office.

Steve was still trying to stay at work, so he just sent them all out back to clean up the yard, while his wife brought him lunch. Weeds had taken over the old equipment there, and he wanted it all cleaned out. The city had been getting on him at every monthly meeting.

Noell put her hard hat on and her gloves and headed out with Bill and Miguel.

It was almost a field. Of weeds.

Rat was already on the mower. Noell raked clippings into piles. Miguel used the weed-eater, and that helped things go faster. Soon they were almost to the back lot line. Trees around and up through old equipment. Tall grass had woven itself in and out of the fence, making it almost impossible to clear. They could hardly tell what was out there.

Bill used a chain saw to cut the trees away … and there stood a little camper trailer. He was the first to get to it and try the door. Locked. He walked around the outside. "Looks kinda old and forgotten, but it's all here. Kinda cute. Pretty small but could be fixed up real easy. Anybody need a camper?"

Noell raised her hand immediately. "I do."

Four guys asked "why" at the same time.

It was tiny. Smaller than her room at Gam's house. She peeked in a window. Too dirty to see inside. But the outside looked okay. Dirty, but how long had it been sitting there?

"Well." She hadn't known she needed a camper until she raised her hand, but already she felt totally sure. "I need this camper." She picked up steam. "I am fixing and cleaning on Gam's house, and I could use it to stay in." She hardly stopped for a breath in case one of the guys would protest. "And a place … uh to put some of my stuff while I fix up the house. She'd been meaning to fix it up for a long time and now I have to do it." She had convinced them and herself. "I need this camper."

She'd laid the 'poor Noell' on thick.

Bill pushed up his hard hat and scratched his head. Rat and Miguel were inspecting the windows and siding—seemed to be contemplating how they would use it themselves. She could almost see the wheels turning in their heads. Ken appeared to be … mad, as usual.

Bill wiped his face and replaced his hard hat. "Well, better go ask Steve. I think he'd just give it to you, and we can help you pull it home."

She knew the perfect spot. Down by the garden, behind Gamma's house. Just up from the little creek that became a bigger creek when it rained. Perfect.

She almost cried.

She ran to the main building, passing Ken on the way back. Where had he been? He still looked mad. "Steve!" She burst into the office.

He jumped. "Oh no. Don't tell me somebody else

got hurt?" One hand was bandaged and in the other, he held a sandwich, meat and cheese stuffed between two slices of bread.

"No. No. Can I buy that camper out back?"

He slowly stood to his feet. "What camper?"

"It's out by the old road."

"You're already out there? You guys have cleaned up all the rest?" He leaned into the window. "Wow. I guess you have."

"About the camper."

"Oh, I see it. Yeah. That's been out there for years … since way before I took over the Roads." He shook his head.

Noell's heart sank. She didn't even know why she wanted it. She just knew she did.

"I don't want anything for it. Just take it. What do you want with it anyway?"

If the story worked once, it might work again. "Well, I am fixing up Gam's house—cleaning it out and stuff, and I need a place to stay until it's all done. Or a place to store some things, too. How much?"

"I said, I don't want anything for it. We'll even help you get it home if you want. Get it out of there!" He turned and smiled at her, glanced at the clock and frowned. "It might have to be tomorrow or the next day, though. Okay?"

Noell kissed his cheek before she thought. "Thanks Steve." Never in her life had she kissed anyone—other than Gamma or Grandpa. Ever. Deep breath. "I'll make it up to you, I promise."

"Hey, I heard you did a great job after they took me to the hospital. You are a great addition to this motley band of workers."

Her cheeks got hot. She quickly turned away, pretending to fiddle with the elastic sticking out from her hard hat and rushed for the door. She rotated. "Thanks Steve. No one has ever … I mean ever … told me I did a great job. Except Gam." Deep breath. "Thanks."

That made two times Steve had told her that.

NINETEEN

June 27, 1937 ~ Dr. Steven's Journal ~ Church. One of the ladies I met at Thelma's invited me to the Lutheran church and I went. Figured it would appease the townsfolk. There are still many who don't want me in town. I could be walking down one side of the street, with someone heading right for me. They might look up and see me and cross to the other side.

Today at church, one man and his wife were shuffling into the pew where I was sitting, saw me and shuffled right out. I didn't see where they ended up.

During the sermon, the preacher seemed to be preaching right to me. And he was.

Why did she even invite me?

Present Day ~ "Attention!" Lisha opened Clarence's door at Hillcrest wide, banging it against the wall.

"What?" Sounded like prison again. The guards woke the inmates every morning with shouts through a microphone of, "Attention! All inmates who want breakfast—that means everybody—rise and shine." Started his day off wrong every time.

"I mean it Clarence." Lisha glanced behind her, down the hall. "We have the new administrator here today, and he is inspecting everything." The whites of her brown eyes were visible.

"New administrator? Why wasn't I told about this?"

"You mean like in ask yo permission to hire him?" She tapped against the door. "Me too. Why wasn't I told about this?" She busted one hip up. "Because we aren't in charge here." She thumbed down the hall behind her. "They are. Now git up."

He struggled to come out of his dreams. "Well, he ain't inspecting everything. Not like in prison, if you know what I mean. Not gonna happen today or ever again."

Lisha raised her eyebrows. "Well, he checked under Mrs. Hatly's nightgown—if you know what I mean. Seems he gots the idee that the residents are druggies."

Clarence half rose from his bed. "He checked Mrs. Hatly's ..." Tears sprang to his eyes. Not her.

Not even the Oust Clarence Brigade ladies. And they'd been after him since they found out he'd been in prison.

Lisha nodded, her chin jutting. Same tears in her eyes.

"I'll get dressed." He threw his sheet off and stepped into slippers beside the bed.

"Hurry. He's in a rampage. Not sure how this'll end." She headed down the hall. "I wish today was my day off."

He selected a shirt and jeans out of his closet and moved to the bathroom, grabbed a washcloth, and turned on the water. "Mrs. Hatly." Reached for his toothbrush and toothpaste with his free hand. He looked into the mirror, his blue eyes wide. The water was still running. "What do I say to …?" He wiped his face. "Oh my God! She is so pure."

He looked down at the water. Both hands were full, so he hung the washcloth back up and brushed his teeth, dropping the toothpaste cap on the floor. He tapped his toothbrush on the sink, harder than usual. He pulled on his clothes, then tossed his pajamas at the door hook.

Who did this guy think he was?

His heart pounded in his chest, and his breathing accelerated. Every time he picked up his phone, he almost threw it. He walked to the window and threaded his belt through the loops.

The spirea bushes lined the parking lot, with full blooms that waved in the breeze.

A visual overlayed the scene outside. A face he hadn't remembered until now. Or he hadn't allowed himself to see.

Mom.

She had been sick and bedridden for a long time. He had been maybe six, so he knew all the hiding places. He'd hidden behind the door until the doctor and Dad went outside to talk. They were only out there for a little bit.

Clarence had seen his chance and tiptoed into her room. He hadn't been prepared for how sick she looked. He hadn't been allowed to see her for a couple days.

He must have kicked something or stumbled, because she opened her eyes and upon seeing him, she smiled. He crawled onto the bed with her and snuggled next to her. She smelled different. He didn't like that smell.

Her hair was strewn around on the pillow. She usually brushed it and tied it back with a ribbon.

Her skin didn't look right—it was white—but sticky-like. She had always worked outside in her garden, the sun bronzing her skin. Freckles even popped out.

He leaned over and kissed her as a tear ran down her cheek. Snuggling in, her watched her chest rise and fall. When her chest didn't rise right away, he'd lift his head to check her face.

She tried to clear her throat. He looked up. She barely shook her head, but the look in her eyes told him what she couldn't physically say.

The moment came when her chest didn't rise again. And she was gone.

Soon after, Dad came in and caught him. He was surprised but not mad. He understood a boy's need for his mother.

He checked her and broke down.

"Daddy." Clarence choked. "Is she … is she in heaven right now? Because she's not breathing. So is she—"

Dad nodded, eyes dripping.

Clarence picked up her hand, but she didn't move. He touched her face. Her eyes didn't open. "Mommy? Mommy?" Something broke in his chest and he let out a long wail. "Mommy! Come back. Mommy—"

Daddy grabbed him and held him; his tears spilled onto Clarence's face. They rocked side to side until sobs slowed. Until they were quiet.

Clarence had taken a long look at her face. The longer he watched, the more peaceful her face became.

And that was the picture that morphed over the spirea bushes outside his window.

Her face.

Michael bowed his head, listened to Lisha get Clarence out of bed to meet Mr. Zee.

Today looked to be a struggle from a human point of view.

Clarence was visibly shaken by what she said. He had kept putting his foot in the wrong pant leg.

"Michael, have you seen the guy? The new administrator?"

Michael nodded. "He doesn't sound like a very nice man."

"Got that right." Clarence stood by the window, putting his belt on and seemed to lose track of time. Back to his memories, Michael guessed.

He stared out the window along with Clarence.

Residents were being rousted out of bed. Groans, as old bones didn't want to move after a whole night of being stationary. Someone dropped a cup or something that sounded plastic. It bounced. Lisha's voice was clear—like nobody else.

He smiled. She was a tough lady. But Father saw her heart. Father knew what no other human knew about her. Her wounds. Her pain. Her joys. Although Clarence was getting close.

Knock. Knock.

"Mr. Timmelsen, I presume."

Clarence wiped his cheeks and turned to see a man handing a chart back to Carol.

"Clarence. Just Clarence."

"Okay … Clarence." The man cleared his throat. "I'm your new Administrator, Mr. Zee." He held out his hand.

Dark wrinkled skin. Thick white spiky hair. Weird black eyes behind black-rimmed glasses. Suit looked like something from another country—Chinese collar—that Nehru guy. Indian. Whatever his name was. Reminded him of somebody else he'd seen recently.

Clarence stared at the dark hand and thoughts of Mrs. Hatly passed through his mind. He shook his head. Not on his watch. Not shaking hands with a guy that treated women that way. Especially Mrs. Hatly.

Carol didn't come into his room, but stayed in the hall, her back to them. That was not like Carol.

Mr. Zee pressed his lips together. Something in those black eyes made Clarence freeze. He had seen eyes like that before—guys in prison who were full of murder. Even his own eyes in the mirror most days. The man seemed intent on an agenda, clearly bursting with his authority.

Mr. Zee glanced around the room and settled back on Clarence. "I see you're dressed and ready for your day. We need to do a little inspection." He pulled on latex gloves.

Clarence looked at Carol.

She had turned around and her face told it all. Eyes were red and swollen. Chin jutted out. But she was in there—that spunkiness was still there. Fighter. Warrior.

Clarence's shoulders and neck tensed. Where was Michael?

"Not on my watch, Mr. Zee. I'm afraid you've got the wrong guy."

"Oh, right." He tapped the chart in Carol's hands. "You're the one from prison. I remember you now." He skimmed his hand over the top of the chest of drawers and nodded to Carol. "No dust." He continued. "I read in your chart you've been incarcerated for murder."

Clarence choked.

Carol stuttered. "B-but he wasn't guilty."

"That's what they all say. Says in your chart you killed your wife—set her up in vehicular homicide."

What had that administrator, Miss Henningway, written in his chart? Little bitch.

Michael nodded to Carol's angel. The new administrator had brought his entourage, and Carol.

Demons on either side of Mr. Zee spit when they saw Michael. Puny little things. Ugly, too. Scars and cuts. One rose up from behind Mr. Zee.

Ahh. Michael recognized that one. From Mr. Wainwright to Mr. Zee.

Michael stood at attention. Please, Clarence, just give the word.

"Not on my watch, Mr. Zee. I'm afraid you've got the wrong guy."

Atta boy Clarence. Now just speak the words.

Clarence's fists clenched. Come on Clarence. We could end this before it even begins.

Michael could feel Clarence's blood boiling. One more level of heat and he could possibly explode.

Sounds of snarling and spitting could be heard from the hallway. Michael stood, feet apart. Standing strong.

Mr. Zee strutted past Clarence's desk. He seemed very interested in papers there.

Clarence gathered them into a pile and flipped them into the top file folder.

Mr. Zee paused, seemed about to comment, his eyes still on the folder, but for some reason restrained himself. "The records tell me you served sixty years. I'd say that's guilty."

Sweat beaded on Clarence's upper lip. He jingled the change in his pocket. Terror he hadn't felt in years crept up his spine and gripped his stomach. This bastard was serious. "Even …" He cleared his throat, sucked in a deep breath, and pushed back his shoulders, head erect. "Even if it were true, I served my time. And how do you remember me? I've never met you."

"Oh, I have your file from Miss Henningway. She left some revealing and refreshing information about you."

Clarence's fists clenched. "Oh, she did, did she?" He wished he'd bought a gun since moving. His whole body tensed.

"Well, I have many residents to visit today, so better get on with this … inspection."

"And what inspection might that be?" Clarence crossed his arms across his chest.

"We check everywhere. I'm sure you're used to that kind of thing, since you were in prison."

"You can check my teeth, Mr. Zee, but anywhere else is off limits to you and anyone else."

"We check teeth, too. Plus, anywhere else you might think to hide illegal substances. You don't have anything to say about it." Mr. Zee smiled a sick smile and opened the closet door, parting the shirts. "Your friend, Mrs. Hatly succumbed, shall we say?"

Two men appeared in the hallway behind him and Carol. Tough sons of bitches. Stout, too. Like professional wrestlers.

He glanced at Carol, but she was keeping her eyes down. She seemed scared to death. This guy must have done something to intimidate her. Was Joe okay?

First Mrs. Hatly and now Carol. His whole body became rigid. Not on his watch.

Mr. Zee opened the door to the bathroom. "Seems clean … Clarence. You keep a simple house."

Crazy thoughts zinged into Clarence's head—some he'd had before, but some didn't make sense. Prison memories swirled. Thoughts, yes about cavity inspections, but about Mrs. Hatly and Harold. Fears of not having enough money to stay at Hillcrest. What if whatever money Clarence had stashed somewhere would be found and confiscated? What if Carol's Joe died? Stupid, stupid, stupid.

His whole life, someone always had taken control. Clarence had never, ever been able to live his own life. Dad was his dad but still had controlled him. Judge Green. Prison warden and guards.

And now Mr. Zee.

Thoughts spun around and around, until he was almost dizzy.

A headache started to pound.

He pointed at Mr. Zee. "You didn't really check Mrs. Hatly in her private—"

Mr. Zee turned and laughed. "Oh, you thought we did that kind of cavity check?" He laughed again, looked behind him at his two stooges and laughed with them.

Ha ha. Funny dorks.

"Oh my, Clarence. We're just not that kind of administration. Maybe Miss Henningway was, but we are not."

Clarence glanced at Carol and met eyes. Her face told a different story. If not down and dirty cavity search, then what? Because she had obviously been crying.

Mr. Zee tapped the desk beside the file folder, scattering papers. "Have a good day Mr. Timmelsen." He started to walk out, but stopped, pulled a candy bar from his suit pocket and pointed to the framed diplomas and certificates on the wall. "Oh, and by the way, you will have to shut down this lawyer crap." He tore the candy open—red letters visible on a 3 Musketeers bar—and chomped a bite. Swallowed. "This is no place for criminals and drug-heads to gather—among innocent elderly men and women."

Clarence blinked as the man walked out, the candy wrapper fluttering to the floor.

Carol met his eyes.

Mr. Zee didn't really know Mr. Timmelsen—yet.

The demons escorting the two men spit at Michael. Low growling alerted him to spirits tucked at each man's feet. They were almost like stick men—like kids drew. But they were real and fiery. Spitting. Claws grew out from their feet and hands. Eyes narrowed when Michael looked at them. Almost covered with a shield or visor.

The men were meant to intimidate. Michael had seen them before, and they were cruel.

The stick spirits stepped to Clarence, loaded tiny dart guns, and began firing on Clarence. Almost laughable if they weren't so effective.

One after another, darts pierced Clarence's head.

Michael stood his ground. Prayers were coming from somewhere. Two more angels landed.

Carol had her eyes closed.

Now, Clarence. They had the enemy in their hands. A prayer warrior was covering this. Give. The. Word.

Clarence opened his mouth.

About time.

He pointed at Mr. Zee. "You didn't really check Mrs. Hatly in her private—"

More stick arrows flew at Clarence, stinging his cheek, his ear, his mouth, and head. Clarence agreed with one enemy thought and three more stick spirits flew in and sent darts flying at that same spot. Michael could see Clarence caving in.

Mr. Zee turned and laughed. "Oh, you thought we did that kind of cavity check?" He laughed again, looked behind him at his two stooges and laughed with them.

"Oh my, Clarence. We're just not that kind of administration. Maybe Miss Henningway was, but we are not."

Michael shook his head as the candy wrapper fluttered to the floor.

Father, give the word. Teach Clarence the ways of Your Kingdom.

TWENTY

June 28, 1937 ~ Dr. Steven's Journal ~ The Pool. Paul was huffing by the time he pulled me to the surface, and he is a big man. There were several more people gathered today. It's humbling being towed out of the water, spitting and gagging, throwing up at their feet. They came for a show and they're getting one—might not be what they expected. Word must have gotten out about the strange phenomenon. Even little Ralph is doing tests alongside mine. Doesn't make sense to him, either.

Present day ~ Today.
At work.

Noell stood taller. The confidence that seemed to bloom from within surely showed to everyone else.

All from a glance from an angel?

She chuckled. And a new, or old, camper? She'd done something so close to the edge, for her, that her whole being, her attitude, every hope and desire seemed attainable—even if she didn't yet know what they were.

Finding the camper made her feel like a queen.

She smiled.

"Hey! No private jokes." Rat grinned as he loaded a shovel and pickaxe.

Noell smiled.

"Well? What gives? You win the lottery?" He opened a pack of gum and offered her one, unwrapping one for himself.

"Don't mind if I do. Thanks!" The gum smelled good. When had she smelled anything so intoxicating? Strawberry? No. Raspberry. She opened the piece and popped it into her mouth. Mmmm.

"Well, did you?" Rat faced Noell, hands on his hips. "Did you win anything?"

"Wha … what?"

"Did you win any money?"

"Money?" She frowned. "What did I say?"

He leaned on the truck. "Kidding."

Blank. "Thought so." Just trying to confuse her. It had worked.

He laughed. "Do you like to fish?" Tinkering with the latch on the utility truck compartment, he cocked his head. "Would you like to go sometime?"

"Go?"

"Yeah. Fishing. Like a fishing pole, line, and hooks."

"Um. I don't … ." Wait. Gamma's boxes. She might have a pole somewhere. She had everything else. There were life vests somewhere. Noell had run into those when she had been looking for work clothes. Gam's hoarding was becoming more and more useful. Not that Noell loved the mess and boxes everywhere. There was no room to move anymore.

"Well, I think I can find an extra pole somewhere. Let's go soon before it gets too hot."

Noell shrugged. "Okay." She just got asked for a date. And she had accepted. Fishing was better than a lot of things he could have invited her to.

Steve pounded the truck door. "Head out!"

Rat climbed in beside her, making her slide closer to Steve. The other utility truck followed behind with the rest of the crew.

"Where are we headed today?" Rat rolled down the window partway. "The old bridge again?"

"Yup. Could possibly get 'er done today. We need to make sure we get all the flashers up and roadblocks out." He chuckled. "Wouldn't want someone to go flying over that at night! Look Ma! No bridge!"

Noell gasped. "Has that happened?"

"Not specifically. Kids will always be kids." Steve gave a sidelong glance at Rat. "Seem to remember something."

Inside the truck grew quiet.

Rat seemed to squirm. "Well, yeah." He chuckled. "I do remember that." He leaned over Noell and pointed at Steve. "But I took the worst part of that one."

Noell pressed back in the seat. "What happened?"

"It was late and I … was drinking." He shook his head. "Woke up to cows mooing and I was parked in their shit pond." He sniffed. "I can still smell it."

She wrinkled her nose. "Did you get hurt?"

"Nope. Too drunk."

Steve stopped the truck just short of the old bridge.

"Why are we taking the bridge out?" Noell straightened to see.

Rat got out of the truck and held the door open for her.

"The state wants it out. It's old, and many of the boards need replacing. It's too old to support new ones, but we'll finish taking it down and then a crew comes in to build another."

She stretched and walked to the bridge. One board was completely gone. That would hurt if someone didn't know it was gone! A tire would get caught.

Another board looked loose.

Ken and Bill picked it up, each carrying an end and loaded it onto the trailer.

The rest of the crew swarmed over the bridge, each knowing their task, except for Noell.

Steve handed her the flag and a roll of yellow tape. "Wind this around the whole bridge but keep a sharp eye out. The people who live out here are used to using this bridge even though it's bad. They don't want to go the long way around the section, so they drive right over it. Make sure no one passes. Okay?"

She grabbed the tape and flag. "Okay." She looked both ways. Clear. For now.

She leaned the flag against the bridge railing and picked at the end of the roll of yellow tape as she surveyed where to even walk, so she could string the tape. Attaching the end to a post one of the guys had driven beside the road she jumped down into the creek.

There wasn't any flow of water so she could step around rocks and clumps of grass to the other side. A snake skittered from between the rocks and slithered away, giving her a start. Thank God she didn't scream.

No one had seen her jump, right?

Dang. Rat was grinning.

Her cheeks grew hot.

Dang, he was cute.

She pulled her hard hat lower on her face and continued to traipse through the creek bed. Those pink boots were the best. They fit great and were super comfortable, but she especially liked how protected her feet were.

She almost laughed. She'd always worn sandals or joggers. She might have turned into a hiking boot fan.

Another snake. Ugh. She let it slither away before proceeding and checked behind and around where she needed to step for anymore. With each step, she disturbed more.

Snake nest.

Only a few more feet to the other side of the creek bed. She could do this.

Just as she reached the other side, a rock gave way, and she began to slide under the bridge pilings where the bridge met the road.

This time she did scream, and it was probably good she did, because she fell into a hole.

Coughing, she brushed away the dirt. Rocks tumbled down with her, opening a bigger hole.

It was a small cave. Gah. What was it with caves and holes these days?

She stomped at the rocks to find a foothold and

discovered that the seemingly small cave wasn't so small. It continued on down under the road.

Something surfaced in her thoughts from the other day—Clarence asking about caves.

Wow. If people only knew what they drove their cars over. They could be driving along and all of a sudden fall right through a hole in the road and be lost forever. She'd seen pictures on the internet.

Rocks and dirt underneath her shifted as she tried to stand, making her slide farther down.

Something slithered.

She screamed.

"Noell? Noell?" Rat yelled from the surface. "You down there?"

"Yes! Yes! Get a line or rope. Anything." She froze and slid down even more. "I'm sliding down into a cave."

Three snakes skidded over her boots.

"Help!"

Gramps had told her if she saw a snake to hold still. Not move a muscle.

"Right away." He disappeared and yelled. "Get a rope. She is sliding down into a cave."

Rustling above her gave her hope.

Until vibrations from above shook her even farther down. And startled more snakes.

She shrieked again. Who was more scared—them or her?

Silence.

"Guys?" Where was the confidence now? "Anybody?"

Steve's head popped through the opening. "Hang tight, girl. We'll get you out." His eyes traveled past her and widened. "We'll get you out."

A rope appeared beside him, and Rat looked in. "Here, catch this."

She reached for the end of the rope, but the movement only made her slide further down.

Splash! Rocks slid and plunked into water somewhere below. Oh God. A pool?

Waves of nausea hit her. One after another.

Layers of pictures opened on top of the dust and billowing dirt. Water rushed over her from below. No! Not now! The water poured in with the dust.

These dreams had to stop!

Sanitizer wouldn't help her now, even if she could find it.

Water rushed and overpowered her. She was drowning. Again. Yellow eyes mocked her. Gnarly hands reached out to her—pulled her down. A mouth opened in a scream that was amplified by the water.

Did she scream?

"Guys. I'm sliding." She shrieked. "Help!"

Vibrations from above turned into rumbles.

"What is that sound?"

Rat looked up from the hole. He hollered. "It's a pickup. Ken! Stop them!"

Footsteps pounded above.

The rumbling grew louder and louder.

Rocks and gravel bounced down below.

"Get me the rope!" She screamed again. "I'm sliding!"

The rope fell right in front of her, and she grabbed it. "I've got it. Pull!"

"Wrap it around your hands."

She wrapped it around and around. "Okay. Pull!"

The vibrations and rumblings had to be right above her. She could hear the guys yelling.

"Stop! Stop!"

"Pull over!"

Just as she began to slide down again, the rope caught and pulled her up and away. Airborne. Her head emerged through the hole. Dirt and dust and rocks tumbled around her and on down to the pool, splashing as they hit water. A snake hung from the toe of her boot. She landed in the creek bed, scattering snakes again.

She kicked and tried to scoot away.

Steve and Rat kicked them away and carried her to the road like she was a feather.

A truck had barely come to a stop at the edge of the bridge, spewing dust and gravel. Air brakes released with a loud whoosh.

The cloud of dust cleared revealing a full-sized semi-truck with a trailer-load of cattle, accompanied by loud mooing and jostling in the trailer. They were just as scared as Noell.

PU.

The driver jumped out.

Noell's legs went limp, and she collapsed where she had been standing. She felt like the wind had been knocked out of her. Like something stood on her chest.

"You okay Noell?"

"That was close."

Miguel and Ken and Bill were all corralling the truck driver, who looked to be a young kid, barely fourteen.

"I didn't do anything wrong. I was just ..." He appeared to, at that moment, see the bridge out signs, the yellow tape, and missing boards, and his tanned face went white. Then he saw Noell sitting beside Rat, and he pointed at her. "Was she? Was she under there?"

Rat nodded.

"I could have ... I could have driven over her. Crashed through the bridge?" He looked behind him at the cattle and visibly shook.

He dropped in the dirt on the road.

Noell stirred.

Rat helped her get her balance. "You okay?"

She nodded. "Yeah." She looked up at him. "Thanks." And at the others. "Thanks. I thought I was going to end up in that hole down there."

Steve leaned down to look. "It seems to go forever." He walked to Noell and put his arm around her shoulders. "You okay Noell? We need to take you to the ER. Get you checked out to be sure."

"No." She kicked a foot and shook her arms. "I'm okay. Really. Nothing broken." She checked again. "And nothing bleeding."

"Just to be safe. We need to get you to the hospital just in case later something starts hurting and then we're too late." Steve thumped his chest, sending dust up in billows. "Your Gamma would never forgive me if something happened to you on the job. She'd come back to haunt me." He pointed. "Rat, take her into town to the ER and tell them it's on the Roads Department, City account."

"Sure." He hooked his arm around hers. "You okay to go?"

"I guess if I have to." She wiped at her face. Gritty and wet. She wiped again. Wet? Tears?

She glanced to the hole as they picked their way to the truck. That could have been her tomb. She could have been buried there.

Under all that dirt.

Drowning in the pool.

Just like Mommy.

Walking out from the ER, Noell shook her head. "I knew I was okay. We just spent city money for nothing."

Rat opened the truck door for her. "I'm sure Steve just wants to be careful. What's the saying? Better safe than sorry? It's worth it to have things checked out."

He shut the door, came around to the driver's side and picked up his phone. "Hey, Steve. This is Rat."

"Good. How did things go? She okay?"

"Yup. She's good. They took blood and did x-rays and everything. She is a little sore, but nothing broken."

"Good news." Steve coughed. "Just take her home, okay? You wouldn't mind doing that?"

"Glad to."

Steve cleared his throat. "Okay. We have everything all buttoned down out here too, so we'll be heading into town. See ya soon."

"Right on."

Truck clock didn't work, she forgot. "What time is it? Doesn't feel like it's time to get off work yet."

Rat checked his phone. "It's 3:37."

"But I can't go home. It's not quitting time yet."

"Steve said to take you home." He looked over at her and brushed debris out of her hair.

She leaned away from him and sighed. "Feels really stupid. The guys will hate me."

"By the look on everybody's face when you fell into that hole, I think they'll be okay with it. I mean …" He stopped at a stop sign and looked over at her. "I can't believe you're okay. That had to be terrifying."

Tears stung her eyes, but she wasn't going to let him see. She looked out the side window. "Yeah. Maybe." Deep breath. "Yeah. Scary. But so quick that I couldn't really think about it. I just reacted. I … every time I moved, I slid farther into the hole. Hearing the rocks splash into water I couldn't really see was … scary." She gulped. "And the snakes."

She felt his hand on her shoulder.

Stay strong. Don't let him see. Don't let him know how crazy—

"I'll walk you up." He pulled the truck into the driveway and stopped.

Visions of the front porch terrified her even more.

She jumped out and lost her footing, stumbled to the ground. He mustn't see that porch.

"Whoa. Seriously. I think you need to slow down." He pulled her up and held her steady.

"I can make it from here. It's okay. I can—"

He grasped her hand and put his other arm around her shoulders.

Even through the work dust and tar, his aftershave provided another layer, taking her to a place she'd never gone before. Usually smells and touches plummeted her into visuals and knowledge she didn't want to know.

But right now, she only saw a morning sunrise and birds rising in flight along clouds. Crisp, sweet air jarred her senses—just about as nice as his after-shave. All very fresh and—

Fletch! He was peeking out through the diamond-shaped window of the outer door.

How had he gotten into the porch? What was he doing in there?

Rat stopped and pointed at the door. "Wait. Is that your brother?"

"No. He's a neighbor." She tensed. What was going on?

Rat turned to her. "You okay? Is he okay?"

She stared at the front door, frowning. "H-he's okay. I just don't know what he is doing in my house."

Rat stopped and turned to her, grasping her arms with his hands. "Want me to do something? Call the police?"

"No. I'm sure it's okay. I just didn't expect it."

The door opened just as Rat's touch activated powerful visions, knocking her back. A lake. Fishing. Rocks being thrown into water. Vicious laughter. Faces too close. Fists pummeling. Cries of terror.

The door swung open.

Fletch's wide eyes. Out of breath. Red face. "Noell." He looked from her face to Rat's. "Who's this?"

"Fletch. What are you doing here?" She stepped inside the house.

Rat stepped in behind her, his hand on her back.

She shuddered at his touch, stepping away.

Fletch backed to the doorway leading into the living room. "I'm getting those boxes out that we talked about."

Noell paused. Boxes? Whew. She must have hit her head falling in that cave. "I … I forgot."

Fletch eyed Rat. He drew up taller and Noell could see the man he was becoming: strong, tall, honorable. All around him, the floor had been cleared. Half of the room, in fact, had been cleared.

Rat stared at Fletch. His black eyes seeming to pierce Fletch's. He pressed his hand into her back, drawing her closer.

Reminded her of a movie—sparing between two gladiators—right in her porch.

"Um, Rat, this is Fletch." She pointed to Fletch, then to Rat. "Fletch, this is Rat, a guy from work." Deep breath. Maybe she had hit her head harder than she thought. She put her hand out on a nearby box, but it slipped. She lost her balance.

Both guys reached for her.

Rat touched her first, and she gasped as Rat's face morphed into a shriveled old man with yellow eyes. Immediately, she pushed away.

When Fletch's hand came in contact with hers, a blanket-like-thing stretched from him and covered her.

So strange.

"I'm okay." She looked at Fletch. "Just kind of had a mishap at work. I went to the ER and checked out fine." She glanced at Rat. "I must have hit my head or something."

"Here. Let's sit you down." Fletch looked behind him into the living room. The only seat available was Gamma's place on the sofa.

Fletch reached for her hand.

Rat's hand still touched her back.

An explosion of emotion crossed her mind's eye. Tension and competition. Torn first one direction, then the other. First Fletch's face—kindness and honor in his eyes—but lacking self-confidence. Then Rat's—excitement, arrogance. Unfamiliar smells pushed into her brain. Even the pornographic mind-pictures from Mr. Grimes down the street hadn't had the hormonal power of this moment.

She heard their voices, saw their faces, but they sounded like they were far away and faces blurred.

Fletch held out his hands, almost bowing. "You need to sit down. You look like you feel terrible."

"I'm okay. I'm fine."

Rat gave her a push. "He's right. Sit down for a minute. I can help him get the boxes out." He stepped toward Fletch.

Fletch held out a hand, pushing him away. "I got it."

Noell looked from one to the other. "It's okay, guys. I'm fine." Not daring to say more, she nodded toward Rat. Seeing him stand against the backdrop of piles of boxes almost made her want to throw up. "Thanks for taking me to ER and home. See you tomorrow. Tell Steve thanks."

"Okay. If you're sure you're okay." Rat looked behind her at Fletch. "If it's really okay." He touched her arm. There was that awful, raucous laughter again. Why was she seeing Rat as so evil? He'd always been nice and polite. They were going fishing together, weren't they?

She glanced behind her at Fletch, who had his hands on his hips. He looked ready to spring. Back to Rat. "I'm fine. Really."

Fletch was staring at Rat. Hard to discern his thinking. Blank face. But his eyes never wavered.

Huh.

Never had she been caught between two men.

TWENTY-ONE

Clarence waved as Mrs. Hatly walked on down the hall.

"Have a good nap, Mrs. Hatly. See you at supper."

"God willing, if I'm still here."

She always said that. Her frail voice always pulled on his heart. Her eyes twinkled, and her laugh sounded like a sweet melody—that Jenny Wren in the spring.

"Silly," he said. "You'll be here. Where would you go?" And yet … what if something did happen to her? He didn't like to think about it, but since he'd been at Hillcrest Homes—six weeks—two residents had died. "Good night, Mrs. Hatly."

"Good night, Clarence."

He watched her walker-dance down the hall. She turned into her room farther down, stopped at her door and waved. Blew him a kiss.

Clarence jumped. First time for everything. He blew her one back just as Harold showed up in his wheelchair.

"Such a love duck."

"Love duck? You weren't supposed to see that." Clarence shook his head. "Is nothing private in this place?"

"Nope." Lisha walked between them. "There ain't nothing private here: your room ain't private, your birthday ain't private, your poop schedule ain't private and your birthday suit ain't private!" Those hips sang her attitude. "Got it?"

Harold chuckled. "So true. Even our sordid past isn't private."

"Hey. Got that right. Mr. Clarence here, rode with Jesse James and his gang. Thas how he got put in prison."

Silence.

Clarence burst out laughing.

Harold wiped his eyes.

Lisha kept on walking past, her huge hips declaring her victory. Up. Down. Up. Down.

Clarence could almost see her sarcastic grin. "Oh, that woman." He snapped his fingers. "Hey, you would be the man for the job." He righted Harold's American flag pin on his lapel.

Harold looked up. "What job?"

"I just got some boxes dumped on me from Pete Malovitch's … uh secretary." He paused. "You know I'm trying to be nice."

"Good job. New territory for you, Buddy." Harold grinned. "Go on."

"Well, one of the top papers from the box has my dad's name on it. I just had time to glance at some of the others farther down, when Carol came in."

"And?"

A couple visuals crossed Clarence's mind at the mention of Pete Malovitch's name—Pete's blood spattered on Clarence's cheek and Pete's angry secretary. "Yeah, well, I was wondering. Since there is a legal case going on right now involving ole dead Pete, who was after me, and that Phil guy who was after Katty, I might need someone with me as I go through this stuff." He leaned against the railing along the wall. "Kind of like protection. You know, where two or more?"

"You spouting Bible at me? You? Preaching?"

Where did that come from? That was what preachers were for, and he didn't want any part of that kind of preaching. He only wanted the preachers that told jokes, or the one that came on Wednesdays and served them hot chocolate. That one he could stomach.

The preachers that used to come to the prison? Now those guys were all business. They didn't take any … crap off the inmates. They were about that Alleluia stuff and getting people into heaven. Whew. At least now at the nursing home, Clarence could walk away. At prison, he had to take it. Listen or …

Clarence shook his head. "Naw. Just sounded right. You up for it?"

"Sure. As long as there's nothing that you want kept private. You know, like family stuff?"

Clarence shrugged. "I can't see that there would be." He spied Lisha sauntering toward them. "Maybe Lisha, here, would bring us some tea and crumpets to ease our work."

She gave them the look—the look that warned of either flying objects or words.

Clarence chuckled and braced himself.

"Me?" She glanced over her shoulder, swinging loose dreads, a brown thumb pointing to her chest. "You talkin' to me?" She posed—one hip up, her pinkie finger up, and one eyebrow up. "I'm thinkin' we all outa crum-pets. We might have some, let me see," she posed again, a finger beside her mouth, "vitamins or some laxatives. Somethin' like tha-t."

The t sound sent a spray, sprinkling Clarence and Harold.

Clarence wiped his face. Had to make it look like he was soaked. What a woman. Why did she remind him of the woman the last day at prison who gave him his beautiful wool scarf? She was nicer than Lisha. She had been precious.

He pushed his hands at her. "No, no. Thas okay."

Her other eyebrow shot up.

Oh-oh. "We'll just drink water, won't we Harold."

"Yup. Water'll be fine for me. Yup." Harold drove his wheelchair behind her, peeked around and motioned for Clarence to come with.

She planted in the middle of the hall. Not much room on either side.

Clarence sidled along the railing, keeping an eye on her. She could move fast, no matter how big she was or how much space she took up in the hallway.

Almost around.

Until she bumped out a hip.

Damn!

She was just a little too close. And she was closing in fast. He could smell her breath—must have had garlic for lunch. He could see her freckles—freckles on brown skin. There was a scar just to the side of her eye. Ouch. He'd never been close enough to see it before.

He pointed. "How'd you ... how'd you get that scar?"

She flinched, and her fingers flew to the place. "What scar?" Her eyes went soft. No, they turned fearful. "I don't have no scar."

Lisha?

He cupped his hands around each of her massive elbows.

They stood like that. Connected. Connected skin-on-skin. Connected eyeball to eyeball.

And soul to soul.

She went almost trance-like. Sucked in a deep breath, trembling. Then she came back to reality. In her eyes, there was still fear, but a new thing. An intimacy? I'll keep your secrets if you'll keep mine? Friendship?

And just as quickly, it was over. Attitude was back. Hip bumped up. But something was different.

"You two have a good afternoon, okay?" She started to walk away. "I'll see what I can scare ya up in the kitchen, though." Bump, bump. She turned back. "Maybe some … soap pads. They're good in a biscuit."

She winked.

Clarence closed his eyes and shook his head. Chuckled to himself.

He popped Harold on the shoulder. "Ready to snoop through those boxes?"

"Yup. Ready."

Clarence flipped on the overhead light in his office. "Here they are." He patted the boxes on his desk. "Amazing Pete had all this stuff."

Harold wheeled into the room. "You said your dad's name is on some of it?"

Lisha popped in with a tray and placed it on Clarence's desk. It was covered with a plastic doily, and on it were two cups of coffee and a Mountain Dew. A pink plate served up raisin oatmeal cookies.

She bowed with attitude. "Now. Don't you two get yoselves all used to this." She wagged her finger in Clarence's face. "But jus know I appreciate you."

She bowed again, grabbed her Dew and a fistful of cookies, and turned to go.

"Hey!"

She turned into the room. "What?"

Clarence stood and gave her a hug. With both hands full, she couldn't deck him.

Her eyes filled with tears. "Jes want you to know. Don't you ever do that agin." She shook her Dew in his face and smiled a very sincere smile. "Ever."

"I won't Lisha." He took a cookie. Only two left? "Ever. And thanks."

Harold mumbled between bites. "I believe. I believe. Now where were we?"

"What are you believing about?"

Harold snickered. "You hugged Lisha and she let you live?"

"Ha! I know. I should lock my door at night!

Watch my back. She's scary!" Clarence bit into the cookie and held it up. "Mmm. Never had these in prison."

Harold parked his wheelchair next to the desk. "Tough in prison, I bet."

He shoved the rest of the cookie in his mouth and brushed crumbs off his hands. Swallowed. "In all reality? Worst thing was losing Annie—she was my angel, my connection to all things good. Prison was," he glanced at the empty plate, "easy, after losing her. It became my home."

Harold stared at Clarence. Nodded. He looked away then stared again. Cleared his throat. "Your home?"

"Yeah. Only two places I called home." He hesitated and counted on his fingers. "Well, three, counting Hillcrest. One with Dad as a kid. Two, Prison—sixty years in prison. And three, here." He opened the box flaps and reached inside. The top papers showed Dad's signatures on a … looked like a purchase agreement.

"Whoa." Clarence blinked.

"What'd you find?"

Clarence handed it to Harold.

He scanned it. "Looks like your dad owned property here." He handed it back. "Right?"

Clarence slowly sat. He scanned the document

and blew out a breath. "Says here that Dad bought that bastard Judge Green's place of residence when he died."

"The judge that—"

"The judge that sent me to prison for sixty years and then set it up for me to be sent here."

Harold let out a long whistle. "The judge's house? Your dad bought it?"

Clarence drifted back. His memory of Judge's house layered over the view of the parking lot outside his window. It had been a beautiful home. Walking up the bricked sidewalk when courting Annie, he had noted every porch and railing, every gable. Upper balconies. The roofline had a dangerous pitch; a turret alone would have been terrifying to roof. Flaunted four bedrooms and two full bathrooms.

Dad always said that was excessive. Some people in town didn't even have one bathroom.

Clarence had always paused just before the bottom porch step to admire the carvings on the portico above the front door. As his eyes lowered, Annie always magically appeared at the front door, the sweetest smile on her face.

It still stirred him after all these years.

Amazing workmanship.

Amazing Annie. After sixty years, he could still see her precious face.

And Dad owned Judge's house? Or had at one time?

"Why would Dad have bought Judge's house, unless ... revenge? Dad got revenge for Judge slamming me in prison?" Clarence whistled out a breath. "Dad, what did you do?"

TWENTY-TWO

Noell looked at the clock after Fletch left with the boxes. Still only four o'clock. Plenty of day left.

She wiggled her toes. Shook her body. She felt okay, just a little wired.

Visions of sliding into that hole passed through her mind. Dust choked her. The minute she had moved her foot or tried to find a stable footing, she slid farther down. And another snake slithered out.

Part of her had been terrified, especially when she heard the plunk, plunk, plunk of rocks bouncing below. But when she heard splashes, her stomach had flip-flopped.

She hit the panic button then, but at the same time, curiosity bit her hard. Maybe not curiosity, but more like destiny bit her in the behind.

Could have been so much worse. She hadn't really been scared then ... well ...

But now, it shook her.

She had been totally at someone or something else's mercy.

She scanned the dining room where she and Gamma had set up the computer. God, she missed Gamma. She needed her right now.

They had laughed so hard when the computer arrived and neither knew what the heck they were doing. Gamma had figured out how to plug it in. Thank God for the telephone guy, who set it all up and gave them an Internet 101 class. Gamma had tried, but this was her first time ever, using a computer.

She got so she could email a very special friend who lived in New York City. When an email came in from the friend, she would laugh and cry. Such a special relationship.

Noell leaned back into the chair and bit her lips between her teeth. She'd had a rough day, so maybe the emotion rising in her right now was just from falling down a hole.

But ... she didn't have a friend like that. She didn't even have the prospect of a friend who would send her funny emails when she was a hundred years old.

Moments passed as she stared out the window.

Gamma had been her only friend and had always been there. Never a day had gone by that Gam hadn't fed her, held her, taught her. Prayed with her.

The reflection of her own face looked back at her in the computer screen. It was all scrunched up. Eyebrows rumpled together. Tears sparkled in the reflection.

How could she go on alone?

Light from the windows illuminated a tear running down the cheek on the face in the monitor.

After the day she'd had, she could sense that if she let herself really cry, she might never surface in life again.

Pictures of Rat and Fletch stirred emotion, too. Mr. Grimes had been scary, but this seemed worse. Rat and Fletch were each so different—made of different stuff, that was for sure. Some days she wasn't sure which one was the good guy and which was the bad.

She punched the on button and after a few minutes, the computer came to life.

She wiped her face and typed in "caves in Osceola, Nebraska."

What was going on with Rat, being so pushy? Gamma would have known.

The webpage turned out to be a site for things to do for kids and had pictures of a kid in a cave, but … not what she wanted.

And was Fletch getting too close? He had been in her house.

"Caves in Nebraska" turned up more. Great photos. Wow. One reminded her of … her cave.

Her cave?

Well, it might as well be hers. She'd almost been buried in it.

Robber's Cave. Cool history. Mostly by Lincoln, Nebraska.

Wow. A depth of sixty feet?

She looked up. How long … or deep was that?

She gauged the room as ten feet across. Take that times six.

She stood and crawled over junk to get to the window. Turning back into the room, she eyeballed the length, then looked outside the window and tried to measure that distance outside. Then again and again.

Sixty feet ought to be from that outside wall to Mr. Grimes' house—the imaginary measuring line running right through the neighbor's house and yard.

As she climbed back over the boxes and clutter again, she shuddered. Was that how deep the hole had been today? And water below that?

She shivered again.

The article said that caves meandered through parts of Nebraska around Lincoln.

She wanted to explore every cave. She wanted to read every website Google found.

All at the same time.

Something stirred in her.

She had to do this.

This was why she … wait.

If people had died even trying to dip water out for their plants, or retrieve a ball, how did she think she would be able to study them? She'd almost drowned so far—twice—once with Mommy and then today.

She skimmed the articles on the computer, not really reading, fussing with a strand of hair dangling over her ear. Twisting it. Winding it around her finger. "A string of pools …" "Depths to … " "Spiritual and magical."

She held her breath. Then let it blow out when she realized she wasn't breathing.

Licking her lips over and over was making them chapped. She dug out her lip gloss and popped the lid off. She applied some and smacked her lips.

Yuck. Full of dirt.

She grabbed a Kleenex and wiped it all off. Gritty.

Noell stretched. She'd been perspiring and wasn't even aware of it. It wasn't hot in the house. It had been shut up all day, so still retained the cool night temperatures.

Good articles.

She wanted to know more.

She was drawn … no, she had been set up to find the caves. She knew in her gut—gut was Gamma's word—that she was supposed to explore. She knew she needed to follow this research. No matter what.

Just having been in that hole today made her even more sure, fear or no fear.

This was what she was supposed to do in life. Maybe not as a scientist.

Wait.

Why not as a scientist?

She needed to follow her heart. God's heart for her. That's what Gamma always said.

God's heart for her.

TWENTY-THREE

Katty wanted to kill. She had driven to Clarence's before she did something stupid, like booze, drugs or … hurt Bea. He could always talk her down. His place was better than being at that crappy trailer. Sometimes, with the new deck out front, it didn't seem so bad. But today … she wanted to kill.

She slammed the laptop closed. She had failed another one. Another test. Why did she ever let Clarence talk her into going to school? Her dad had always told her she was stupid—

"Katty?" Clarence looked up from the file he was reading. "What's wrong?"

Her face burned. She wanted a fix. A drink. Whatever made her think she was smart enough to be a paralegal for him?

"Katty." He put the paper down and leaned in. "Tell me."

Her eyes burned now, too. "I failed another test. I can't do this. I—"

"You can do this, Katty." Clarence stood, shuffled around the desk and sat on the chair next to her. "What was the test on?"

"Words." She glanced up at his face. "Just vocabulary." She opened the laptop again. "Affidavit. Adult. Ad—"

"I can teach you those." He looked at Bea watching educational TV. "How do they teach the little ones?" He pulled a yellow legal pad close and clicked open a pen. "Let's start with … five words. Adult. Adultery. Adopt. Affidavit. And … apple." He tried not to smile, but his right eye twitched.

Goofy man.

He pushed the list to her. "And next week, we'll have five more." He nodded and held her gaze. "You can do this."

Bea crawled up on his lap. "I want a list."

He chuckled. "Okay." He tore off a corner piece from the yellow pad and began to write. "Red. Rose. Bea." He handed it to her. "And just like Mommy, learn everything you can about those words—what they mean, how you use them in a sentence."

"But one is me." Bea pointed to her name.

"Well, that's the most important one. Then find

out everything you can," he tapped her chest, "about you."

Katty watched, mesmerized, then added her own name to the list he had shoved at her.

She stapled a couple sheets of paper together and skimmed the contents. Then glanced at the boxes in front of her. "Clarence, what am I looking for? These look like some kind of legal documents ..." She shook her head. Those boxes were stuffed with papers. This could take forever.

Clarence leaned closer, picked up Bea and sat her on his lap. "Hmm. Court proceedings." He motioned for her to flip over the page. "Signed by my dad." He scanned further down the page. "Clynder. Ted Clynder. That's the name of the lawyer we always went to for legal needs." He wiped Bea's nose.

He sat her down. "Set those aside with Clynder on them. Just put them in the same pile."

"Here's more." She flipped the page to read the signatures. "Signed by your dad." She put the papers down. "What was he like, anyway?"

"Who? Dad?" Clarence leaned back in his chair. "He was a great man. An artist. Creative. Great businessman." He sighed. "Mainly a master of wood working—a master at his craft. And known for it. People would come a long ways. One family wanted him to go to Chicago to build their home. Wish I would have had more time with him." Clarence looked out the window. "Robbed of the best years of my life with him because of that bastard, Judge Green."

Bea looked up from the TV. "What's a bastard?"

Katty looked at Clarence.

Clarence looked at Katty, then Bea.

"It means … well, that he was not a nice man."

"Was your dad a nice man?" Bea rolled on the floor and kicked the TV.

"Bea, stop kicking." Katty moved Bea away from the furniture.

"Uh, yes." Clarence grimaced. "Do you want to get some ice cream, Bea?"

Katty chuckled. "Skirting the issue. Good lawyer tactic, Clarence."

Clarence wiped his eyes.

First time she had seen him blush.

He pulled Bea to her feet, took her hand, and closed the door behind them.

Huh. Shouldn't have said that. She might have hurt his feelings.

She was so messed up. Even now. Especially now.

She used to be messed up because of the drugs and booze—really messed up. But since she had met Clarence, he'd helped her get cleaned up and given her this chance. Being his legal assistant would be hard—he was tough—but it had already been so rewarding. Helping Carol with hard issues with her husband Joe. Even the Sheriff had enlisted Clarence in on some very interesting cases.

Just because a lawyer was fresh out of school didn't give him or her the experience Clarence had— what with his years in prison.

She looked at the closed door and sighed. She sat in Clarence's chair that he hardly ever sat in.

She was still messed up. Even though she wanted a drink in a bad way, she also wanted truth. She'd have to be careful where to use it. Like just now with Clarence. Several times with Bea, she'd caught herself demanding truth. Being perfectionistic. Bea was only four.

She wanted so badly to be a good mom. But who did she have to learn from? Her own mom had been .... Visuals of being slammed against the kitchen table. Of being pushed down the steps. Never outside. Always hidden from the outside world. The sting of a hand against her tender cheek. A reflection in the mirror of red welts that couldn't be disguised or hidden. There was no make-up that ever hid the scars deep inside.

Katty wiped her eyes.

She glanced at the closed door. Bea deserved a good mom.

Eyes closed. Elbows on her knees. Face in her hands.

"Help me Jesus. I can't … do this." She opened her eyes. "I want to be like Carol. Mrs. Hatly." Deep ragged sigh. "God, I want to be … help."

She leaned her head back against the cushioned headrest of Clarence's chair and watched the door.

Maybe they'd bring her an ice cream cone too.

Someone knocked on the door and pushed it open.

"Clarence in here?"

Carol. Her beautiful green eyes had more in them than just color. She radiated love. How, with all she had … work, Joe.

Katty wiped her face. "Uh, no. He—"

"Ice cream, right? He took Bea for some ice cream?" Carol turned to the hallway. "I'll find him." She looked back at Katty. "You okay? You seem …"

Katty nodded. "I'm fine."

"You sure?" Carol's eyes softened somehow. Glistened.

Something passed between them. She had just prayed to be more like Carol and here … she was.

She shivered. That didn't just happen.

"Well, if you ever need to talk, Katty, I'm here." Carol raised her eyebrows and smiled.

The door closed softly behind her.

Had stuff like this happened before and she was just too drunk to see?

Papers became visible again. Stacks and boxes of papers.

She wanted to stay and wanted to run.

Help.

Huh. More documents with Dawes Timmelsen's name on them. "553 Hawkeye Street." Another piece of property purchased by Dawes Timmelsen. She picked up another sheet. Dawson Retrieval: Reclaim Systems. Who was Dawson? Or what? Clarence's dad's name was Dawes. This was on a legal document, and this was taken to Polk County Court, so it couldn't be his dad. His name was—

High sing-song voice and a bass voice burst into the room as the door pushed open.

Katty laughed. "What on earth are you two singing?"

Clarence handed her a styrofoam cup of ice cream covered in rainbow sprinkles, spoon claiming rights to the mountain. "Ice cream courtesy of me. Sprinkles are all Bea's."

"Aren't they pretty, Mommy?" Bea licked her cone. Her cone was covered with about as many sprinkles as Katty's dish.

She shook her head. "They are pretty. But do they taste good?" She took a bite and shivered. "Yum! Yummy!"

"I knew you'd like them Mommy. Clarence didn't think so, but I know you."

Katty blinked. "Who is this little girl who sounds so much like me?"

Bea stood up straight. "I'm me!" She pointed to her own chest. "I'm Bea! That's who!"

"Are you finding anything of importance?" Clarence sat and swiveled to face Katty. "Maybe we should just stack those boxes over there on top of the other boxes from prison." He stuck his spoon back in the ice cream and shrugged his shoulders. "That way we'll know where they are."

"Don't you want to know what's in these? Why Pete had them?" She wiped a sprinkle from Bea's cheek and fed it to her, licking her fingers. "What were they doing in that old building of his, anyway?"

Clarence shrugged and licked his spoon. "I don't know. And I do want to know what all this is, but I probably should get at Noell's Gamma's stuff. Get that settled for her." He shook his head. He stood and closed the door. "She doesn't realize it yet, but she is a wealthy young woman."

"With all that stuff in the house, you mean? The hoarding?"

"Well, there may be some good stuff in there." He shook his head. "I'd hate to go through it all. That was one good thing about being in prison—you couldn't keep much stuff. There just isn't room in a cell."

Katty glanced at the boxes of books. "Where did

you keep all those, then?" She leaned back in her chair and scooped a bite.

He chuckled. "Since I was a lawyer, I had a small office." He looked from one wall to the opposite wall, waving his spoon as he eyed the room. "I guess it was a fourth of this room, but it provided privacy for any clients. Prison has big ears."

She shrugged. "Then what else did her grandma have? I know she worked a lot of years, right? At the telephone office?" She pointed to a drip on Bea's cone. "Lick that up, Bea."

"She did work and leave a nice pension, but she had also purchased land." He opened a file folder. "Her husband started before he died to buy up a section or half a section at a time. She just kept it up."

"Here in Polk County? Or where?"

"All over." He pointed to another drip running down Bea's cone. "Lick that. There." He shrugged. "Even in other states."

"Wow. Does Noell know?" Katty grinned as Bea licked around the outside of the cone and took a bite of the crunchy wafer.

Then her grin faded. What did she have to leave Bea?

Not. One. Thing.

She sucked in a deep breath and closed her eyes. She could do this … this life.

What was Mrs. Hatly always saying? Everything always works out.

Each day, Clarence taught her a little more. Every day, she learned from Harold, Mrs. Hatly and from Carol. Even Lisha.

If she started now … well, after she got through school, she could start then.

She opened her eyes. No. Now. She'd start now.

She tossed her empty cup in the trash and picked up a pile of documents. Some were stuck together and when she peeled them apart, a candy wrapper was in between. 3 Musketeers. Nasty. She threw it away. Names seemed highlighted on the papers: Judge Green, Dawes Timmelsen, Clarence Timmelsen. Dawson Retrieval: Reclaim Systems again.

She compared several documents, and they all had those names on them. "Where's the legal pad you just had, Clarence?"

He slid it to her. "What'd you find?" He scraped at the inside of his cup. One last bite.

She began to copy addresses down and soon had a list of twenty or so. She took out her phone and tapped on the screen.

She looked up to see him watching her. "Who's Henry Green?" She flipped a page. "I get Judge Green and I know what your dad's name is. But who is Henry Green?"

He shook his head. "I-I don't—" He threw his cup away.

She spread out several papers in front of them. "Do you know you own maybe," she counted on her finger, "most of downtown—plus?" She pushed the papers to him.

He choked. "I own what? Do we have a map of Osceola?"

Katty tapped on her phone and passed it to Clarence.

He checked back and forth between the papers and the map on the phone. He looked dazed. "Damn. I own three-fourths of the whole town!" He stood and spread the papers out, moved the boxes to the floor to make more room. "Even Judge Green's house?" He plopped down hard on his office chair, rolling backward.

What do you say to a millionaire? Maybe even a billionaire?

He rolled forward again, pushing off with his good leg, both elbows on the desk. "What did you do, Dad? And I thought you were just a carpenter."

Katty scanned the papers in order by date. "He bought the town, piece-by-piece." She pointed to each sheet. "Day-by-day. Block-by-block."

He wiped his face. "And Judge Green's house was the crowning glory, I'll bet." He closed his eyes and leaned his head back against the chair. "Revenge.

I bet he did it all to get Judge back." He opened his eyes. "And for me. He did it for me."

Bea climbed on his lap. "Do you own the swimming pool?"

Clarence laughed, then stopped and looked at Katty. "Do I?"

"Well, if you do, you own the park, too."

Bea chimed in. "And the swings?"

Katty laughed. "Oh, you are too funny."

Clarence started digging through his pockets. "Where is that article?" He patted his shirt.

"What article?"

He stood Bea on the floor and pulled it out of his jeans pocket. He opened it and read out loud. "It seems his assistant Henry Green, fell into a pool in a cave they were studying near the Old Ridge Road."

Katty had never seen Clarence's eyes so serious, except when she had first met him in the park, and he had protected Bea from her. "What? Who is—"

"Henry Green?" He finished her question. "Could Henry Green be … Judge Green's brother?" He checked the documents, his fingers tapping the desk. "I think they were brothers. Judge Green's brother drowned in a pool?"

He looked down at his leg. "In that pool? What else was that Judge guilty of?"

TWENTY-FOUR

The next day, Bill and Rat pulled up saplings growing around the camper, and Noell tried the door.

"Locked. I forgot to ask Steve for a key."

A saw buzzed behind the camper. Small trees flew into the air.

Bill walked up beside her. "I bet it's not. Bet it's froze shut—just stuck real good." He yanked on it, but it held tight. "Well, maybe not. Maybe it is locked." He looked down at her. "So, no key?"

"I forgot to ask." She scratched her head under her hard hat and settled it on her head again.

"Here. Let me." Rat threw a tree onto the pile and shoved his way between them. He planted his feet in front of the camper door, took one hard yank on the doorknob and the door broke free. The doorknob came off in his hand. "Oh-oh." He dropped it in her hand.

"Now, what do I do with this?" she asked.

Bill picked it out of her hand and examined it, holding it up to the door. "Aww, we can get this fixed in no time." He ushered her inside. "Take a look at your new abode, Little Princess."

Noell stood there a minute absorbing what Bill had just called her. Somehow it fit. She was living in a fairy tale, and this was her kingdom. This was her coronation day. Well, it was just an old camper, but she knew big things were happening. This was the day.

She shivered as she stepped inside. Dark. Kinda creepy, but not bad. A veil of cobwebs barred her entry until she swiped them away. They added another layer to her already dirty orange shirt. Stuck like contact paper. Where they draped over her arm, her skin tingled. Strange stuff—spider webs.

The camper smelled, but not as bad as she expected. Musty, but not dirty. Except for stale air from being closed up for … a hundred years, it wasn't too bad.

Kind of warm, too, but it wasn't anything like it would be come August.

A little kitchenette: oven, cook top, tiny sink, ice box—really a cooler. In all its glory. It was beautiful. Dirty yellow curtains were the reason she hadn't been able to see through the window. A long bench across from the kitchenette was upholstered in some kind of flowered vinyl. A built-in eating area.

She clapped her hands. "So cute!" Rich wood lined every surface that was not a bed or kitchen. "Sweet. Sweet. Sweet." Even after this long, the wood still looked fantastic. A good wiping down would restore it.

A calendar dated 1937, advertising Thelma's Eatery and Diner, hung on the side of a … she opened the door … bathroom! This thing had a bathroom? Cute little sink and potty. Checkerboard tiles on the floor. Oops. Some were loose.

She opened a cupboard door beside the oven, and a pan fell out.

Bill stuck his head in. "It comes stocked? Awesome."

Rat stepped in, and the trailer leaned with his weight on one side. "This is cool." He laughed. "Pint sized for a pint size girl." He opened the bathroom door. "You got your own restroom." He looked down at her. "How you gonna do that? How you gonna dump that shit?"

Leaning against the doorframe, Bill nodded his head. "We'll find a way. It'll be fine."

Noell popped her head up. "You'll help me?"

"Of course, Little Princess. This is a piece of cake. Or pie—like in apple."

"I could do that. I could bake you a pie—with Gamma's recipe. She was a great pie baker." She started to jump up and down but stopped, knees bent, her hands spread out like she had just landed square off a balance beam in gymnastics. "Will we break through this floor?"

"Bet not. These things were pretty sturdy." Rat checked with Bill. "Unless there's a rotting issue." He jiggled and danced. "Feels okay."

"Once we move it out, we can check for rotting. It happens in the best of houses."

Hah, Bill. She was beginning to love him almost as much as Steve. Rat, though, seemed to be another kind of guy entirely.

"Thanks, you guys for helping."

Bill scrunched his face like Grandpa used to and nodded. "Sure thing. But should I put my order for apple pie in now—just to be sure, ya know?"

She laughed. "You better. Once I … we … get this home and moved in … I mean this settled … I might just be too busy to bake." She opened an over-head cabinet, and a book fell out on her head. "Ouch."

Rat picked it up and handed it to her.

She flitted through it and exclaimed, "Wow. Comes with my own personal library." The leather on it was embossed with a cross on the front. If only she wasn't at work—she'd sit down and study it. She stuffed it back in the cabinet and slammed the door quickly. "Should I clean it out first, before we move it, or wait?"

"I'd wait," Bill said. "Then you will have all the time in the world to go through things. You might find some treasures. If that calendar isn't a replica, that's even antique." He adjusted his hard hat. "Plus, moving it to your place would stir up dirt, I'd think. Might be junk in here you don't want and then you'll have the time to decide."

"When do you think we could move it?"

"Rat, you free after work today?"

Rat grinned and nodded. "Yup. But I don't think she can bake a pie that fast."

"I'll owe you both." She clapped her hands again. "I am so excited! I have always wanted my own little place. Tiny place," she corrected.

"Well, now you have one." Bill knocked on the outside wall. "Now that you have a camper, you'll need a fishing pole."

She stole a glance at Rat, but he didn't seem to pick up on it what Bill said. Good. She had reconsidered their fishing date.

Lots of work in store for her. Not as bad as Gam's house, but still work. But this was going to be fun, no doubt about it.

Bill clapped his hands. "Back to work, guys.

Steve won't be happy if we don't get this lot cleaned up."

The afternoon lagged, but they finished cleaning the back lot. It wasn't nearly as boring as running paper through a copy machine.

The sun was warm. Swallows dive bombed Bill's hard hat. The guys bantered back and forth, even picked on Noell, with laughter in between. Except for Ken. He just sulked, raked a little, then sulked some more. At the end of the day, Noell realized she hadn't thought of germs or hoarding once. Amazing. Must be good for her to get outside and experience real dirt, instead of people's germs.

When Steve let them all go for the day, they headed out back to get the camper hooked up and ready to travel. Anything that could fly around on the inside was shoved into a cupboard. Not many were empty.

Bill backed up his pickup to the camper hitch. It wasn't even the right size; it was so old. He rummaged around in the compartment behind his seat and held up several. "One of these'll work."

Rat laughed. "Wow, Bill, you have everything back there. You are the handiest guy to have around."

"Wife says I need to clean it all out. Now I have witnesses. I really need all that … junk." He grinned as he knelt at the hitch. "Even if we have to pull it with a rope tied onto my truck, it'll work. It isn't that heavy, like campers are nowadays."

"You think? It has a lot of wood in there." Steve tapped on the siding. "Even this siding is heavier than the plastic stuff they put on now." He looked back at Noell. "Pretty neat find, girl. This is cool. If this doesn't work out for you, I'll take it off your hands."

"Wait a minute." Ken stepped in front of the camper. "How long has she been working here? A week? If that?" He threw off his hard hat and crossed his arms. "I could have been using it for fishing." He pointed at Noell. "How come she gets it when I've been here for six months?"

"Four months." Steve corrected him. "Because she asked. You didn't. Simple as that."

"Ask and you get," said Miguel.

Steve nodded. "Right, Miguel. Something like that." He looked at Bill ready to pull away in his pickup and waved his arm. "All righty. Let's see what this truck of yours will do."

The screeches and groans of the camper would have made great sound clips for a spooky movie as the truck strained to pull it out. Steve motioned for all to get behind the camper and push. Tires had sunk in so deep she couldn't tell if they still held air. Eventually it released, standing pretty as you please, the late afternoon sun reflecting off the chrome. White—or dirty cream colored top half. Gold colored bottom half. Nice.

Ken stood aside, a frown on his face.

Only problem was four flat tires.

"It's not going anywhere like that."

"Oh no. I don't have money for tires." Noell shook her head. "You couldn't even tell they were flat when they were still buried in weeds and dirt." She hung her head.

Steve sidled up to Noell. "I think I can find some old tires somewhere. Maybe even the right size." He elbowed her arm and pointed to the old boundary fence. "Lookie there. There're a few spare ones, to boot."

"But—"

"I told you to clean this place. Cleaning out this camper and those tires." He held his hand up for a high-five.

She barely tapped his hand with hers and wiped her eyes. How could she ever repay this man?

Miguel and Rat pushed and shoved each other as they ran to the pile of tires. Were they still in high school? Ken lagged behind.

Rat pulled a tire from the weeds and rolled it to Miguel. Miguel lobbed it to Ken, only it knocked him over. They dove and wrestled for the tire. Rat ended up with it around his shoulders.

Noell lost it. Belly laugh. All the way from her toes. Laughing had never, ever felt this good.

Steve caught her as she misstepped, still laughing. What a blast! She caught her breath.

She had friends.

And six tires. Wow.

They rolled a couple to the back of Bill's truck and bounced them in, one by one.

"You get bonus tires."

"Hey, I need some for my car." Ken finally acted interested when it came to something for him.

"There's two left over." Steve took a vote. "Anybody have a problem with that?"

"Yeah." Rat spoke up. "Ken just bought new tires. Miguel needs them more than him."

Miguel grinned. "Really? I can have the tires?"

Noell pipped up. "He can have them all … Miguel, if you need them."

Miguel shook his head. "No. No."

"Okay." Steve clicked off each man. "Everybody okay with the two extras going to … Miguel?"

"Aye."

"Yup."

"Where do you want the rest?"

Steve pointed to the camper.

"Cool." Rat grabbed one and rolled it toward the camper.

Bill kept it going to Steve and waited for the next one.

"Hey Bill."

His head popped up from behind the ever-faithful backseat storage compartment. "Found my jack." He walked to the camper, carrying it over his shoulder. "I had no idea this would be so much fun."

With four guys changing tires and Bill's endless supply of tools, it took no time to get the new tires on. Wheel covers were kind of rusty and lug nuts were tight, but they had what they needed for the job.

Bill honked at them. "Come on. Let's get this done!" He waved them to the back bed of his truck. Rat held the passenger door open for Noell. She tossed her backpack in and jumped onto the seat. Rat got in and slammed the door, pounding on the outside with his hand. "We're off!"

Steve followed in his truck with Miguel and the others, except for Ken, who walked behind, still frowning. He wasn't cute anymore.

Noell was squished between Bill and Rat, and she had never felt more a part of something than now. Like a family. Everybody pitching in just to help her was overwhelming. No one except Gam had ever taken it upon themselves to do something so nice for her and to help her.

Well, except Fletch.

They pulled around a corner and the camper

dragged to the left, right at the corner of the park where the old highway crossed the railroad tracks. Ahhh no.

Bill hopped out. "Flat tire."

Rat hopped out.

Noell kind of slid out, not wanting to see the damage.

Steve knelt to check. "Good thing you stopped. These rims are really strong, harder metal than they make nowadays, but better to stop and check instead of ruining them." He looked up at Noell. "Sorry the tires weren't the best of deals."

"It's okay." She shrugged. "Getting a camper for free, some ... tires, and the help to get it all home is amazing."

Rat inspected the little area of the park. "Hey. What if you left it here? It's not on park property, I don't think. You'd have bathrooms down there at the park if you needed them—showers too, I think—and a very nice little piece of ground to live on. Lots of trees and shade." He stopped and looked at Noell. "Or do you need it to be on your gramma's lot?"

Noell raised her eyebrows and stuttered. "Well, I ... Gam maybe wouldn't like me to sleep here. She might need help in the night or something."

Silence.

Oh God. Gamma's gone. She wiped at her eyes.

Steve stepped to her, his hand on her shoulder.

She blew out a deep breath. Oh, to run away right now.

"You okay with it here for a while and see how it goes? Otherwise, we can throw on a new tire and keep on going to your … your place. It's up to you."

Noell thought a minute. "Seems okay here. For now." She spied Ken, lurking on the other side of the road.

Steve saw him, too. "Maybe we'd better get it over to your place. You never know who might want to pay you a visit when you're least expecting it."

Bill entered in. "Yup." He let down the gate to the bed of his truck. "Let's get another tire down and switch them."

They again made quick work of the tire change and were on their way to Gamma's. The place would never be Noell's. Forever Gamma's.

As they drew near, Bill pointed. "Okay if we back it over there? Kinda between the two houses. Your door would open facing your house. And it's kind of secluded from the road and the neighbors."

"Sure. Looks okay." Hard to know.

Bill was great at backing in, and soon the little camper was in place. They all got out and unhitched it. "We can come over and jimmy it around for you if this doesn't feel right."

Noell shivered as she looked at the little camper, her new little home. Settled with a row of trees behind it, a backdrop of the old trellis framing an entrance to the garden that Gams hadn't used in many years.

Her own secret garden.

Goosebumps traveled up her arms and she rubbed them. It all seemed perfectly planned and ready for her to thrive here.

"Anything else we can do for you, Madam?" Rat bowed low, faking a plumed hat and sword.

She laughed in delight and curtsied. "No, my lords, all is well." She clapped her hands until she saw Ken following their trail. "Thank you all so much. I am so excited. I'll have to learn to cook so I can repay you somehow."

"Pie. Apple."

"You may repay at any time, M'Lady."

"I could buy you pizza," she offered.

The guys all perked up at that.

Bill held up his hand. "Wait a minute. Let's let her get this thing settled first. Let Noell get things put together and then we'll talk pizza. Okay guys?"

"Deal. Thanks again all."

Bill stepped away from the door. "I think that'll do it." He rattled the doorknob. "It is good as new."

"Uh … well, … uh, we'd better be going, right guys?" Steve stepped up to her and jingled a set of keys in front of her face. "I found 'em. Here you go, and may you have fun with this new adventure."

"Thanks Steve." She took them in her hands and flipped them over, reading the numbers and the inscription on them. There were markings—

Bill honked as he drove away.

Noell waved at them, even at Ken as they pulled away from the house. She shoved the keys into her pants pocket.

Gamma would have loved this.

She would have limped out with cookies in her walker basket, a delighted grin on her face.

Oh, Gamma.

TWENTY-FIVE

Mr. Zee stood by his window, scanning his new office space. It was not the best in the world, but it was better than it had been. The nursing home board, people from the community, hadn't agreed to all renovations, but he had found ways to expand his budget. And of course, it was at the expense of every resident and staff in Hillcrest Homes.

The board had proposed a new resident and staff dining room and he had convinced them that the leadership of the nursing home was at risk if they didn't approve his new addition instead. Well. It was a little more dramatic than that—he had dropped the hint that their precious stipend would end if they didn't approve his plans. Wherever did they get the idea that the board was in charge?

Staff, unfortunately, had to sacrifice raises indefinitely. There weren't enough funds to do both, which didn't go well for the staff's team spirit. But there was always back-biting among the nurses and aides, so he enjoyed stirring that up as an added sidelight.

Loretta, the receptionist, had been promoted to his personal secretary, so she had no problem with his decisions. She loved her new space. New designer carpet with rich golds and browns—very plush. New equipment and computers, office furniture. Beautiful paintings of families engaged in … family things—like Thanksgiving meals, reunions. That sort of thing. Something he had no experience with. Nice facade.

Even the words on his coffee mug fed into his mounting ago—The Boss—and it was due for a re-fill. Ahh. Coffee aroma was always good, but this im-ported stuff was over-the-top.

He stepped to the window and sipped. He had a perfect view of who was coming and going at the front door. He had purposely designed the addition so he could enjoy the new landscaping—roses, bushes, trees, garden sculptures.

Deep sigh. Mmm. Delicious coffee. Beautiful day.

Who was that limping down the sidewalk? Splint on his leg. Cane. Longer gray hair.

Mr. Zee leaned into the glass.

Clarence.

Clarence was getting into a red truck. Couldn't

see the driver. He didn't have any relatives. There was that younger woman … what was her name? She had a kid. Unless she had purchased a newer pick-up, that wasn't her.

Back to his desk. He keyed in Clarence's name on his computer. "T-i-m-e-l." Back-space. "Two m's." When the file opened, he scanned the records and nurses' notes.

Nope. No known relatives. Even that young woman wasn't related.

One note was dated when Clarence was first admitted. "Repeatedly escapes to explore the town. Seems harmless. He grew up here in Osceola."

He keyed in a different date. "Came back with rusty pipes today. What the heck?"

Pipes?

Later date. "Always talking about a Michael guy." Huh. Mr. Zee glanced toward the window. He knew they worked together on a building in town.

Another date. "Angry old man." Ha. Lisha's notes.

Back to the window. The red truck drove off

Clarence was escaping again.

TWENTY-SIX

Clarence tucked the yellow legal pad Katty had written addresses on under one arm and lifted the cane with the other hand. This cane stuff took co-ordination. Made sense though. Cane on his right side to protect his right leg.

He limped his way from the front door of the old people's home to the street. Felt good to be outside, even with the damn cane. Air smelled better outside. Of course, he might be part of the stink indoors. Maybe.

Cane down. Right leg down. He had practiced in the hallway inside, but it still felt strange and unbalanced. Cane down. Left foot step. There should be a video teaching this because it didn't come naturally.

There was Michael in his new red truck. An automatic. Clarence chuckled even now about the many grinding rides he'd taken with Michael. He was going to miss those.

He paused to view the scenery before him. It had been a while since he had escaped to explore the town. He'd get back to it once this leg healed. The park to his left, where the pool was, looked mowed up and beautiful. In front of him in the distance, the courthouse rose majestically above every other building downtown. He shook his head. Wished he owned the courthouse. That was one fine building.

He jingled change as he remembered addresses, mentally pointing out the buildings. "That's mine. That one's mine. The old Town hall is mine." He whistled. "Never saw it coming. Dad." Dad. According to Katty's map on her phone, he even owned many of the houses surrounding the town square. Many of the properties.

Ha. Including Judge Green's old lot. Would have been nice if the house hadn't been torn down, but he could identify with his dad for ripping the damned thing apart, no matter how beautiful it had been.

Clarence gulped when the enormity of what his father had done, hit him. He blinked. Blew out a deep breath and blinked again. How Dad must have suffered. His only son being dragged off to prison—never seeing him again. Clarence could forgive him for not coming to visit.

One of the hardest days, next to Mom's death,

was when they had hauled him off to prison. He'd never, ever forget Dad's face. The pain in his eyes. Horrible even now. Horrible.

The hardest day of all—the day Annie died. A lump rose in his throat, even now. Had to swallow it down like always. Sixty years.

Michael drove up and parked in the handicapped spot. He climbed out and hurried around the truck to help Clarence in, opening the door. "Michael, hi. You don't need to help me. I can get in myself." He proceeded to trip over the cane and Michael caught him just as he fell into the door. He leaned into Michael until he got the cane out of the way and his feet straightened. "Well, maybe I do need help."

"I'll say you do. You just about crashed." Michael eased him into the truck and closed the door. He walked around the front of the truck and got in, shifted into reverse. "So, the courthouse today? That where you want to start?"

Clarence nodded. "Yes. I can't remember if you were in my rooms then or not. But Katty started digging out one deed after another yesterday. All from that bastard, Pete's boxes." He paused. "Thank God his secretary dumped them on me." He glanced at Michael. "Might have never known what Dad did back then." He fumbled with the legal pad. "Did you know, Michael?"

Michael started to shake his head no but stopped.

"I knew, but I have no right to interfere without Father's command ... or yours."

Clarence pointed to his chest. "Mine?" He turned in his seat to face Michael as much as a bench seat would let him. "Like in, I could command you to do something?"

Michael stopped at the stop sign and looked directly at Clarence. "Yes, Clarence. But only if it's Father's will."

Clarence stared back. "Why didn't I know this sooner? I would have commanded you to release me from prison. To fly me home on your wings. Take me back in time before Annie died."

"I'm not an airplane, Clarence."

Clarence chuckled. "But you could have, right?" Why didn't he know? He'd gone to church all his childhood, well, after Mom died, it became sporadic, but they had gone every Sunday before she got sick. "What can I tell you to do, Michael?"

Michael glanced at him out of the corner of his eye. Back to the street as they stopped at the Railroad tracks. Glanced at him again.

"What. Did Father command you not to tell?" Clarence grinned. "You're afraid I'll tell you to do something ..." He searched the sky and their surroundings. A train blasted its horn. "Something like jump in front of that train."

The train chugged in front of them.

No comment from Michael.

They bumped over the tracks after the train passed.

"Or rob the bank for me. Clean 'em out." Clarence laughed again as they pulled into a parking space in front of the new bank.

Michael shook his head. "I couldn't break into that bank."

"Against your religion?"

"No. It's fortified with steel girders and the vault is impenetrable." Michael pointed to the front windows. "Says so in their brochures."

"Michael. Y-you read their brochures?"

"Well, what else am I supposed to do while I wait for you? It's a new bank and I wanted to find out more about it." Michael looked in the rear-view mirror to behind him. "Looks as good as the courthouse does. Or vice versa."

Clarence struggled to see behind him. "It does, doesn't it? I should get in there before they close."

Michael pointed to the bank. "There?"

Clarence pointed behind him. "No, the courthouse." He tapped his list. "Need to find out if my name is actually on the deeds registered in there." He opened his door. "Let's go."

They got out and jaywalked across the street—Clarence cane tapped, and Michael followed.

"This is a great building, huh, Michael," Clarence

said. "Do they even build them like this anymore?" He pointed at the level above them. "The windows still look great. The brick is solid. Everything looks well done."

A woman met them, coming out of the building.

Pete's secretary.

She didn't smile. In fact, she did the opposite, like in a soft growl. Her eyes could have penetrated the bank vault that Michael had been talking about. She'd be prettier if she smiled.

Clarence watched her stomp down the sidewalk and into Pete's old insurance agency. "Guess they're closing the place up, huh." He looked again. "How does she walk in those spike heels? I'd break my … well, it's …"

Back to the courthouse. Huge pillars. How had they done that back then?

A man pushed open the door from inside and held it for them.

Clarence nodded. "Thanks." He stepped into the entrance. "Wow. The marble. It shines. Stunning." The stairs curved up forever. "Look at these steps." He looked up at Michael. "Is this one of those times I can command you to fly me upstairs?"

Michael grinned and hooked Clarence's arm with his. He took a step at a time, with Clarence by his side.

"Woah. We are flying. Kind of." Clarence moved

each foot, but he didn't need the cane anymore. Felt like he was floating. "Michael."

"What?"

"Michael, are you doing this?" They made it to the first landing and Clarence got distracted by the marble. He paused to run his hand along the step above. "Look at the curve on this one. How did they cut this? Whoever built this was a fine craftsman."

Michael glanced above him, seemingly lost in the beauty, his face peaceful, beautiful.

"What are you thinking? It's beautiful, isn't it?"

Michael flinched. "Uh, yes, but that's not what I was thinking of. It is beautiful, though."

They reached the top step. Clarence wasn't even out of breath or tired. He turned to enjoy Michael's expression again. "What were you thinking, then?"

Michael helped Clarence move out of the way of a person heading downstairs.

"What, Michael?"

Michael glanced at Clarence and then quickly tipped his head toward the Clerk's office. Back to Clarence. "I was with your dad when he registered the deeds to the plots he purchased back then."

Clarence swallowed. "How?" He slid down onto a nearby bench.

"I was assigned to you from before you were born to this earth." Michael sat beside him. "And I have been with you ever since." He watched a man in overalls walk out of the Treasurer's office and down the steps.

The tap, tap of the man's boots echoed throughout the building. The door downstairs clicked shut.

Michael spoke again softly. "But when your dad purchased all the lots, Father sent me to him. He was grieving badly for you and your mom. But for you."

A tear slid down Clarence's cheek. A ragged breath escaped.

"That day, the day he walked into that office there," Michael pointed, "and registered each deed in his name, he didn't rejoice. He didn't party." Michael dropped his arm in his lap and bowed his head. "He wept." Shaking his head. "And wept."

Clarence finally found his voice, cleared his throat. "Revenge didn't help."

Michael shook his head, still bowed. "He loved you so much."

Clarence leaned forward, his face in his hands. The cane clattered to the floor.

He wasn't sure how long he had sat like that—probably seconds, maybe minutes—but as he straightened, his eyes landed on a portrait of some guy from the early days of Osceola. Clarence didn't know who the guy was, but he must have done something good, been someone so upstanding, that he had gotten his portrait on a wall in the courthouse.

Was there a wall of fame at the prison? Kind of. Either bad or good, it probably was in a guard's heart, or the dietary woman's memories of how she had been mocked, ridiculed, insulted. Or how an inmate made that life-changing, split-second decision to not go over the wall, or not throw that first punch.

He must have done something right. Dietary lady had made him a scarf—he still had it.

He knew he had made bad decisions. Hence the memory the day he left prison, of William Austin pacing along the cell bars, flipping him off. But the finger was nothing compared to the evil and hatred William had fired at Clarence. The scar on Clarence's cheek, mostly obscured by his beard, tingled. He rubbed it, remembering the brutal and bloody battle.

He glanced at the portrait again. Eighty years of living and the only acknowledgement for a life well lived was a wool scarf. It was beautiful, but the only thing he'd ever done right for that dietary woman was to tell the ringleaders in prison to leave her the hell alone.

The man in the portrait passed judgement on Clarence. He swung the gavel down in conviction.

A Pearly Gates moment.

Who had he become?

It wasn't about the acknowledgement—the scarf and the time it had taken her to make it—it was about the heart.

And that arrow pierced the deepest.

As he sat next to Michael on this now very hard bench, the question was asked—the handwriting was on the wall—who had he become?

Michael picked up the cane and patted Clarence's back. "And now, you get to go in there and receive what you rightly own. Fair and square. All legal. Because your dad loved you. He couldn't get you out of prison and believe me, he tried."

Clarence looked up at Michael. "He tried to get me out?"

Michael nodded. "For years. He hated Judge Green—that hatred and grief are what killed him. When he couldn't get you released, he decided an undercover sort of thing might do just as much damage."

"Sounds like revenge." Clarence tapped his cane on his foot. "Sounds like me."

Michael nodded again. "Like father like son."

Clarence slammed his cane onto the marble floor. "But it didn't help. It didn't get me out of prison. I was in that damn place sixty years." He shook his head. "Revenge doesn't work." He searched Michael's face. "Does it."

Michael shook his head, paused, then shook it again. "Never has. Never will."

"What works then? We just get to live here on

earth mad at each other? Bitter?" He swallowed. "Angry?"

"Read the instruction manual and find out." Michael stood. "Let's go in and get your inheritance."

Clarence struggled to stand. "The instruction manual?" He followed Michael through the door. "The Good Book? The Bible?"

A woman stepped to the counter. "Hi. Can I help you?"

Clarence, still in that moment, pulled out the yellow legal pad, placed it on the counter and spun it around for her to read. "Yes Ma'am. Evidently, I own most of Osceola, Nebraska."

TWENTY-SEVEN

Growl.

Noell had been so caught up in exploring her camper, she had forgotten it was suppertime. One last peek inside and she locked it up. She faced the camper, walking backward on her way to the house. It was so cute, she couldn't quit looking at it! And it was hers!

In the kitchen. Cereal for supper. Today felt like she'd been living a fairy tale. She poured the milk and mindlessly ate. She could just barely see the back end of the camper if she moved her chair a little to the right.

Ahh.

A knock sounded at the back kitchen door. Fletch let himself in. His curly blondish-brown hair was even curlier—Nebraska humidity was beginning to rise. His shirt hugged his body. Why hadn't she noticed that before? How old was he?

He pointed. "What's that in back? It's really cool." He nodded at Noell. "Is it yours?"

She nodded, a lump in her throat. It still felt unreal. "Yes. It's mine."

"Where'd you find it? It's a little jewel."

"It needs a lot of work. It was behind the office at the Roads Department in the trees along the fence. We were cleaning out since we were between jobs. Steve told us except for certain pieces of equipment, we could have whatever we found, and I found … that."

Fletch raised his eyebrows. "So, it's … yours?"

Noell nodded, holding her breath.

He stepped to the window in the kitchen and looked outside a long time, nodding. "Pretty cool."

"Thanks. This has been my dream for a long time."

"It's been your dream to have a camper?" Fletch turned around and half-grinned, his eyes crossed.

Noell laughed. "No, silly. It's been a dream to get out on my own, or at least out from under … this." She waved at the house. "But I can't afford it yet. So that," she motioned in the direction of the camper, "is a way I can make it happen without any … or much cost." She turned back to him. "The Roads guys helped me pull it out, and Steve gave me some old junk tires. All free." She bowed her head slightly. "I know it's kind of an eyesore right now. I'll clean it up, so it doesn't look so bad. I hope you aren't mad at how it looks." She fidgeted with her hair. "Do you want to see it?"

"I thought you'd never ask." Fletch opened the door and held it.

Noell ran ahead and unlocked the door. "And I present … my new tiny home!"

Fletch stepped inside. "Oh cool!"

"I know. It needs a lot of work and cleaning, but—"

"Look at all this wood." He smoothed his hand against the trim. "They don't make 'em like this anymore. They're all plastic. Or vinyl." He tapped the stove. "And look at these vintage appliances."

"Yeah. Well." She eyed them. "I still have to find out how everything works."

"Propane. If you cook with electricity, we could find a hot plate somewhere. That would be better. Make it so you can use either one." Fletch was already inspecting the plug-ins, then he ran outside. He must have been checking the connections and exhaust on the outside.

She brushed the counter and checked her hand. "Pretty dirty. I can't believe I just did that."

She sat on the flowered bench seat. "I just swept my hand over that dirty counter." Deep ragged sigh.

"Oh Gam. I wish you were here. I wish I could show it to you, too." She studied everything. "The wood just glows—even dirty like it is now. Think what it will look like when it's clean."

She tried to imagine what Gamma would have said had she been here still. Gam was almost visible. Almost.

Noell could almost hear Gamma's voice.

"You brushed the dirty counter with your hand." Gamma patted the seat for Noell to scoot beside her. "I've seen you when you come home from work, from school. How you place the paper towel down, then your book bag down and change your boots into slippers."

Noell stared—she could see her now.

Her face burned, and a tear slid down her cheek. She wiped it away. "Gam I'm sorry. I didn't mean to make you think I don't like it here. I—"

"Little one, I know why you do all that—why you are afraid of germs and other people's dirt. It's because you were abandoned."

"I wasn't abandoned. I have you. I've always had you. You …" She started to sob.

Fletch stuck his head in. "I found …" He went back outside.

"Oh, Gam. And now you're gone."

She had almost been able to touch Gamma's hand, her face.

Almost.

She could pretend Gam's fingers were caressing hers.

"Honey, when a momma leaves her baby, something happens, no matter how good the caregiver is, something breaks. Does that make sense?" Gamma dried Noell's eyes and touched her cheek, pulling her close.

Almost.

Noell cupped her hand around Gamma's. "It does make sense. But how do I stop being afraid?"

"It's not something you can do on your own."

"So do I have to go to a doctor?"

Gam shook her head.

"Take some medicine?"

"No, Little One. He is the Way."

Noell leaned her head onto Gamma's shoulder.

Only, she was gone. Gam was gone.

That fragrance.

"Hey, uh, … sorry, but there is someone out here that wants to buy your camper." Fletch stuck his head in the door and pointed behind him.

"What? I just got it here." She wiped her face, stood slowly, and looked behind her where Gamma had sat. Had that really—

"Sorry, Fletch. Can you tell them I'm not interested? I'm not selling it."

He looked behind him and shook his head. "Not

for sale. Thanks." Stepping inside the doorframe, he smiled. "This is really the sweetest little camper I've ever seen. It's really old too, but in such great shape. What a find for you."

Noell slid her hand along the wood door to the little bathroom. "I know. I can't believe it. It has everything I would ever need." She swirled around taking it all in. "Not big, but I don't need big, just … mine."

"Well, I'll let you get on with exploring your new digs. I have some things Mom wants me to do, but if you ever need help, I'd love working on this with you. I mean—I don't want to intrude, but this would be fun to … well, you know what I mean." He waved as he jumped out onto the ground.

"Thanks, Fletch. I will ask. I'm sure I'll need it." She stuttered. Words wouldn't come out right when he was around. Her face got hot just thinking about him. She knew him, but she didn't know him. She knew he was always willing to help. She knew where he lived. But she didn't know his mom, his family. Him.

She opened a cupboard, and a pan fell out. A can fell out too, almost hitting her on the head. "List to make. I need a step stool, cleaning stuff, trash bags. I'll probably just need to toss everything."

She ran into the house and found trash bags and supplies. It would be so cool to sleep out there tonight, but she needed time to clean. She'd need fresh sheets and blankets.

Hmm. She remembered a box inside Gamma's house somewhere … the dining room … where there were boxes full of sheets and blankets and comforters. Maybe hoarding wasn't so bad after all. She might have everything she needed. All she had to do was go in and find it.

And wash it.

When she returned to the camper, she started digging through all the cupboards, doors, and all the little nooks and crannies.

Books. Notebooks, newspapers, photos.

She took them to the dinette table and sorted through them. She wouldn't throw anything away until she'd had a chance to really figure out what this all meant. Kind of felt like hoarding, but something might be valuable.

Huh. Osceola Record. From … when? 1937. Pictures of a man who wore a shabby straw hat in every picture. A Dr. Walter Stevens.

Huh? A scientist. Researcher? Like in geography or what?

A newspaper article had a picture of him and another man.

She scanned the caption.

His assistant. They were standing beside a small pool of water. He had presented new information about the pool and the water. The assistant looked creepy, standing almost behind the doctor, but to the side, fully visible to the camera.

Something about his eyes.

Reminded her of … someone. Weird.

There was a map too. She wasn't sure, but it looked like Osceola. Couldn't be. There wasn't anything to discover here.

Was there?

She wasn't getting any cleaning done, but she couldn't stop looking at the journals and notebooks. Intrigued. This was an amazing find.

Did this guy—she looked for the right name, Dr. Walter Stevens—had he lived here in this little camper while studying whatever it was that he studied?

Wow. Maybe he was famous.

She grinned. Or not.

She opened the door to another cupboard, and something fell out and hit her on the head. Again.

A book.

She slowly sat.

Bound with soft brown leather. A ribbon had been tied around it to keep it closed, but the ribbon was shredded, falling off in her hands. The knot was still there, though.

She opened the book carefully. It was maybe four inches by six inches—just a small leather-bound notebook. Real leather. Not what they advertised today. It was soft, old.

An old-style cross was burned into the cover. A regular cross—not skinny—not chunky, with a round coin-like piece covering the center. The coin had what looked like a thumb print pressed in, but a daisy-like flower was inside that.

She glanced through the pictures and articles scattered on the table, hoping for a reference.

What a unique cross.

Stains added to the beauty of the old leather. Probably coffee or tea stains.

Or was it … blood?

Oh, her imagination could run away sometimes.

As she opened the book, she held her breath hoping dust wouldn't make her sneeze or her allergies flare up. But she promptly forgot about any germs as she read the first page.

"I can't believe what is here. Henry wants to go in but I can't let him. There are reports of a young boy of eight years old falling in as he tried to retrieve his brother's ball from the back of the cave. He never returned. He couldn't be found. As searchers were called in, they dredged the pool as far as they could, but nothing touched bottom. Heart-breaking. His brother had sobbed and sobbed until their mother arrived and found him. Then there were two broken hearts. An older woman had tried to dip water out for her garden and plants. She believed the water contained some sort of magic minerals or potion to make her vegetables grow big. She fell in as she tried to fill pots with water. Again, rescuers tried to find her body. It never turned up. Where had these people gone? The human body floats because it is seventy percent water. They should have floated to the surface. They were never found."

Noell gasped. This was in Osceola?

Wait. Bill at work the other day. He remembered caves and drownings. This might be what he was talking about.

She flipped through the book even more slowly, wanting to read every word. Maps and directions, sketches of the pool and of the surrounding areas, must have been part of Dr. Steven's research. He even had sketches of people he had interviewed and places he had visited. A Mr. Bowman. Someone named Mrs. Bertrand—wasn't that the antique store lady's last name? Maybe her mom.

Bill. Bill at work had been talking about a cave. He remembered drownings … back …

She glanced up at her new little home in the camper. She had to go through the whole thing very carefully and slowly—every nook and cupboard. She couldn't miss a thing.

And who was Henry? Somewhere. She'd heard that name. Lately. Henry. She tapped the table.

She needed to visit the library to research every newspaper from back then to now, check every fact, every date. What a mystery presented by these journals and notes. She had to follow the trail.

"Henry. Where?" She tapped her forehead. "Somewhere." Her head bounced up. "Clarence's wall of frames! The newspaper article!" She shook her head. "He was studying it. I should—"

But a pool would have germs, bacteria. And water. Water was what took her mom away. Water was her nightmare.

She stopped at another page and read. "The water in the pool is the strangest I've ever seen or tested. Seems to be able to radiate light, to make a person turn inside out—I don't know any other way to describe it. I've seen things, too. Things that should not be in that pool—things from my past, my parents, a brother that died when he was seven and I was eight. How is that possible?"

How could she ever explore along the same path of this ... this ... Dr. Stevens, when she was terrified? She'd almost been on the threshold of digging out of her fears. Now she could feel them return, almost touch them.

At the opening gate was that stupid terror. It was almost ... real. Like a person. Standing there in front of her. Guarding against any freedom she might experience.

As she entertained thoughts of exploring and following this path, her mind tingled. Her flesh got goosebumps.

But at the same time, thoughts of the unknown crippled her.

The germs. Disease. Death. What had killed his assistant … this Henry guy?

There was a distinct pulling inside her. First one way, then the other.

The battle.

Which would win out? Determination and adventure? Or fear and torment?

She gathered the articles and journals into a pile, putting the newspaper photograph on top. Dr. Stevens stood in front of a pool, in Osceola, Nebraska, what, seventy-some years ago.

Where was that pool?

TWENTY-EIGHT

Mr. Zee locked up his office and turned toward his secretary. "Loretta, I'm going downtown. Gonna find out a little more about this town, the history and such. Might be able to drum up more benefactors for Hillcrest."

"Sure, Boss." Loretta tapped on her computer keyboard, her eyes scanning one monitor to the next as she worked. Up to the minute technology.

He had been surprised at her abilities—especially with computing. Never put a blond down.

The wiring for this addition had been a nightmare, but he hadn't backed down when the installation guy had complained. There was no way he would give up his bank of monitors. He needed to stay on top of things in Hillcrest.

So far, it had been a frustrating morning. After

he'd seen Clarence leave, there had been two staff dis-
putes, a decision on where to have the family carnival
in July—since he had taken the customary space for
his addition, and a resident complaint. The woman's
daughter had insisted her mother be given dining
room privileges, a better view from her table. Why
wouldn't she want to be seated next to the kitchen?
She got her food faster than anyone else. Picky-picky.

He walked to his car and unlocked it but noticed
a spot on the paint, beside the door. Oh-oh. Dirty. He
licked his finger and wiped at the spot. Stepping
back, he scanned the whole car—a Porsche—he had
always dreamed he would own one. Beautiful black.
People said black was hard to keep up, but he didn't
think so. Carl, the maintenance guy, hand washed it.
He'd have him do it when he got back.

Truth be known, today he wanted to find the perfect spot for his new home. He had decided he liked
Osceola and needed his own presence, other than the
small temporary apartment he lived in that was connected to the facility. He needed to put down roots.
What was the saying? Rule where you're planted—
something like that.

He backed out of his personal parking space.
There were a few lots in town he had spied that might
be the perfect place for him to settle in. One, on the
top of a hill, would need a house taken out. The other

was perfectly flat—the house had already been torn down, and a line of trees provided privacy he required.

His car almost drove to the flat lot by itself. He was always drawn to this one. Hmm. Maybe today was the day to find out. He pulled over and got out. The trees cast shadows that played across the grass. Bricks were imbedded in the grass and seemed to line a path. He followed them to almost the center of the lot and rotated full circle. Oh, the house he could build here. And right behind the nursing home. Convenient.

He pulled out his phone and snapped pictures. He had an architect in mind to design it.

Time to go to the courthouse to see who owned the land and to make it worth their while to sell.

As he drove downtown, he realized that if he was to capitalize on his time in Osceola, he'd better get on the ruling boards and commissions. It'd be easy to get voted in, since he was administrator of Hillcrest. It was a natural progression in his career.

Hillcrest and Osceola were only the beginning.

The courthouse was an amazing building. Columns on either side of the entry were massive. When was this built? Amazing feat to put those in place when? There. The cornerstone read 1922. He'd have to do some research to find out how they accomplished that back then. Inside, marble lined every wall. Steps, too. He was smitten.

He needed marble for his offices.

He straightened and blinked. For his house.

The clerk's office should have information on who owned his lot.

A bell jingled as he opened the door, evidently startling the woman at the front desk. "May I help you?" She walked to the counter, a file in her hand.

"Yes." He loved name tags. "Shirley, I need to find out who owns some property here in Osceola."

She dropped the file onto her desk. "Do you have the address?"

"Well, there's no house on the lot, but it's on Ridge Street." He pulled out his phone and showed her the photos. "It's right next to the big Victorian." He pointed out the trees. "Nice weather break already there."

She checked the map. "Here. Hmm." She tapped the document. "No. Here. 530 Ridge Street."

"Could you please find out who the current owner is?" He tapped the address into his phone.

"Sure." She took the map with her into the back-room where two other ladies worked. Laughter and whispers echoed from the small room. One woman peeked out at him, then backed out of sight. More whispers.

Shirley walked in, a smirky expression on her face. Map and notes in her hand.

"What did you say your name was?"

Shoulders back. "Mr. Zee." Cleared his throat. "Otto Zee." He couldn't resist—his chest pushed out. "Administrator at Hillcrest Homes."

She tilted her head. "Well, Mr. Zee, we have had several inquiries on that property recently. In fact, someone was just ... Sorry, I'm not supposed to say." She put the map on the counter in front of him. "Just to make sure I have the correct property ... is this it?"

He scanned the area on the map under her painted fingernail. He tapped on the same area. "Yup. That's it."

Shirley slid a post-it note in front of him. "The current owner is a Mr. Timmelsen. Mr. Clarence Timmelsen."

Goosebumps skittered up his arms and down his legs. "C-Clarence Timmelsen?" His chest was on fire. "Mr. Clarence Timmelsen?"

Shirley nodded and checked the address. "I believe his address is at the nursing home. You are new there, but I bet you might know him."

He shuddered. "I bet I do." Heh. Clarence was so close, he could almost smell the rat.

He wasn't done yet. "Um ... curious. Who owns the lot next to it?" He shrugged. "Maybe he wouldn't mind being neighbors."

Shirley walked to the back room again. She returned, carrying the logbook. "Probably not supposed to bring this out, but I had a feeling. I've been doing this a lot lately." She turned it so he could see and pointed. "Here. He owns that lot, also."

He began to fume. "And the next one?"

She leaned over the book. "Appears that Mr. Timmelsen does owns that, too."

Later as Mr. Zee walked down the outside front steps, he did what he was good at—he put on a mask of contentment, and not what he felt inside—rage.

Clarence Timmelsen had to die!

TWENTY-NINE

Clarence sat at his desk. He had talked the county clerk out of a blown-up map of Osceola and taped it to his wall on top of the framed documents. A little obvious, but he had to see what he owned.

Shirley was the clerk assistant's name. She had run back and forth between him at the front counter and the logbook in the back room, when finally, she brought it all out front so they could work together. She'd cleared a desk off and pulled up a chair for him. "Maybe this isn't legal, but it's more convenient than me running back and forth."

Three hours. During that time, he'd heard all about her kids, her grandkids, her dogs and cat. Why her husband never fixed the toilet—he had been traumatized as a child when his older brother flushed their pet mouse down the toilet. Important things like that.

Before he left, he had been invited to her family reunion August 5th.

When he had asked her for a map, she printed it off in sections, and he and Katty had taped it together. No questions asked.

Well, there had been plenty of questions—how did your dad buy all this property? What had he done for a living? Did he have a girlfriend? Her elderly mom needed a man—or a bank account. Did Clarence have a girlfriend?

Some questions of his own had now been answered. But many more continued to gnaw at him.

Even though he had proof of his ownership of the properties. Even though Dad had destroyed Judge Green's credibility.

What had happened to Henry Green?

Why had he gone into the pool?

And where had Judge Green gotten the power back then to send Clarence to prison?

Now that he thought about it, hadn't there been anyone other than his dad, with the clout or authority to find out the truth, so Clarence wouldn't have had to spend the last sixty years in prison?

He slammed his hand down on the yellow legal pad.

That was the real question.

"Michael." Clarence squirmed in his chair. "Michael, please help." Didn't seem to be around right now. "Where are you?"

He'd dropped Clarence off at the front door not too long ago and Clarence had been so busy taping the map together, he had lost track of where Michael went.

Back to the question. Where had all Dad's clients, who had seemed so loyal, gone? People Clarence himself had built furniture for. He had pounded nails into their homes. He had helped put a roof over their families. Had anyone shown up at the court proceedings in support of Clarence?

He tried to go back in time. He'd relived the court scene every minute of every day when he'd first been incarcerated. He'd mentally scanned every row in the jury box, examined every face. Was there no one who would stand up to Judge Green on his behalf?

He'd thought about this all, every sixty years and why now did it seem so important? After all these years.

Why did the name of Henry Green stir up so many questions now?

Clarence found himself staring at the boxes from Pete's as he tapped on the desk with his pen.

Had Pete's secretary gone through those boxes herself and decided which papers to give him and which ones she didn't? Did she know she had brought Clarence his inheritance?

Probably not.

He limped over to one, dragged it back to the desk and opened the flaps. On top was one of the warranty deeds with his dad's name on it—one of the first ones that had started Katty digging for more.

Something surged in him, pushed at him and he stood, cleared off the desk and began to methodically dig through the box.

Lisha knocked on the door sometime later. "Supper, Mr. Clarence. Dinner bell." She shook her head. "What a mess."

He glanced up. "No time tonight for dinner, Lisha."

"You are chasin' those bunny trails, I can tell." She crossed her arms, stood beside the desk and watched him for a minute. "I kin bring you a plate."

He looked up. "A sandwich maybe?"

"Sure, Mr. C." She walked to the door. "Milk and some cookies?"

He nodded but didn't look up. He'd go through each and every paper—not miss a thing. The newspaper clipping. Why had that popped in his mind, now? He looked at the wall. There it was, tucked into a frame. He shuffled over and slipped it out, placing it in his shirt pocket. Not losing that.

An hour later, halfway through the box, he found

it. He stacked the empty plates and chugged the rest of the milk.

Someone knocked. He groaned until he saw who it was.

Katty and Bea.

Bea walked in, holding up a bandaged finger. Her eyes were red.

"What?" He threw up his hands. "What happened to my girl?"

She had on a pout and was ready for a good cry if he'd give her just a minute of sympathy.

He could do that. He held out his arms.

She ran to him, letting the waterworks dam open. He held her on his good knee and let her cry it out.

When he looked up, Katty just stood there, still in the doorway.

Oh-oh.

He scanned the desk. Not one thing on this desk was more important than these two.

He caught Katty's eye and tilted his head, motioning for her to come in.

She just stood there.

"Katty."

Her waterworks opened too, as she stumbled into the room.

He pulled the client chair close to his and she sat, her head on his shoulder.

Just as Lisha came in the door.

All she did was put her hands on her hips and raise her eyebrows. She didn't say a thing. Just stepped into the room, picked up the plates and glass, and walked out the door. But not before giving him the biggest smile he'd ever seen on that beautiful brown face. Big teeth and all.

Bea hiccuped. She had stopped crying and now sat up and wiped her face. She jumped down and picked up the box of tissue. First to her mommy, then to Clarence who took one to blot his wet shirt. Then she helped herself and blew her nose but really blew out from her mouth.

He chuckled and Katty looked up.

One corner of her mouth lifted up.

Clarence had learned a few things since having girls. One—to never ask what was wrong, before it was the right time. And two—to remember that girls were different from boys. Period.

He wiped Katty's eyes and hugged her. "Well?" He looked from Katty to Bea.

Katty looked at Bea. "I had a melt-down." Tears trickled again. "I shut her finger in the car door." Her chin quivered. "I didn't mean to, I was just … I wanted a beer."

Silence.

Katty's face crumpled. "Bad." She started crying again. "I wanted it bad. I was trying to hurry her into the car. Just one beer." She shook her head. "And I slammed her finger in the door." She covered her eyes with her fists. "And she wouldn't quit screaming."

Bea's face crumpled too.

Clarence gathered Bea on his lap again, his cheek on her forehead. He pulled Katty close.

She straightened and looked into his eyes. "I didn't hit her though. I promise." She bit her lips.

"I believe you, Sweetheart." Oh, these girls, how he loved them like they were his own. In a way, they were. He found himself staring at Pete's boxes again, containing his own inheritance. Maybe he should make it official.

Katty leaned against him again. She started to relax there and soon she began reading out loud. "Today sealed the deal. Judge and I made sure, since Timmelsen was knocked out in the accident, he would never know the truth—that he was supposed to die, and not Annie." She straightened and looked up at him.

He had followed along with her as she read. His chin twitched; eyes filled with tears. Not crying now. He hadn't cried then and wasn't starting—

Bea crawled onto her lap.

"Clarence?" Katty tapped the journal. "What is this?"

He swallowed. He read the next sentence.

She peeked around Bea's head and continued

reading. "But she was thrown from the car." Her voice softened as she read those last words. "The evidence against him stuck, plus the testimony of well-paid witnesses. Judge set it all up. Timmelsen will go to prison for life."

Clarence choked. His body shuddered. Head bent as he wept.

Bea hugged into him.

"Even if he goes before a parole board for good behavior, he'll never be free. Judge also passed down a decision that Clarence will be sent to Osceola nursing home when he turns eighty years old. Serves him right. Timmelsen was supposed to die, and I was to marry Annie."

Someone gasped.

Carol had her hands over her mouth. Her eyes popped, as she moved closer. "Clarence." She pointed with both hands. "What is that?"

He shook his head. Never in his wildest dreams. His chest wanted to burst. He was sure his head would.

Carol slowly sat.

Katty read on. "Judge is brutal. I've seen evidence from years ago, that he screwed his own brother out of his inheritance, and we know how Henry ended up. I need to watch my step. Judge paid people to keep their mouths shut in Timmelsen's trial, too. He paid them all off. Even the preacher got a new Sunday School addition for his church."

No one had come forward except the neighbor with her cookies.

He buried his head in Bea's hair. Little girl sweetness filtered into his heart.

The newspaper article. He reached into his pocket and unfolded it. "Henry Green," he muttered, "fell into a pool …"

Henry had been robbed, too. Just like Clarence. Robbed of a whole life of living.

Judge had caused his own brother's death. He'd literally murdered his own daughter, Annie. And he had sent the wrong man to prison. Three lives robbed. Four lives—there'd been a child—Judge Green had murdered his own grandchild.

He breathed in the presence of Katty and Bea, so close he could smell their fragrance—their essence. He might have missed this … these precious—

"I have to get to the pool."

Katty jerked her head away. "Get to the pool? Clarence that doesn't make any sense."

"We're swimming?" Bea hopped down.

Carol stood. "Clarence, you already hurt your leg there." She shook her head. "What if something else happens?"

Katty picked up the journal. "They wanted you dead back then. What if …"

He took the journal from her. "What if … what if those demons come back to haunt me?"

He blinked. But they had.

He whistled at the realization. They had.

"I have to. There's something I have to find out there." He owed it to Henry.

He folded the article and stuffed it into his pocket.

"I have to go back to that pool."

THIRTY

His walking stick. Dr. Steven's walking stick. Score. That was a prime find.

What else was in the closet? Old straw hat.

Lots of straps. Ropes. One still appeared muddy.

Noell's imagination went wild with that. Fear prickled down her back. Had he been tying himself to something—a tree or rock beside the pool so he wouldn't drown?

She shivered. Goosebumps again.

She stepped away from the closet, still holding onto one strap. She shook her hand free and brushed her hands together. Something in her wanted to slam the closet door shut and run out of the camper, never to enter it again.

Sanitizer. Sanitizer.

Too late.

A kaleidoscope of colors and scenes rotated in her mind. Memories overlaid water movement.

Unfamiliar settings and faces. Exotic buildings. Spicy smells and snippets of music—either Egyptian or Israeli singing.

A flash of Mommy's face as she offered Noell a baby spoon of applesauce, layered on top of the exotic dancers, created an unholy mix of brain flashes.

"Here you go." Mommy's voice.

Noell slid to the floor. Oh Mommy.

Sunshine glinted off a rear-view mirror. Mommy's laughter tinkled like bells in a breeze.

"Noell?"

Water flowed in a river. Bubbled over rocks. Gurgles from the river matched her own baby sounds.

"Noell? You out there in the camper?"

Her head popped up and she blinked. Fletch's voice.

Back to present day. She was in the camper again. Still on the floor. The closet door still stood open, luring her into more incredible discoveries. Drawing her into the river of this research, this flow of what happened long ago.

And something else.

This camper, the books and journals—all dared her to break free. Dared her to break out of this bondage of fear.

She could sit here stagnant and helpless, run back

to her room, clean and sterile and live out her life, hiding.

At that word hiding, she hugged herself.

That was what she was doing. Hiding from her life, her destiny.

Knock, knock.

She jumped, coming back to the present again with a gasp.

Fletch peeked in the door. "You in there?" Blond curly hair. New T-shirt. Cute.

"Oh. Yes. Sorry." She struggled to stand. "I guess I was somewhere else."

"You hungry? We got pizza and I … saw you in here so I figured you might be hungry." Still standing just outside the door, he offered a paper plate piled with Supreme. Her fav.

The pizza aroma pulled at her.

"Yeah. You were on the next planet." He grinned.

"Uh." Noell was still partly trapped in her thoughts of a moment ago. Mommy. Water. Terrified to break out and really live. "Maybe. Maybe … I was on the moon?" Hiding. Oh yes, hiding.

"Yeah. That'll work. You were on the moon and couldn't hear me calling!"

Noell relaxed a bit and smiled. She really looked at him for a change, instead of quickly glancing away when he spoke.

He had a mole on his left cheek by his nose.

Didn't only women have those? His blondish brown hair tumbled in thick waves to almost his shoulders. Deep-set blue eyes framed with dark lashes.

Those eyes sparkled and as Noell looked deeper, they became Mommy's blue eyes. Laughing. Gentle. Loving.

Then terrified.

Noell blinked.

"You okay?" Fletch stepped into the camper and slid the paper plate onto the table. "You seem far away today."

"Um, yes. Yes, I'm fine." She glanced up at the closet yawning wide at her. "The stuff I'm finding here is awesome." She reached in and pulled out the cane. "This must have been Dr. Stevens' cane or walking stick. Pretty cool to think about where this has been."

He surveyed the camper. "He had a great little house here. Seems like it has everything a person needs."

Noell circled. Kitchen. Dining, living, sleeping space. Bathroom. "It's really sweet, isn't it?"

"Have you dug through everything? Any rich discoveries? The pot of gold? Fountain of youth?" His eyes twinkled again.

Noell chuckled, nudged out of her fog. Corners and edges returned to their usually clear details. She wiped her hand along the wood of the nearest cupboard. "Yeah. Some great finds. Can you sit down awhile?" She pointed to the plate. "Have some pizza with me." Her stomach rumbled. When had she eaten?

He grinned. "Sure. I was kinda hoping …"

Noell laid the cane on the bench and sat at the table. "I want to show you what I've been finding in here."

Fletch eased onto the seat and examined the table, the seat, the cabinets, the floor. "This is so amazing." He caressed the tabletop. "What happened over this table back then, you know? Who sat here? I mean, what history happened?" He knocked on the table. "Right here?"

Noell sighed. "I know. It's pretty cool." She opened the leather journal and held it up. "Now this. This is amazing." She took a slice of pizza.

"What is it?" He cocked his head. "Looks like someone's drawings or notes." He looked up at Noell, as he took a bite. "What is this? Whose is it?"

"Dr. Walter Stevens." She waved around the camper. "He was some kind of professor or researcher. And this is … or was … his camper." She licked her finger, spun the book around and found a certain page. "Look at this."

A beautiful drawing of a small pool.

"That's awesome. The guy was an artist." Fletch took another bite.

Noell turned a few pages back.

"A map." He turned the book around so he could read it. "What's it of? Where?" He grinned. "A treasure map?"

Noell tapped on the upper corner.

"Osceola, Nebraska!" He looked into Noell's eyes. "You don't mean … did he explore here? Osceola?" He scratched his head. "Why?"

"I guess … there were caves here. And pools in them." She shuddered at the thought. Pools. "He was hired to investigate some drownings that had no basis, no reason." Another shudder. "These are his findings." Noell flipped farther in the book. "I don't know why all this stuff and this old camper were just sitting in the back lot of the Roads Department, but I'm determined to find out his story."

He tapped on the book. His blue eyes met hers. "Maybe this is your calling. Stuff like this doesn't just happen."

"I know. I just happen to find a camper where I work. And I just happen to get it for free. And all his journals and research just happen to still be in it." She checked her phone. "Time to go to Clarence's." She sighed. "Find out … what … from Gamma." Whatever could it be other than the house, this lot? She'd rather have Gamma anyway. "Sorry."

Fletch slid out of the booth. "You okay, Noell?" He hesitated. "I mean, anything I can do?"

She shook her head. "No. I'll be okay. Thanks for the pizza."

"Then I'll see you later." He stepped outside, only to come back in and give her a quick hug.

"Fletch. Thanks."

He nodded and closed the door. And he was gone again.

She wiped her eyes. Fletch was so nice. Huh. Always seemed to be around when she needed someone to talk to.

She scanned the camper, opened a cupboard door. Opened another. Still so much to explore. Her own little treasure hunt.

Another cupboard. An old mug. Another way in the back.

She checked it in the light. "Thelma's Eatery & Diner." Cute. Might have to start drinking coffee.

She gathered the treasures together and slid them into the oven. The only place right now that was uncluttered. She shook her head. How fast had her life changed? From Gamma dying, getting this trailer and now an inheritance? And Fletch? What next?

Gamma. How she wished for one more day with that precious woman.

She stepped outside. Beautiful day to walk. She locked up the camper and stood still. A bird sang from somewhere close by—Gamma had always called it a Jenny Wren. The sun warmed her skin.

It wasn't an all-is-right-with-the-world moment though. The pain in her heart was more than she'd ever experienced. Gamma had been her world. Even though there had been differences—hoarding, germophobia—what were those, but the same fear?

She stopped.

The same fear.

Just expressed in a different way.

The camper seemed God-sent, or Gamma-sent, to help her through this time … but to jog her fear of germs loose.

It had gotten warmer since she had been inside the camper. She surveyed her yard—her yard--and shook her head.

Help me do this right, Gamma. God.

This was a perfect place to park her camper—very convenient to the house and a bathroom. Her idea of a place by the creek could wait.

Onward to Clarence's to see what he had found.

Katty loved helping at Clarence's on a regular basis. She loved time with him. She might never feel like she was smart enough to help him, but he always made her feel like she would make a great paralegal. She had already learned so much from him—almost more than in her online class.

She glanced at the line of boxes on the floor. Still a lot to dig through, but they were making progress.

Knock, knock.

She jumped up, but Clarence beat her to it. How could he do that with a hurt leg?

Clarence opened the door. "Hello Noell."

She peeked inside. "Is … is this a good time? I thought I'd check to see what you found out … if you're not busy."

Clarence shook his head. "Found out?"

"Yes." She adjusted her backpack. "A-about Gamma's will?"

"Oh. I'm sorry."

"I can come back. I just thought—"

He opened the door all the way. "No. No. Come on in. We were just doing research. I just told Katty here … sit down." He closed the door.

Katty jumped up and cleared a space on the desk. "Hi Noell." Noell was so pretty, even in her orange T-shirt and ball hat. No make-up. "I forget. Where do you work?"

Noell sat and hung her backpack from the chair." At the Roads Department. I'm a flag girl. Among other things."

Huh. She was pretty even after working in tar and dirt all day. "Nice to be outside on a day like today." Time to practice being Clarence's assistant. "Want some ice cream … or something to drink?"

Noell shook her head. "No thanks. I'm okay."

Bea climbed on Clarence's lap. "I want some ice cream."

Katty laughed. "You stinker. You just had some."

"Hi Bea." Noell smiled at her.

Bea snuggled into Clarence and hid her face.

Clarence patted Bea's back and shifted her to his other knee. "Noell, your Gamma and I'm sure Grampa were very smart people."

Katty passed him the file folder.

He opened it and showed Noell. "They had put everything in a trust with you as the sole beneficiary."

"What does that mean, exactly?" She leaned over to look.

"Katty?"

Uh-oh. A test. "Beneficiary." She could almost envision the word on the page. "It means you receive everything your Gamma owned."

He nodded. "Right, Katty."

Whew.

"Since it's a trust, it means no court dates, no pro-bate." He pointed to the information in the file. "Everything passes to you as their named heir." He pulled out one sheet. "Here is a list of what you in-herited."

Poor girl was gonna need tissues.

Noell was quiet as she read the list. Her eyes

slowly moved up, first to Clarence's face, then to Katty's. "They … I own land? A-and," she counted with her finger, "five bank accounts?"

Katty nodded and pushed the tissue closer. "Seems you and Clarence own the town." Oops. What did her online class say about being discreet? She stole a look at Clarence.

He appeared overwhelmed, too. "I just learned that not only did my dad buy the judge's house—the guy that put me in prison all those years—but he proceeded to buy whatever your grandma and grandpa didn't own." He wiped his face.

Noell seemed to be absorbing the news that she was a wealthy young woman.

Clarence shook his head. "I spent time at the courthouse earlier. Finding out what I own, but also what you own, Noell."

Katty fiddled with the box of tissue. Clarence was a wealthy man. Noell, according to the documents, was rich, too. No worries. When bills arrived in their mailboxes, they could pay them.

She slumped. She couldn't even pay for Bea's new shoes.

THIRTY-ONE

Mr. Zee stood, scanned the room, and faced the staff. "Yes, I've called this meeting to address certain problems that have come to my attention." If he had his way, they would build a whole administration wing with private offices and upscale conference rooms. Chandeliers. Real wood—oak or mahogany—desks and tables. Plush chairs. The best.

For now? This. The crowded room was pathetic compared to the dining room that the residents got to eat meals in. This would have to do until—

"Sorry I'm late." Lisha burst into the room and barely squeezed between chairs and the wall, her body bulging over the chair backs. "I was givin' a bath and couldn't just leave her." She found a chair at the end of the room.

That aide had to go. One of the first things he

needed to do was clean house. People had to go. If there was any staff that might block his plans, boom! Gone.

Carol, sitting to his right, opened her files, making notes here and there.

She might be the first to go. He could find a good director of nursing anywhere. More than anyone else, she might be the main person hindering him. And no one must stop his work, his plan.

One last nurse scooted in, lidded coffee container in her hand. The only place left to sit was on Mr. Zee's left. She skirted behind him and slowly lowered herself to her chair, as if any motion might set him off. Today anything might.

He cleared his throat. "Thank you all for coming." He cleared his throat again.

"It's not like we had a choice or anything." Lisha sat with her arms crossed as far as she could across that massive chest. No, maybe she was the first to be kicked out.

Mr. Zee looked down his black-rimmed glasses at each person there. A couple men, but mostly women. The men were part of his entourage—planted to befriend, to infiltrate and spy.

When he had them all squirming, except maybe Lisha, he began. "I have completed my inspection of this entire facility. The building is old. It has had several updates and remodels. The grounds have become overgrown, although Carl has done an exemplary job of maintaining and pruning things back."

Carl bowed his head and nodded.

"Oh, you want us to clap for him?" Lisha broke out in wild applause.

Tandy joined her until she realized no one else was clapping. She slowly stopped and clasped her hands together, glaring at Lisha.

"If we are to get through this meeting without having to stay here all day, there will be no more outbursts. Clear?"

Lisha rolled her eyes.

"Am I clear?" His blood was beginning to boil. These people would have to learn some respect and he was the one to teach them.

"Residents' rooms are fairly clean. I don't have much problem with the grounds, the condition of the buildings. That can always be updated," he paused. "I do have a problem, though, with resident safety." Pace. He wanted to pace, but even he couldn't squeeze between the walls and chairs. "As I have read through the files and reports given to me by each department head, it has come to my attention that there have been many accidental falls, inside our building and outside."

Carol began tapping her pen on the file, ever-so-gently. He was getting to her.

He pushed on. "I have consulted with my board,

and we have come up with a solution that we really don't like to implement, but for the safety and peace of all, we feel it is necessary."

Lisha started rocking forward and back, again and again. Her dreads flopped with each movement. She squinted, nostrils flared.

He could almost smell smoke. After Carol was gone, Lisha was next.

"For now, there are just a couple residents that this would affect, but we will be diligent to watch others, to make sure they are safe, and their families are assured of that." Good sob line.

Carol had her eyes closed. He didn't think she was sleeping.

Not good.

"So." Louder than usual. She still didn't open her eyes. "The first resident that is badly in need of medication and activity changes is Mr. Timmelsen."

"Oh, he ain't gonna like that," Lisha said. "He—"

"He has no say in the matter. He has no blood relatives." Calm down. Deep breath. Lower the voice. "Since he has been escaping regularly, and especially since he has hurt his leg, it is imperative that he be restrained."

Carol stared at him. She blinked, frowning.

Restrain was maybe too harsh a word. "I propose he be confined to his room and medicated so he cannot harm himself again."

Many staff were now at full attention. Some with glee, like Tandy and Carl. Others appeared horrified.

"We're only doing this, so he won't fall again and harm himself even more. We all know the woes of the elderly as they are injured—one thing after another until … they go on to heaven." He almost choked on the word. He must be catching some virus—all this choking and coughing.

He handed the nurse on his left a printout. "Please, would you be so kind as to pass these out?"

She stood slowly, reading as she backed her chair into the wall, bumped her coffee but righted it before it made a mess. She continued to read as she passed them out. By the time she got to Carol, she was shaking her head. She sat again, slowly, her eyes never leaving Mr. Zee's face.

"Now as you read through this, we will need to be extra careful with charting so we can adjust these amounts if necessary."

"These amounts are enough to kill a cow." The woman who said it, ducked behind someone.

He'd find out who she was. She didn't have a chance to remain anonymous, sitting between his two goons.

"This is the reference sheet that you will use for Mr. Timmelsen, Mrs. Hatly, and Harold Dexter."

Lisha rose in indignation, her chair hitting the back wall. "Thas murder! You can't do that!"

"Lisha, one more outburst and you will be cast out from this room." He locked eyes with the goons, and they stood in unison. They pushed the women beside her to their own chairs and proceeded to sit in their chairs.

"Lisha, dear. Mr Timmelsen must be protected from himself. He is falling. He is sneaking out of Hillcrest. He needs to be restrained and medicating him is the safest way to do it."

Heads began to nod.

"He has a violent temper sometimes."

"That's how he got into trouble before—he kept sneaking out."

That's the way. Light a match and the fire burns.

THIRTY-TWO

"Michael?"

No answer.

Clarence searched the cave. "Where'd you go?" He hobbled around to see the whole cave.

No Michael.

Sure. Dump me off and then leave.

Clarence peered into the water.

It had seemed the right thing to do back in his room. But now … well, the pool had lost its appeal.

But he had to know its secrets, its mysteries. Even if … if he didn't return to Hillcrest.

Flashes of dear Mrs. Hatly played through his mind. Her twinkly eyes.

Katty.

And Bea.

Something touched his back and he turned in time to see Michael.

"Michael, no! Help me. Don't let me …" Clarence fell into the pool with a splash. Had Michael pushed him?

He gulped, swallowed. Gagged. The water tasted like sewer.

He thrashed his arms and legs. His head broke the surface and he roared for help. He couldn't have been above water for more than a split second, but the sound of his roar reverberated against the walls of the cave.

Michael!

Father. I trust Your plan.

Michael watched as Clarence went under, bubbles breaking on the surface. It crushed him to have shoved him into the pool.

Father why'd you make him so stubborn?

Michael bowed his head. Some people never realized they even had an angel.

Being Clarence's guardian angel had not been boring.

Before Clarence went under water, a visual imprinted in his mind.

Michael started to glow in his angel costume—his wings spread wide, golden belt around his middle, wielding a huge sword left and right, stabbing into the air in front of him.

He didn't appear in costume unless something big was happening.

Michael had been there when no one else had.

And now …

Was it all a lie?

A sob burst from Clarence's chest. His eyes scrunched. Pain inside exploded in another roar that amplified in the pool, sound bouncing off the rock walls. The water circled about him in waves—a monster closing in for the kill.

Michael was still visible—his glow shimmered through the moving water. He seemed to be flying; his wings fluttered with the ripples of the waves.

Clarence kicked and dog-paddled, holding his breath, feeling every minute of his eighty years. He had always held his breath so as not to smell prison odors—and then nursing home smells. This slimy water was no different.

He broke the surface again, gasping for air.

"Michael?"

His skin crawled, and goosebumps made him shiver.

He'd only been under a few seconds.

This wasn't the same cave.

Making a conscious effort to slow his breathing, he groped for a handhold along the side.

This cave was darker. And the air had turned frigid. So had the water. The other pool had felt like a bathtub.

Two connected pools? Two different atmospheres and temperatures?

Got to get back to Michael.

He primed his breathing, taking several deep breaths, then dove.

He dove deeper, eyes open. Cold. Amazed by the amount of light under the surface.

In spite of the muck, his eyes wouldn't stay closed. His fingers followed the rock walls. There had to be another opening.

Was this what Henry Green had seen?

Carvings and writings extended along the underwater passage. Some glowed. Tiny gold speckles glistened from the rock walls, lit up his fingers as they traveled the walls. It had to be gold—real gold.

Memories flooded: Annie—he hadn't killed her, prison—evil men had intended to harm him in ways his young and mostly innocent mind could not have fathomed, and his life—becoming the rough-edged, angry, stubborn ex-con because of it all.

And now the nursing home—realizing he was a good man.

He shivered. The deep cold hurt his bones.

Colder. Colder.

Which way was up? Or down?

The water pressed against his chest. It felt like a giant had one hand on his chest and one on his back, pressing it's hands together. Tighter and tighter.

Something … two eyes glowed from the side of the wall. Couldn't be. Just something in the rocks flashing a reflection.

They blinked.

He jumped, kicking away.

Still, he held his breath, but began flailing, treading, panicking. The eyes watched him and glowed ever stronger.

Something grabbed his hands. It pulled him down, down.

He couldn't find anything to hold onto. No tree roots or hand holds. Just cold stone.

A face—nose-to-nose with his. He screamed and he was sure that it could be heard at the nursing home and the grocery store. He pushed away. That face. Dark wrinkled skin. White hair.

Screamed again. Bubbles stormed around him, from his mouth, his nose.

If only this was a dream.

He sucked in water, gasped, then sucked in more.

His eyes bugged out. Arms and legs cramped. He was sure his body was turning inside out.

The pool was winning.

He was losing.

Bubbles escaped his mouth and floated upward in a magical dance, making their own music. The colors of the pool appeared more vibrant, more beautiful than before: greens, purples, blues.

The waving and rippling of the water mesmerized him. No better lullaby. "Sleep my baby, sleep." Deep sigh. His mother's voice drifted in and out.

The water temperature turned warm.

He drifted, slowly, calmly.

Fear was gone.

He hiccuped and sucked in more water.

Deep breath in. Breathed in the water. Reason said it was impossible. He breathed in again.

He coughed and choked, but soon it wouldn't matter.

There was no question as to how this was going to end. A person had to die somehow—sometime. He'd wanted to die ever since he'd come to Hillcrest.

He sank farther down—deeper. His arms floated out from his body, his legs limp in the water. Fabric in his clothes rippled around him.

He didn't struggle.

Light beams diminished. Not only did the water

grow colder, but his body shuddered as temperatures plummeted.

Sounds were still amplified through the water, but they seemed more distant.

A melody gently rose and fell with the water. His mother's pure voice seeped into his heart, his soul. Her hands caressed him, combing through his hair, massaged his wounds.

Or was it the water as it followed his movements? The activity of the ever-present demons in his soul?

Drowning wasn't that bad.

He was ready. He wasn't afraid. He'd see Annie and his mom and dad. Doubtful he'd see prison inmates he knew. They were too mean to get into heaven.

What happened after death?

Heaven? Probably just a myth.

So many lies.

His thoughts drifted.

Voices. Melodies.

A small boy, eyes of concern.

A hand.

A face like nothing he'd ever seen before.

Liquid eyes, and not from being in water. Kind eyes. Eyes so full of love that Clarence choked. He gasped and sucked in more water, but it didn't matter. His body was now so waterlogged his lungs and skin couldn't hold anymore.

Just as his toes touched bottom, the hand drew him closer.

I've missed you, my son.

Clarence half smiled. Had to be hallucinating. Even in his relaxed state, there was no one else underwater with him. All part of … dying.

I thought you'd never come.

Clarence's eyes drooped.

Almost gone.

A burst of electricity shot through him, jolting his arms and legs straight out. His eyes popped wide. His fingers shot out, vibrating and trembling. Even his inner organs shuddered. Every part of him throbbed.

What he saw shouldn't have shocked him.

Michael?

Not Michael.

A powerful energy penetrated, radiated. Waves of peace and love.

Son …

Son?

Clarence stirred.

Dad?

Waves rippled, drew him, pulled at him.

A power traveled through him.

Enveloped him.

One.

THIRTY-THREE

Noell left Gamma's house after work. Today she would find that pool. With each step, she traced an imaginary path on Dr. Stevens' map. Her backpack bounced against her hip as she walked.

She wound her long blond hair into a bun on top of her head—it felt good to be free of that hardhat. She still had her orange T-shirt and overalls on. She figured if she ruined them, she had another twenty shirts back at Gamma's—and a couple more pairs of overalls.

She stopped and studied the map for the thousandth time—Dr. Stevens had even drawn the warning signs in: Keep Out and Witch Hole. The signs had probably fallen apart long ago, but the meaning still held—this was not a place to play.

She nodded. Three people had drowned in that pool.

Her steps slowed. So why was she looking for it?

He had drawn signposts on the map too: a tree that since then had probably been cut down, the Boy Scout cabin, and the railroad tracks.

She skimmed a journal entry: "A man … keeps repeating that the pool was of the devil … over and over … someone shushes him … city needs to fill in that pool." Dr. Stevens added: "I'm not sure dirt will keep demons in."

The day was warm, but chills traveled up and down her arms.

Dr. Stevens had parked his trailer—her trailer now—under a cottonwood tree. She knew what kind of tree that was. Grandpa had taught her that they had big shiny, almost heart shaped leaves that clapped together in a breeze.

The signposts today? Boy Scout Cabin—still intact. Railroad tracks—how timely that a train was chugging through right now. The horn blast made her jump. The engineer even waved. And a huge old cottonwood tree stood guard—still. The rough bark ran in deep channels up and down the trunk. The leaves applauded Noell.

This had to be it. Noell studied the map in Dr. Steven's journal, closed it and shoved it into her backpack.

She might have found the pool.

Others had been there. Footprints of different sizes and shoe-types trampled the dirt.

She climbed inside the cave and her stomach did flip-flops. There really was a pool.

An argument rose in her: one side really wanted to go in the water, but the sensible side wanted to go home and hide in her bed. She'd done that plenty in her lifetime—always taken the easy way.

Even as she climbed into the cave today, thoughts tried to dissuade her from ever dipping her big toe in the water.

But here she was.

She dangled her necklace in the water. It didn't seem to change the metal or anything or dissolve any part of the chain. The cave had a smell about it that caves normally had—dank, moldy, damp. As she dipped her hand into the water and let her fingers swirl around in it, something zapped her, like an electric current or shock from an electric fence when it's grounded. She jumped and jerked her hand out.

What was that?

Part of her was still terrified, but that jolt felt like when she had flipped a light switch and had gotten shocked. The electrician had said there was a faulty ground wire.

Huh. Whatever was in the pool felt like real electricity—a sort of buzzing. And there appeared to be a layer of something on the surface, like oil on water.

She dipped her necklace in again and the cross began swirling in a slow circle, stirring the water, making concentric circles flow on the surface from the necklace to the perimeters of the pool.

She tried to hold her hand still, to hold the necklace still.

She couldn't. That swirling wasn't anything she was doing.

A jolt buzzed her hand again. It seemed to follow up the necklace from the water, stronger and stronger, until she dropped it.

She shrieked. Her fingers hugged her neck. She had worn it ever since Grampa had given it to her when she started high school. "My cross. No!"

She stuck her hand in the water, trying to hook it.

She searched the edges of the cave. Spotted an old branch. Grabbed it and fished where the necklace had dropped.

Nothing.

Again.

No necklace.

Gah. She couldn't lose it!

The branch hadn't touched the bottom. She swished it again. Why wouldn't the chain catch on the twig?

She fished again, sticking the branch in as deep as she dared reach.

Nothing came up but a few strands of hair.

Her eyebrows went up.

Hair?

When she searched around the side of the pool, the walls of the cave caught her attention.

Writings. It didn't look like English. Old American Indian? But they used mostly pictures, didn't they?

A big tree root poked up from under the surface. Maybe her necklace had caught on it.

She stretched down into the water trying to reach it. It was only a couple inches away.

"I want my necklace!" Splashing the water, she willed her necklace to appear in her hand.

Nothing happened, of course. Her hand automatically found its way to her neck again. No necklace.

Hugging her knees, she scanned the cave. The interior seemed the same as any cave. Partly dirt, mostly rock. It seemed to be sparklier than usual cave walls, glowing and sparkling. Kind of like gold.

She should go in and find her necklace. A slight shiver and butterflies in her stomach told her no, don't go in.

She stuck her hand in. Not too cold. Almost like the sun had been warming it for her.

What was she thinking?

This would never work. An old lady and a kid had already drowned. And Henry, the assistant.

She stretched to touch the tree root—almost there —almost touched it.

And in she went! Splash!

Terrified, she kicked hard. Her lungs wanted to burst. She needed to open her mouth and breathe.

She swam with all the strength she could muster but couldn't find the surface. There! Her necklace hung from a rocky finger at the edge. One gasp and she sucked water. Another push and she … but it wasn't her necklace, it was a tree root.

She paddled frantically, trying to find a place to climb out. Her hands slipped on the wet, slimy rocks. Her feet couldn't find a foot hold under the water. She couldn't get to the edge fast enough to push her-self up and out before—

It started. Her mind played frames of visuals over and over, like a cinema. A boy floated. Balls bounced. Children splashed, then were chased away. A woman fell in but didn't fight the pool. An angry man swam deeper.

Noell screamed in her heart.

Sanitizer! Sanitizer!

Something grabbed her and pulled at her. She was just conscious enough to feel the hand and arm around her throat, pulling her out of the pool.

The instant she opened her eyes, she sat up, and

looked around. "Fletch?" He had suddenly appeared when Gam died.

Her voice merely echoed off the walls of an empty cave. She wiped her eyes and tried to look around.

Someone or something had just saved her life.

Her breathing returned to normal.

Shivering, she eyed the water. She sat on the edge of the pool and wiped her eyes again.

She looked to the cave opening. Felt like the same time of day she had fallen into the pool. She remembered her necklace and looked up. There it was, hanging from the root, the dim light from the cave opening reflected off the metal cross, causing rays of light to burst on the walls of the cave. A slight breeze must have blown through, for the necklace began to twirl and swing as if a fan had blown on it. Beautiful.

Noell got lost in the beauty as the rays spun around the cave, highlighting the carvings and writings on the walls. Things became clearer. A cross carved into the rock drew her attention. She edged closer. It was the same cross as the one on the front of Dr. Stevens' leather journal! Another sign. He had to have carved it here.

Dots were being connected.

Something had changed.

She had never felt more powerful in all her life.

Fear had always crippled her, caused her to give up before a victory.

Gam had always said it was because her mom had drowned. Strong ties were supposed to glue the bonds between a mother and child. Growing up the way she had—no dad around for sure and seeing her mom drown when she was two—no wonder she had fears.

But today.

This minute.

She could change the world.

She studied the water. This pool brought back the terror she still remembered when her mother drowned.

But it also stirred a feeling of power, but more of … a sense of Destiny. Of being who she was meant to be, following God's plan for her life. Gam had always prayed, "Be all God wants you to be."

What was her prayer? Jesus help. That was it. Two little words.

She sat up and pulled her necklace from the branch and dangled it in the remaining rays of sunlight that were peeking through a crevice in the wall. The necklace sparkled. She strung it around her neck and clasped it. The cold metal cross sucked to the skin of her chest—almost burned into her as the dampness helped it seal to her skin.

Sealed to her heart.

THIRTY-FOUR

Something moved at the far end of the water. Shadows snaked back and forth, leaving a bubble trail. A powerful tail slapped against the water with each twist and turn, pushing the water against Clarence, sending him tumbling against the wall behind him. Voices, like a radio blaring from across the hall at Hillcrest muffled through a head cold, reached his ears. Only he couldn't distinguish any words.

Even in the water, chills ran up and down his body.

The shadow swam closer. It wasn't a snake or water creature. It was a woman.

Someone else was in the pool.

The blue and purple and green water highlighted her red-brown hair. It flowed and billowed, swirled about her face. Pale clothes fluttered around her body as she swam back and forth. The water cast a bluish tint on the translucent skin of her hands as she treaded water.

Beautiful.

She swam closer, until she was right before him, her brown eyes wide open.

Annie! He reached to touch her face.

She cupped her hands around his, smiled and kissed them, turning them palm side up to kiss the scars.

A spark of light zinged from both hands and a deep shudder vibrated throughout his body.

But this wasn't Annie.

Mom?

Had she come for him at last?

His chest no longer burned. Breathing water worked as well as air. Songs played in the background from his memories.

It was time to go wherever it was that dead people went.

She caressed his cheeks and spoke to him from her eyes.

Clarence! We don't have much time. Father has sent me.

Dad sent you?

She smiled and shook her head. No. Father.

God sent you?

She nodded. Her hair billowed out. I never got to tell you, and Dad didn't know how.

Is Dad here now?

She held her hand against his mouth. Hush. There is one thing you need to do before you leave this earth.

Anything.

But instead of explaining she blurred. The water around them became violent, surging up and down, like the inside of a washing machine. Waves crashed into him, pushing him away from her. He couldn't lose her. Not now. It had been so long …

He struggled to hold onto her.

He would not let her get away. Her hair was still tangled in his fingers. Not letting go. He'd follow her to the next world wherever that was and back again.

She seemed to float away, but he sensed her coming back for him. She slipped her arm under his chin and towed him up, up. He was weightless. He couldn't feel his arms and legs.

His lungs no longer wanted to burst. He didn't need air to breathe. His thoughts were clear. His mind refreshed and revived.

As they reached the surface of the pool, he saw Michael through the water. He had never felt such vigor.

His head burst above the water, and he gasped.

Choked. Air in his lungs didn't feel right. His lungs were filled with water.

Somehow, she pushed him to the edge. Gasping and sputtering and choking, he gripped the hard rock. He threw up and threw up, coughing. Couldn't be any water left in the pool.

Mom!

He turned.

Blue eyes. Blond hair stuck to her face, plastered to her shirt, still tangled in his fingers.

Noell!

Wings pounded in front of him, as Michael flew across the water, commanding the host. Powerful, beautiful wings. There were many. A host of many.

And there was One.

Him.

Face to face. Inches apart.

Those eyes.

He was real.

Clarence gasped.

Such love.

Sobbing, he breathed Him in, into his lungs, his heart, his bloodstream.

Every cell.

"Father … "

Then He was gone.

Noell caught Clarence just as he blacked out, hooked her arm around his body and struggled to pull him out.

Dead weight, water-logged body.

She cried out. Help me! God! Help!

The water in the pool billowed and surged, bubbles swarmed. Images floated.

The pool seemed to vomit them onto the bank.

She rolled him over. He wasn't breathing. Water-wrinkled skin emphasized burn scars on his palms as she checked his pulse.

No pulse.

Long-forgotten skills kicked back in.

Check his throat. Tilt his head back.

CPR classes became automatic. Clarence was only the dummy from class. Glassy eyes open. Pasty gray skin.

God help!

She went through the motions of CPR, counting, her hair dripping onto his face. "One-two-three-four …"

"Come on. Breathe!" Drips from her hair became tears pooling around his closed eyes, his mouth. Each count became a cry—a prayer.

As vision blurred, his gray hair blended with her mother's wet blond hair, splayed around her head.

Noell's two-year-old voice replayed the awful truth. "Mommy! Mommy! Beathe!"

Hands held her away as a fireman leaned over Mommy, pushed on her chest, breathed in her mouth.

The fire chief leaned in and pulled the man away from Mommy. "Ted, there's nothing more we can do. She's gone."

Both men had looked at Noell—even a two-year-old could discern pity on their faces.

She wrenched herself free and pushed on Clarence's chest. Counting. "Breathe Clarence! Come on! Breathe!" Push, push, push. "One two three." Push, push, push. "One two three."

She glanced up. Back in the cave.

Michael. With wings on.

"Michael! Help me!" Sobbing now, she pushed again and again, counting. "Michael, do your stuff!"

Michael glowed as he knelt beside Clarence, his face crumpled. He beat his chest with one hand. Tears coursed down his cheeks. "Father. Father." His head lifted, eyes closed, voice louder. "Father, if it is Thy will." He focused on Clarence and Noell. "If it's Thy will."

Noell sat back and screamed. "Father!" She shook her fist at the sky. "You took my mom. You can't take Clarence too!"

She looked to the heavens, fist outstretched.

Motion and sound became one; her scream matched the force of her fist as it slammed down on

Clarence's chest. Like a mallet meeting a railroad spike, it drove the Power into Clarence.

He gasped and rose partway off the ground, as if a medic had attached paddles to his chest and shouted, "Clear!"

His eyes opened wide.

A roar burst from his mouth.

It took a long time to come back to full awareness. Was this heaven? No, there was mold on the rock wall. Clarence didn't figure there were spider webs in heaven either. Angels would keep it cleaner than that.

There was his wallet, where he'd hidden it before he fell into the pool. He started to reach for it.

Michael peeked into the cave.

"Michael. Michael." Clarence puked up more water and mucus, spitting and foaming. "God, that water is terrible. It's burning my throat."

Noell! Where had she gone?

There. She sat panting in a corner, watching him. Her long blond hair hung wet in her eyes. An orange T-shirt with a big X printed on the front clung to her young form, mascara smudged under her eyes. He pointed at her. "You. That was you." He choked again. "Not my Annie. Not my mom." He slumped against the rock wall. "I was sure it was Mom …"

Noell crawled to him and pushed his hair out of his eyes. "I'm sorry. I'm so, so sorry. About your Annie. Your mom." She cupped her hand around his jaw and stared into his eyes.

Locked eyes with him until he wept.

Something had changed. There weren't many people he let look into his eyes—his heart.

"You." He swallowed and gagged. "You saved my life."

Then he remembered more. He fell back on the cold rocks, sobbing.

He struggled to speak. Sobs broke in. "Angels." He searched the cave for Michael, finding him sitting against the cave wall near the opening, face crumpling as he looked at Clarence.

Clarence crawled to him. "Michael. There were angels all around you." Clarence reached him and grabbed his leg. "You were … you were in command."

"No, my friend." Michael pointed up. "He is in charge. I'm only a servant."

"But you were … He was here." He sobbed again. "He was here."

His face dropped into Michael's hand, and Michael's fingers curled around his jaw. His sobs echoed in the cave. Waves in the pool crashed against the sides. Every sob seemed to speak to the water, making it rush to and fro in response.

Clarence lifted his head. "He looked at me. He …
looked into me." Hiccuped and tried to talk. "He
touched me … everywhere." Pointed to his chest.
"Here and … here." Hiccup. "Everywhere. He
showed me who I w-was. He showed me everything I
ever did."

He sobbed again. "I saw my mom." He turned to
look at Noell. "I saw my mom."

He collapsed, unconscious.

———

Noell started to cry.

I saw my mom, too.

I saw her die—again.

THIRTY-FIVE

Mr. Zee held his arms out, pushing people in wheelchairs and walkers back against the wall. "Give him some space." He had to make way for Clarence to be transported to his room on a gurney. "Let him through, poor man."

Mr. Zee was so close to ruling in this region. Not only was the receptionist his now, but Hillcrest would also be—soon. After that, the town of Osceola. The people, the businesses, churches, the farms? All would be his.

"Sir, this man needs to be transported to the hospital." The EMT checked straps on the gurney and patted Clarence's shoulder, checking his pulse. "He has been in and out of consciousness and his color is terrible. Considering his age, I think he should be admitted to the hospital. I don't understand why you redirected us here."

Mr. Zee stepped in front of her, toe-to-toe, looking down his black-rimmed glasses at her. When he spoke, it was an icy whisper. "Because I said to bring him here."

She blinked and stumbled back, trembling. She held her hands up in a kind of surrender. "You're the administrator."

Atta girl. All according to plan.

Mr. Zee raised his voice, like a preacher getting ready to deliver the final point of a sermon. "We have competent staff here—nurses and aides—who are very capable in caring for his needs." He beckoned them to follow, then hesitated. "I appreciate your concern though." Nosy little biddy. He'd better make sure she wasn't around for what came next.

They proceeded around the corner and were stopped again, by several people crowding the hallway.

"Oh, it's Clarence!" Harold leaned over his walker. "Clarence! Hey Buddy!" When Clarence didn't respond, he searched Mr. Zee's face and reached for the EMT. "Is he going to be okay?"

"Mr. Harold, maybe back up a little." Lisha stepped in front of him. "Give 'em some room. When he's settled in, I'm sure he'll need your comp'ny." She smiled, her eyes never leaving Mr. Zee's face. "Okay?"

Goosebumps on her brown arms. Mr. Zee was sure now, that even Lisha was understanding his power and authority.

Harold did the walker dance backwards—shuffle, lift, shuffle, lift.

Mr. Zee nodded. "Good job, Lisha. We don't want our residents to become agitated." Or suspicious. He escorted Clarence's gurney and the EMTs down the hall to Clarence's room. He glanced at the EMT's name tag and hovered an arm above her shoulders. "Just between you and me, Sally, and all HIPAA aside, he has a do-not-resuscitate order on his chart. So," he paused, "we believe it's important for our residents to be able to … direct their own passage into the next life."

"Of course." She nodded to her partner, who was pushing the stretcher. "You were right, Aldo. I thought we should go right to the hospital."

Good. She was now under his power.

Mr. Zee locked eyes with Aldo briefly, and an energy zing snapped between them. Aldo had complied with all the instructions of the plan precisely. Mr. Zee motioned for them to follow.

Glad Aldo was on the same side. A good plan needed a good team.

When they reached Clarence's room, Tandy and Carl were already waiting. Loyal subjects.

Carol had raised the bed and turned down the covers, so they could slide Clarence across the gurney to his bed.

He groaned when he landed.

They'd have to work fast if they were to complete the plan before Clarence became fully awake. If he became fully recognizant, their window of action would be closed.

Mr. Zee needed to get Carol out before she suspected anything. Lisha, too.

He helped push the stretcher into the hall. "Carol. Lisha. Would you please take Sally to the office so she can sign our release forms? Thank you."

Carol glanced at Lisha. "I need to be here, taking his vitals." She tapped a chart. "I've documented his return, but," she stood taller, "by law, we need to take his vitals and record them."

He firmly pushed her and Sally out of the room. "We've already recorded them on the Master Chart."

Carol balked. "What Master Chart?" She faced him. "I have never, in all my time here, heard of a Master Chart." Hands on her hips.

That woman was trouble.

Lisha stood behind Carol, hands on her hips.

She was even more trouble.

Mr. Zee alerted Aldo and Tandy with a blink.

"Well, there is a Master Chart, and it is in my office. But I don't have time to argue." This was going to be tough, but he was not quitting, Carol and Lisha, or not. He motioned to Tandy.

The town must be his.

Tandy glided across the hall and met Mr. Zee, pulling out the syringe—ready. He had trained her well on oranges and other residents. Just a couple people had actually died. She was quick, too.

Only Carol wouldn't cooperate. Lisha either. They seemed to be glued to the old man.

Aldo bumped into Lisha and began to flirt with her. Should have warned him about her—that kind of thing would not work. Bet she could deck a man faster than a cat on a grasshopper. And she did. She disengaged her hips and swung at Aldo, sending him flying against the opposite wall.

Not a problem. Tandy slipped Mr. Zee the syringe and she distracted Carol by shoving old Harold to the floor.

In the midst of a Lisha-brawl and Carol's cries alerting other staff, Mr. Zee had his moment of opportunity.

He turned to Clarence's bed, syringe poised, just as Noell skidded into the room and tackled him. She knocked him to the floor then shielded Clarence with her body.

"You're not going to kill Clarence." Noell kicked at Mr Zee. "You'll have to get through me first!"

Mr. Zee pushed off the floor. "I can accommodate you." He turned, syringe in Noell's face, just as three cops rounded the doorway into Clarence's room.

Mr. Zee tried to hide the syringe up his sleeve, but the cops lunged at him, and the syringe bounced up, spinning in the air. Hands grabbed for it as it flew, end-over-end.

Noell sucked in a breath.

Mr. Zee's eyes grew wide. He dodged left and right—the cops tried to contain him—until the needle finally landed in his arm. Handcuffs clicked over his wrists.

Michael removed his fingers from the syringe. The demon had shuddered when the needle pierced Mr. Zee's skin.

With wings unfurled, Michael stretched up and out.

The demon screamed.

It appeared to have been so involved in Mr. Zee's plan to kill Clarence, it had forgotten all about Michael—something no demon should do.

It hissed and snarled, kicking as Michael drew his sword and plunged it into the demon's body.

Clarence's bed was bouncing.

Muffled voices.

He squinted his eyes open.

Noell was sitting on his bed close beside him and Mr. Zee was in handcuffs beside the bed, surrounded and restrained by three cops.

Wings billowed. Michael, in full dress angel costume, glowed—his sword extended to Mr. Zee's chest. His stature was twice the size as normal, his skin glistened, a golden belt gathered his white robe.

Bea and Katty stood outside in the hallway. Bea pointed. "Clarence was too swimming, Mommy. He's all wet."

Clarence tried to sit up, but Noell patted him down on his bed.

The cops ushered Mr. Zee out, his right leg giving out every other step. He growled as he passed Michael, his eyes fluttering almost closed.

"Whatever was in that syringe was meant for you, Clarence." Noell pulled Bea up on the bed. "And look what it's doing to him."

Clarence shook his head. Images confused him— memories of the pool and now this chaos.

Carol helped Harold onto Clarence's sofa, a pillow to prop up his leg.

Lisha held both Aldo and Tandy in a death grip on either side of her. They struggled to get free as she marched them away.

Carol turned to the bed. "Clarence. You're awake." She checked his pulse.

Michael pushed his sword in its sheath, metal ringing against metal.

Clarence blinked. "I …" He cleared his throat. "What happened here?"

Noell scooted to the end of the bed to give Clarence more room.

Carol pressed her hand onto Noell's leg. "Noell, how did you know?" She fluffed up the pillows under Clarence's head as he pulled himself up. "You ran in here like a lion was chasing you. What happened?"

Noell met eyes with Clarence and wept.

Bea crawled onto her lap. She reached for the tissues on the side table, almost falling off the bed.

Katty sat beside Harold, holding his hand.

Noell blew her nose. In front of everybody. First time ever.

She looked at Carol, then the others. "I … have this curse. But maybe, now it's a gift." She hesitated.

"When I touch doorknobs, or handles, or cups … I see stuff."

"Like you can see this tissue?" Bea swung her legs back and forth, handing Noell more, one-by-one. "Like when I saw you and Clarence in the pool?"

Gasp. Bea had said that days ago.

Clarence's eyes were as big as she guessed hers had to be.

It was now or never. Noell swallowed. "No. Like when I touch, say a handle—whoever touched it before me, leaves their handprint or molecules … or germs … and when I come into contact with it, I see their face, things they've done, where they've been."

Clarence cleared his throat. "Like when you touched my hand when we first met." He tapped Bea's shoulder. "You saw Bea."

Noell nodded and wiped her face. "Yes."

Carol pushed Noell's wet hair out of her face. "What did you see this time?"

"When I touched the entrance door, I saw Mr. Zee giving people here in Hillcrest shots, and those people died." Tears dripped.

Bea handed her one more tissue. "You have to stop crying now. We're all out." She held up the empty tissue box.

Noell smiled. "I knew he was after you, Clarence." She turned to him and touched his fingers.

Oh-oh. Where was her backpack?

Sanitizer. Sanitizer.

What had she been thinking? How could she have forgotten to protect herself?

Only, what she saw when she touched him, was the pool.

And an angel.

Clarence leaned forward. "Noell."

Tears dripped from her eyes before he could say anything else. "I was so afraid he was going to kill you."

Bea dropped the tissue box. "We need more tissue."

Noell laughed. "I'll stop crying."

"Noell." Clarence reached for her hand. "Dear Noell." His blue eyes were wet, too. "You saved me —twice. Once, at the pool. And again, just now."

Bea held up her hands. "Now Clarence is crying."

He laughed, then stopped and wiped his face. "How can I ever repay you, Noell? You gave your life for me."

She nodded. "Maybe it's not a curse."

He nodded, too. "Oh, it's a gift." He kissed her cheek. "You used it well."

Lisha pushed Mrs. Hatly into the room.

Mrs. Hatly unloaded a big plate of cookies from off her lap. Then held up a box of tissue. "Somebody in here need this?"

Bea bounced on the bed. "We do!"

Clarence leaned back onto the bed.

Bea laid on his chest. "Where's Michael?"

He lifted his head and looked around the room. "He's here somewhere. But if you can't see him, I guess he had to do something or to maybe help with that bad guy, Mr. Zee."

She combed through his hair. "Your hair is still wet. Did you really go swimming? In a pool? Do you own the swimming pool?"

"Yes, I went swimming. Yes, in a pool. And no, I don't own the swimming pool." He hugged her. "So many questions."

"I wish the swimming pool was yours." She lifted her head and patted his cheek. "Can you buy it? What did you do in that pool? Did you have water fights? Were there diving boards?"

He chuckled. "Well, no, not exactly." He stroked her hair. He couldn't answer right away. What would make sense to her? "I ..." Title deeds from properties he now owned flashed in his memory.

His head popped up. "I must go do something, Bea. I know what my mom was talking about."

"Your Mom? She was in the pool with you?" Bea sat up. "Is she wet, too? Does she own the swim—"

Katty stepped to the bed and lifted Bea down.

"Baby Bea, not so many questions. Maybe Clarence is tired."

"No, he's not." Bea pointed. "He's getting up."

Noell jumped off the bed. "What's the matter, Clarence? Where are you going?"

He swung his legs over the side and stood. A little wobbly at first, but Bea and Noell helped balance him. "Katty, would you drive me?"

Carol stepped in front of him. "I don't know Clarence. You've just been—"

He cupped her face with his hands and spoke softly, just loud enough for her to hear. "Remember when we were talking about Joe and … well, you remember. You said something about forgiving him?"

She nodded.

He swallowed. "I need to forgive that bastard … uh, Judge Green." His throat began to burn and tighten. Tears rolled down his cheeks. "If there is one good thing," he glanced at Noell, "no, there are many good things from my time in that pool. But one is … God … He showed me I need to forgive." His face crumpled. He leaned his head down and kissed the top of Carol's head. "Like you forgave Joe."

Clarence sat in the front passenger seat in Katty's car, looking out at the green, tree-lined lot.

Bea had just been shushed for the fifth time and Noell, who was sitting in the back seat with her, was trying to distract her.

In his memories, he could envision the huge mansion from when Annie was alive. It had been massive. Window glass sparkled. The porch furniture beckoned. The bricked walkway led him to the front door, where Annie had always waited.

He opened the car door and stepped onto the asphalt street.

"Can I come, too?" Bea kicked the back of the seat in front of her.

"No!" Katty's voice grew louder. "And quit kicking my seat!"

Clarence closed his door and limped around the front of the car, holding onto it for balance. Using the cane in his left hand still didn't come naturally, but at least now, he knew how to use it.

Katty rolled her window down. "Want some help? You okay?"

"I'm okay." He glanced back at her. "But thanks."

Some bricks were still imbedded in the grass, still drawing him. Where they stopped was probably where the porch had started.

The weight of what he was about to do, almost crippled him. He'd always carried hatred and unforgiveness like a badge, a shield. Don't come too close. For sixty years. Maybe … he turned around and motioned for them to join him. If he fell, they'd come running anyway.

Car doors slammed and Bea skipped toward him, her hair flowed with each step, her brown eyes sparkled. Too much ice cream? She was so cute. How he loved her and Katty.

He looked beyond.

And Noell. He could tell she was concerned about what he was about to do. With all she had been through why wasn't she angry?

And why not have them all here? Why not let them hear? He had no secrets … well—

"Clarence!" Bea hugged his leg. She always managed to hug his injured one, but he didn't mind. She just forgot.

Katty caught up with her. Noell was right behind her.

He wiped at his eyes. "I have something I must do."

"Build a swim—" Bea started.

"Bea. Enough. Quiet." Katty picked her up and hugged her. "Clarence has something he wants to say, and you need to be quiet."

Bea hid her face in Katty's neck. "Okay." She peeked at Clarence. "Sorry, Clarence."

He smiled and nodded. "I forgive you, Little One." He stepped away, then turned to face them. "Years ago …" He swallowed. "I'll make it short."

He searched the grass as if he'd find the words there. "I'm here today to forgive Judge Green. For … doesn't matter what. For everything." He licked his lips. "And so Judge Green, wherever you are … I forgive you."

Bea began to squirm again. She whispered something to Katty.

Katty shook her head.

Clarence cocked his head. "What does she want, Katty?"

"Michael is here!" Bea burst with the news and wiggled out of Katty's arms. "He's got his wings on!" She hopped and skipped toward Michael.

Clarence turned just as Michael raised his sword straight up. His wings glistened in the sunlight, each feather iridescent. "Michael. Where have you been?"

Michael's sword transformed into a beam of light as he aimed it at Clarence's chest, cutting into his flesh.

A roar of pain broke out from Clarence, echoing across the mowed lawns.

Bea was in mid-stride and fell to the ground. "Oh, no. Clarence." She screamed, "No!"

Clarence gasped. A jolt of power went through his heart, his whole body.

A thick, black shadow swirled out of Clarence's chest and floated to where two angels waited, ready to bind it with long golden threads.

Bea crawled to Clarence's shoes, sobbing. "Clarence. Don't die."

Clarence opened his eyes, staring into Michael's —eyes he had looked into for months now—as a friend, a confidant, and a protector. And right now, Michael's eyes were filled with pain.

A warmth began to fill Clarence's chest. He looked down where the sword had pierced, and blood seeped there. He stared at it, hands covered it, wanting to bandage the wound, to stop the flow. "Help me, Michael. I'm bleeding." He lifted his eyes to Michael's, not for a moment blaming him.

But the being in front of him was no longer Michael.

It was Jesus, His arms open wide.

Clarence dropped to his knees. "Lord." His cane was forgotten.

Bea crawled to his lap.

Katty and Noell on either side, arms around him.

Clarence began to weep. He wiped his face with his sleeve and picked up Bea, drawing her onto his lap.

She touched his chest. "Where's the blood?"

He looked. Patted his chest all around. No blood.

He looked up and now instead of Jesus, it was Michael. No wings. No golden belt. Just the usual jeans and T-shirt on his overgrown body. He walked toward them and knelt on one knee.

Again, he and Clarence locked eyes.

Clarence spoke first. "Forgiveness is messy."

Michael smiled his half-smile. "Yes. It is."

Clarence looked out across the grass and shook his head. "Why didn't I see? It was eating me alive. It was …" He patted his chest. "I feel so free, now. I'm … so clean."

He looked down at Katty and Noell. "Help me up, can you?"

Katty helped lift at one arm and Noell the other side.

One foot on the ground, then the other, until he stood upright. "That's harder than it used to be." He patted his leg. "Feels better though." He hugged them. "Let's go eat Mrs. Hatly's cookies, shall we?"

Bea stood and hugged Michael's leg.

He picked her up and threw her onto his shoulders and carried her to the car.

"Can we have ice cream, too?"

Katty shushed her. "I think you've had enough."

"Aww."

Clarence felt a big hand on his shoulder and he turned. Michael was beside him.

The huge angel knelt on one knee, his arm across his chest, head bowed.

Katty and Bea were arguing about who had dumped the water bottle again. Noell was tickling Bea while she strapped her into the car seat. Bea was telling her she didn't need to be strapped in—she was a big girl. Katty told her she could walk, then.

Clarence chuckled and dropped his hand onto Michael's shoulder. "This is us, Michael. We're family." He looked out at the empty lot. "Thanks Dad. We'll build something here just to piss that Bast … uh, Judge Green off. Wherever he is."

They clasped hands, Michael's huge one and Clarence's old one.

Warrior Brothers.

THIRTY-SIX

July 11, 1937 ~ Journal of Dr. Walter Stevens, Professor of Agriculture ~ Osceola, Nebraska.

Just one month to the day.

What began as the worst assignment of my career just one short month ago, turned out to be the most enlightening.

I sit here in Thelma's Diner, where it all began.

The pain.

The people who had lost loved ones.

Henry.

Fear.

Depression.

Did I find answers?

Not really.

I was able to do the Professor of Agriculture things, like analyzing the water and soil. I helped the farmers find ways to push back the threat of losing their farms and livelihoods, due to drought. Makes it all worthwhile.

I was able to help people find closure.

These people will forever be in my heart.

I could say I'll be back. But deep down we all know that I'll go wherever the adventure leads.

The last month has been anything but fun. Oh, there have been laughs. But living life with the people of Osceola, Nebraska has been raw at its worst, and precious at its best.

Last night I gassed up the truck. Battened down my little camper at Paul's place—leaving it here since I must drive to Lincoln to take care of some business. Even tucked this little journal in the camper. I put the final touches on the leather cover—a cross and a flower over God's thumb print. I'll be back. I figure leaving it here will insure my return.

The town came out to say good-bye. Literally, the town did come out, all except Mrs. Martin. She had the flu and is hereby excused.

One-by-one, starting with Frank Linder and Tommy Porten, people stepped forward from the crowd surrounding my little homestead in the park and gave their Testimony of the Pool.

Most had experienced a drowning of sorts. A reversal of life into death. I know that's opposite of most messages from the pulpit. But unless we die, we can't truly live. Something happens when we give Him our very breath. Life becomes precious.

I'm ready to go back to University. Back to my students.

But this experience will forever be imprinted on my mind and heart. These people let me dig into their memories and pain—only to find my own transfiguration and renewal.

AUTHOR NOTES

Caution!! Warning!! Something I want hammered home (we are building a house, so wording naturally takes on construction terms) is that our local nursing home in Osceola, Nebraska, Good Samaritan Society is a wonderful place. The leadership and staff are caring and professional and the facility is one of Osceola's lasting entities and businesses.

Remember! Most of this book is written through the eyes of Clarence, an eighty-year-old ex-con, and a demon-infested Mr. Zee! Mr. Zee especially, isn't a nice person. So, if you read something that isn't true about our own Good Sam, it isn't. It simply isn't true! This is fiction!

There. I hope I made myself clear.

Whew.

Some of you wanted more of Michael. I hope you won't be disappointed.

If any of this makes sense, it's because God and many people had their eyes on it! I fully take responsibility for any mistakes or blunders.

And I want to make it clear that there is not salvation in a pool, but only through Jesus Christ as Lord and Savior. He is the Way (John 14:6). He is the only answer to every question!

ACKNOWLEDGMENTS

Thanks be to God, Who is the Instigator of all ideas worth pursuing! You are my Source!

Thank you Dearly Beloved, kids and grandkids, family. I could not do this without your encouragement and support. Thank you for believing in me.

Friends and prayer warriors—thank you. It's the people who surround me in love and prayer, that help birth the words that touch a reader's heart.

Thank you, readers. Thank you for your encouragement—it keeps me on this sometimes very rocky road of writing, gets me past the moments of self-doubt. Thank you for your interest, your questions, suggestions. When you ask, "How's the book coming," and I get this look of sheer panic, that's a good thing! Keeps me on deadline.

Thank you, Kathy Tyers Gillin, my editor. I shake my head at what I put you through. I send you a manuscript that is upside down and inside out, and when you send it back, it all makes sense! I can't thank you enough! I will learn commas. Thank you for your patience.

Thank you, Jane Dixon-Smith. You are a wonder to work with. You take my scattered synopsis/ideas and make those covers sing. Very gifted woman.

Thank you, beta readers: Cathy and Cynthia. I know how much time that takes! Be brutal!

And thank you, Jan. Again—over-and-above. Post-it Woman.

Thank you to all the people I have asked weird questions of. "Would Dawes have come into the Clerk's Office at the Court House to register deeds in a private real estate sale?" "Do they allow Coke (as in soda) in prison?" "Does this character need a Power of Attorney if I kill him off?" You know who you are!

Thank you, retailers. Independent Bookstore Owners. Thank you for taking a chance on independent authors. Never give up!

Thank you, libraries. As an Independent Author, I had been told that libraries would not stock my books. I have found the opposite to be true. Every library I have approached, has been welcoming and encouraging. Of course, that's because there are very warm and kind people running those libraries!

Thank you NWG (Nebraska Writers Guild). You put on the best conferences ever! The people, the connections, the venues, are all top-notch!

We are so blessed to be living in this time and age. Freedom to write--if we choose. Freedom to publish. Thank you to all who have gone before, stepped out in faith to try this thing call indie publishing!

THANK YOU, READER,

Thanks for reading Rescued. Look for other titles, short stories, novels, kids' books in the future.

Book 3 in The Great Escapee Series is due out 2017.

You are always welcome to email ~ bonnielacy@bonnielacy.com for any news or events—with any questions or suggestions.

Look for Released, Book 1, in The Great Escapee Series, wherever books are sold.

Visit me online: www.bonnielacy.com and Instagram: @bonlacy

Sign up on my website to receive newsletters. I only get them out once a month, if that! Just to keep you up on what, when, and why!

Yay God!